The highwayman's eyes were not cruel and pale, but a warm honeyed brown, and his gaze was steady and strong and compelling, holding hers so that she could not look away. She felt her heart miss a beat and a shiver shimmy all the way down her spine.

"What the hell do you want?" her father snarled at him.

The highwayman glanced away, releasing her gaze, and only then did she realize that he had a pistol in each hand and both were aimed at her father's heart.

"Stand and deliver." The man's voice was quiet and harsh, as if half whispered.

"You'll rue the day you picked me to thieve from, you scoundrel."

"I think not." He cocked his pistols. "I will kill you if you do not give me what I have come for. And once you are dead, I will be free to take that which you seek to protect…without reprisal."

"Papa, please, if you have any knowledge of what this villain wants, I beg you to deliver it to him. Do not risk your life."

Both men looked at her. Her father's face was strained and haunted. And the highwayman's eyes held the strangest expression.

"Run, Marianne," her father said, agony in his voice. "Run and do not look back."

And she understood in that moment what it was that the highwayman wanted even before he said the words.

"For what does a father love best in all the world but his only daughter?"

* * *

His Mask of Retribution
Harlequin® Historical #1105—September 2012

Author Note

You first met Lady Marianne Winslow and her rather sinister family in *Unmasking the Duke's Mistress*. Marianne was always going to have her own story, and you, the reader, an explanation for her father and brother's behavior in that earlier book. But I needed a very special hero for her. I found him in the tall, dark and handsome highwayman Rafe Knight. If ever two people deserved love and a happy-ever-after...

So here is Marianne and Rafe's story. I really do hope that you enjoy it.

His

Mask

of Retribution

MARGARET MCPHEE

HARLEQUIN®

entertain, enrich, inspire™

Recycling programs
for this product may
not exist in your area.

ISBN-13: 978-0-373-29705-4

HIS MASK OF RETRIBUTION

www.Harlequin.com

Printed in U.S.A.

For E

Chapter One

Hounslow Heath, London—1810

It was the perfect day for a wedding.

The October morning was crisp and filled with sunshine. The sky was a cloudless blue. Hounslow Heath was a rich green, and the surrounding oaks and beeches that peppered the heath had turned the prettiest shades of red and gold. But as the solitary dark liveried coach sped across the heath Lady Marianne Winslow noticed nothing of the beauty.

'We had better pray that Pickering is still waiting in the church. I would not be surprised if he has suffered a change of heart and gone home. And who could blame him? He has his pride, after all. What on earth were you doing in your bedchamber for so long?' George Winslow, the Earl of Misbourne, pulled his watch from his pocket and flicked open the gold casing.

Marianne wondered what her father would say if she told him the truth—that she had been staring into the peering glass for the last two hours, wondering how she might bring herself to marry a man she had met only twice, was almost as old as her father and scru-

tinised her as if she were a prize filly. But her father
did not wait for an answer.

'Forty-five minutes late and we have yet to reach
Staines.' He snapped the watch case shut and returned
it to his waistcoat pocket. 'Good lord, girl! We cannot
risk losing Pickering after the fiasco with Arlesford.'

'Papa…marrying Mr Pickering…I am not at all sure
that I can…'

'Marianne, as your mother has already told you,
what you are feeling is nothing more than wedding-
morning nerves, which are perfectly normal in any
young lady. We have been through all of this before.'

'Yes, but…'

'But?'

'I thought when Mr Pickering and I were first betrothed that I would grow used both to him and to the
idea of marriage. But I need more time. It is barely a
month since he gave me his ring.' She glanced down
at the heavy signet ring upon her finger.

'A month is more than adequate for a betrothal,
Marianne.'

'But, Papa, I barely know him.'

'You will come to know him soon enough and Pickering is not a demanding man. He will be kind to you.'

The gold of Pickering's ring glinted in the sunlight.

'I can understand that he may not be the most ap-
pealing of bridegrooms,' said her father, 'but he is
steady and solid and reliable. Not only is Pickering's
fortune vast and he highly esteemed within the *ton*, but
he is a man of influence and power. No one can question the sense of the match.' He paused. 'The wedding
must go ahead. You will say no more of it and do as
you are told, my girl.'

She stared down at the wedding posy clutched in the

clamminess of her hand, at the pale pink roses delivered fresh from a hothouse in the country that morning and the tiny white babies'-breath flowers. She knew all of her father's arguments and knew, too, that they were right. Yet it did not make the prospect of marrying Charles Pickering any more palatable.

The coach took a bend in the road too fast and Marianne reached up for the securing strap to stop herself from sliding across the seat, her posy tumbling to the floor in the process.

'Papa, please, can we not at least travel a little more slowly?'

'The time is too short, Marianne. If Pickering walks away from this, there will be the devil to pay.' He glanced away, a strange expression in his eyes. His mouth tightened as she watched and then he seemed to remember himself and continued. 'John Coachman is under instruction to make up the time. Besides, Hounslow Heath is hardly a place to be dallying, even in daylight.' Her father retrieved her posy from where it rolled in the dust and returned it to her.

Marianne gave a little shiver. 'You cannot think that the highwayman—'

But her father cut her off. 'Neither sight nor sound has been had of the highwayman for over two months. Now that the Horse Patrol has been put in place to catch him he has likely taken himself elsewhere. And even were he still around, the hour is yet early. He would be lying drunk in some tavern, not waiting upon the heath especially for us. I will not risk losing Pickering.'

'It always comes down to my marrying,' said Marianne with a heavy heart and looked away.

'Marianne.' Her father gave a sigh and took her

hand between his own. 'You know you mean the world to me, do you not?'

She gave a nod.

'That I would only ever do what is best for you?'

'Yes, Papa.' It was the truth.

'Then believe me, my dearest, when I tell you that marrying Pickering is for the best.'

She nodded again. She would marry Mr Pickering because her father had arranged it and it was the right thing to do, even though the thought of becoming the man's wife filled her with dread.

The carriage slowed to a crawl to cross a narrow bridge and the sunlight shone through the window, illuminating her father's face as he smiled at her. She could see the specks of dust floating in the sunbeams, could see the gentleness of her father's eyes. His hands were warm around hers. Everything in the world seemed to quieten and calm. The wheels fell silent. Even the birds ceased to sing. It was a moment of pure tranquillity in the golden light.

And then the shot exploded and all hell broke loose.

The grooms were shouting and the coachman yelled a curse before a loud thud sounded. The horses whinnied. The coach lurched, then stopped. Something hard and big hit one panel, making her jump. She stared at the side from which the noise had emanated and, from the corner of her eye, saw the dark shadow move across the window. There was galloping and screaming and running feet. Then silence.

Her father scrabbled for his pistols in the pocket of the door and sat ready, a pistol primed in each hand, his eyes flicking nervously from one door to another, waiting.

She could hear the thud of her own heart and the heaviness of her father's breathing.

'The highwayman…' she whispered. 'It must be.'

Her father's jaw was clamped tight. He gave no response.

'Give me one of the pistols, Papa. Please.'

'Do not be so foolish, Marianne,' he snapped and his knuckles were white where he gripped so tight at the pistols' handles.

They waited, and there was nothing.

They waited, and the seconds dragged; the fear and the dread were almost overwhelming. Her father must have felt it, too, for he muttered beneath his breath, 'Come, show yourself.' But whoever, or whatever, was outside did not heed him.

Nothing moved. Not even a flicker. The air was so thick with tension that she felt she might choke with it. Time held its breath as surely as Marianne.

Nothing happened.

She wondered if their assailant had fled, whether they were alone. Her father must have thought the same, for he looked across at her and gave a slight shake of the head, she knew that he meant for her to remain silent and say nothing. She nodded and watched him edge towards the door…just as it swung open.

Her father's pistol fired, a deafening noise within the confines of the coach, so loud that her ears hurt from it and her eyes watered from the cloud of blue smoke. The stench of it was acrid, filling her nostrils, catching in her throat. She made to move, but her father's hand caught hard at her wrist, thrusting her back down on to her seat.

'Stay where you are, Marianne!'

The silence in the aftermath of the pistol shot

seemed almost as loud as the shot itself. It hissed in her ears and seemed to vibrate through her very bones. Through the smoke she saw a shadow flit across the open doorway and heard the taunt of a man's harsh whisper.

Her father fired at the shadow with his second pistol and launched himself out of the open doorway.

There was a thud against the carriage panel at the side of the door and the coach rocked as if something had been thrown against it. She heard a grunt of pain and then an ominous silence that made her stomach drop right down to her shoes.

'Papa?' She checked the door pockets for a spare pistol, but her father had taken no such precaution, so she hoisted up her skirts and scrambled to the door, trampling on the pink-and-white posy in her desperation to save her father. The smoke was clearing and the scene was quite clear before her as she jumped down from the coach.

The horses had been cut loose. Of the coachman, grooms and footmen there was no sign. Her father was leaning back against the side of the coach, his face powder-white, a trickle of blood seeping from the corner of his mouth, staring with angry black eyes filled with the promise of violence. Marianne knew that the highwayman was there, knew that he must be watching her at that very moment, but she could not look. Her heart was thudding hard; the fear was pounding through her blood and she was afraid to look, even though she knew that she must. Taking a deep breath to control her rising panic, she slowly followed her father's gaze to the tall dark highwayman.

He was dressed in black, wearing a long shabby greatcoat and, beneath it, a pair of buckskin breeches.

His boots were scuffed, the leather cracking in places with age and wear. Even his gloves were dark and old, well worn. On his head was an old-fashioned tricorn hat; it too was black to match the rest of his outfit, and under it she could see his unfashionably long hair, the colour of rich dark mahogany. All of this she absorbed in an instant, with barely a glance, for her focus was fixed firmly on the dark kerchief that was tied across his lower face, hiding his identity.

Her stomach was clenched small and tight, and beneath the ivory-and-pink-patterned silk of her skirt her legs were trembling. Her eyes lingered on the piece of cloth for a moment, then she screwed her courage to the mast and, with slow deliberation, she raised them to meet his.

The highwayman's eyes were not cruel and pale, but a warm honeyed brown, and his gaze was steady and strong and compelling, holding hers so that she could not look away. She felt her heart miss a beat and a shiver shimmy all the way down her spine. She did not know whether it was from shock or relief or fear, or a combination of all three.

'What the hell do you want?' her father snarled at him.

The highwayman glanced away, releasing her gaze, and only then did she realise that he had a pistol in each hand and both were aimed at her father's heart.

She knew that he smiled at the question, even though she could not see his mouth behind the kerchief. He smiled, but there was nothing of mirth in his eyes as he looked at her father.

'Stand and deliver.' The man's voice was quiet and harsh, as if half-whispered.

'You'll rue the day you picked me to thieve from, you scoundrel.'

'I think not.' He cocked his pistols.

'My daughter is on her way to be married.' If her father had thought to reason with the highwayman then he was mistaken, for the man's eyes did not so much as flicker. His gaze remained hard and relentless.

'I have a purse of money.' Her father scrabbled in his pockets, pulling out the small brown-leather pouch. 'Here.' He threw it in the direction of the highwayman. 'Take it and be gone.' The purse landed on the grass between them.

The highwayman did not even look at the purse, heavy and bulging with coins though it was. 'I do not want your money,' he said in his harsh half-whisper, his eyes fixed unblinking on Misbourne's.

Her father looked at the highwayman for a moment, as if unable to comprehend the man's answer, before speaking again. 'There is my diamond cravat pin and my watch; both are gold.' Her father's fingers were trembling slightly as he unpinned the diamond and threw it down to lie on the grass by the side of his purse. The stone glinted and sparkled in the sunlight. Then he took the watch from his pocket, unfastened the fob and offered the watch and its dangling chain to the highwayman.

But the villain made no move to take it.

'Marianne, take off your pearls and throw them down by my purse,' her father commanded, adding beneath his breath, 'Pearls before swine.' But for all his bravado, his brow glistened with sweat as she reached for the clasp.

The highwayman shook his head. 'Nor your jewellery, Misbourne.'

Her fingers stilled, then dropped away, leaving the pearls intact around her neck.

Her father frowned and she could see the suspicion and fear that flitted across his face. 'You know my name?' His voice was sharp.

'I know a lot more than that.'

The two men watched one another. The silence was heavy, pregnant with foreboding.

'Then what *do* you want?' asked her father at last.

There was a pause before the highwayman spoke. 'We'll come to that in time, but for now I'll take from you the same I took from the others—that which is most precious in the world to you.'

Every last trace of colour washed from her father's face. His beard and moustache, grizzled and grey, stood stark against the pallor of his skin. Across the heath a blackbird was singing, and in the background was the gentlest whisper of the wind. Nothing else stirred.

Her father forced the semblance of a laugh. 'You mean to kill me?'

'No!' Marianne stepped forwards in alarm. 'Do not harm him! I beg of you! Please!'

The highwayman's eyes met hers and they looked almost golden in the morning light. 'Rest assured, Lady Marianne…' how shocked she felt to hear her name upon his lips '…both your father and I know that it is not his life of which I speak.' His voice was that same stony half-whisper, devoid of all emotion, but the look in his eyes was cold and hard as the deepest winter and filled with such implacable determination that she shivered to see it. He turned his focus back to her father. 'Don't you, Misbourne?'

'No.' Her father's voice was little more than a croak.

The denial was weak and something about his expression made her think he knew exactly what was meant.

The highwayman made a small movement with the pistol in his right hand. 'I will kill you if you do not give me what I have come for. And once you are dead I will be free to take that which you seek to protect... without reprisal.'

'Papa, please, if you have any knowledge of what this villain wants, I beg you to deliver it to him. Do not risk your life.'

Both men looked at her. Her father's face was strained and haunted—he seemed to have aged a hundred years in those few moments—and the highwayman's eyes held the strangest expression.

'Run, Marianne,' her father said, and there was agony in his voice. 'Run, and do not look back.'

She shook her head. 'I will not abandon you to him.'

'Do as I say and run, damn you, girl!'

And she understood in that moment what it was that the highwayman wanted even before he said the words.

'For what does a father love best in all the world, but his only daughter?'

'You are wrong,' she said. There was her mother and her brother. But she knew in her heart that he spoke the truth. Her father had always loved her best.

'You shall not take her from me, you fiend!' Her father threw himself at the highwayman, but the villain was taller and stronger and younger. In an instant his pistols were uncocked and out of sight. He caught Misbourne's punch as easily as if it were that of a weakling and, in return, landed a hard fist to his face and then his stomach. When her father gasped and doubled over, clutching at his belly, the highwayman pushed him away and he stumbled back, hitting

the side of the coach. He collapsed on to his knees, his right arm still wrapped around his belly. Blood was seeping from a cut on his cheek and his face was already beginning to swell.

'Papa!' Marianne made to rush to him, but the highwayman was quicker. He caught her around the waist and hauled her to him. 'No!' She kicked and punched and fought for all she was worth, but her captor was too strong. In an instant he had her held in his grip and facing her father.

Misbourne scrabbled to his feet from where he knelt in the dirt, the blood trickling down his poor injured face to darken and matt the grey hair of his beard. She tried to go to him, but the highwayman's arm was firm around her upper arms and *décolletage*, restraining her, pulling her back until her spine tingled with the proximity of him, even though their bodies were apart.

'What will you give for her safe return, Misbourne?'

'Anything you wish.'

'Anything?' The highwayman's voice was low and grim.

Her father nodded. 'Money. Gold. Silver. Jewels. Name your price.'

Behind her she felt the highwayman move, although his grip upon her did not slacken. He threw a folded sheet of paper to land on the ground before her father. 'My price, Misbourne.'

Her father retrieved the paper and opened it, and Marianne watched his expression contort with sudden shock and horror. He made not one move, spoke not one word, just stared at the piece of paper as if he could not believe the words written upon it. His eyeballs rolled up and he swayed before stumbling backwards. Only the panel of the coach door kept him upright—

that and his stubborn will-power as he leaned, visibly shaken, against it.

'Papa!' She struggled, but the highwayman's grip did not yield. 'Papa!'

So much sweat beaded on her father's forehead that his hair was damp from it. His face was ashen as a corpse. He looked old and weak, all of his usual strength and vitality exposed for the fragile mask it was. Yet the highwayman showed no mercy.

'The exchange will be today, Misbourne. Be ready.'

Marianne felt his arm drop to her waist and then the world turned upside down as he swung her up and over his shoulder, balancing her there as if she weighed nothing at all. She wriggled and tried to kick, but the blood was rushing to her head and his grip tightened, securing her all the more.

'No! Do not take her from me! Please!' her father cried and collapsed to his knees as he tried to stagger towards them. 'I beg you, sir. I will give you what you want.' She had never heard her father plead before, never heard his voice so thick with emotion.

But the highwayman was unmoved. 'Yes, you will,' he said. 'Watch for my message.' Then he whirled around and, in the blink of an eye, was upon his horse, sliding Marianne to sit sideways on the saddle before him. The huge black beast reared, impatient to be off, and she found herself held hard against his chest, gripped so tightly that she could not move.

'Who sent you? Was it—?' her father shouted and she could hear the fear and trembling in his voice. But the highwayman cut him off.

'No one sent me.'

'Then who the devil are you?'

The highwayman's arm was anchored around her

waist as he stared down at her father. 'I'm your past come back to haunt you, Misbourne.' The horse reared again and then they were off and galloping at full tilt across Hounslow Heath, leaving behind her father, white-faced and bleeding, the horseless coach, and the battered remnants of her wedding flowers blowing in the breeze.

Chapter Two

Rafe Knight pushed the horse hard, all the while keeping a careful hold of his most precious cargo. He could smell the sweet scent of violets from the girl's hair and feel the soft curves of the slender body pressed against his. He regretted that she had to be any part of this, but she was Misbourne's one weakness: the only hope of finding what he sought.

It would not be long before the coachman, groom and footmen reached the inn and summoned help. He did not have much time. He headed west, as if travelling on towards Staines, until he was out of Misbourne's sight, then he left the road and doubled back across the wild heath land towards Hounslow and London.

Callerton was waiting exactly as planned, hidden from view within the derelict farm buildings on the outskirts of the town. The doors of the great barn were wide open and Knight rode straight inside, slid Marianne Winslow down to his friend and servant, and dismounted.

The highwayman's masked accomplice placed Marianne inside a dark coach that waited within the barn,

then assisted the highwayman in harnessing his horse as part of the team. Her throat was so dry that it stuck together, making it difficult to swallow. Within her chest her heart beat in a frenzy and every muscle in her body was racked tight with tension. The fear was so great that her breath shook from it and her palms were clammy. She squeezed her eyes shut and slowed her breaths, counting them to control the panic. When she looked again, the men had a flask and a rag and were washing the distinctive white flare from the horse's muzzle. They were focused, hurrying, intent on their task. Marianne gathered the remnants of her courage. A deep breath in and out, then she curled her fingers round the door handle.

Her blood was still rushing, her heart beating loud as a big bass drum. The door opened without a sound, letting her slip noiselessly to the ground and edge towards the rear of the coach. Once there she stood, her back pressed against the empty boot, while her eyes scanned desperately for an escape route or hiding place. She held her breath, ragged and loud as it had become, fearing they would hear it, fearing they would notice at any moment that she was gone.

Time seemed to slow and in that tiny moment of waiting every sense seemed sharpened and more intense. She could smell hay and horse sweat and leather tack, and the damp scent of autumn and brambles. She could hear the jangle of the harness and the shuffle of hooves as the horses grew impatient. Against her face the air of the shadowed empty barn was cool. There was nowhere to hide: not one hay bale, not one cart. Her heart sank. She knew that she was going to have to take her chance. Taking a deep breath and lifting her skirt clear of her ankles, she eyed the great, wide,

opened barn doors. Outside the sky was blue and clear, the sun lighting the heath land as if in invitation. She hesitated no longer, but ran for her life.

Three paces and there was a yell and a sudden swift movement and Marianne gasped aloud as strong arms enclosed her. Within a second the highwayman had her backed against the coach door, both wrists secured behind her back, as his eyes glowered down into her own.

'Not a good idea, Lady Marianne,' he breathed, in that harsh half-whisper of his.

He was so close that with every breath she took she could feel the brush of her bodice against his chest, so close that she could smell the scent of the sandalwood soap he had used to wash with. She had not realised that he was so very tall, or how much he would dwarf her. She felt overwhelmed, by him, by shock, by fear. For a moment she could not speak, could not even breathe as she stared up into his eyes. Her heart was pounding, her mouth dry. She forced herself to think of what he had done to her father, forced her anger to override her fear.

'Scoundrel!' she hissed. 'What did you expect? That I would just sit there waiting for you to come and beat me as you beat my father?'

'I do not beat women.' His eyes were hard and angry as they held hers.

'Only old men who have done you no wrong.'

'You know nothing of the matter, Lady Marianne.'

'You did not need to hit him! You did not need to make him bleed!'

'Misbourne got off lightly.'

'What has my father ever done to warrant such treatment?'

'Your father is a thief and a murderer.'

She shook her head in disbelief, stunned by the declaration. 'And you are a madman, or drunk on wickedness.'

'I am as sane and sober as you are, my lady.'

His gaze bore down into hers and in the shadowed light of the barn his eyes were the colour of her father's best tawny port and clear and lucid as he claimed, and when she looked into them she could not prevent the shiver that ran through her. He was still holding her in place against the door, her wrists secured in his grip, his body too close to hers. There was an aura of such danger surrounding them she could scarcely breathe.

'It is you who is the thief. And, for all I know, a murderer too.'

He stepped closer, his eyes intent on hers, and she saw the flare of fury in them. 'It is true I have thieved, but as for murder? When your father grovelled in the dirt before me I could have done it, Lady Marianne, so very easily. I confess I was tempted.' His hushed voice was so harsh and so filled with anger that she caught her breath to hear it. 'An eye for an eye is what the Bible says. But murder…' He shook his head. 'That is your father's game, not mine. I'll settle to see him brought to justice in a hangman's noose.' The force of his words flayed her. Then, as suddenly as he had captured her, he released her, stepping back to open up a space between them.

'My quarrel is with your father. You need have no fear. I shall not hurt you.'

She moved away from the coach and rubbed her wrists—not because he had hurt her, but because they still tingled from the feel of his skin against hers. 'Then what are you going to do to me?' Her heart was thumping fast and hard. Her lips were stiff with fear but

she asked the question even though she was so very afraid to hear the answer. She waited with legs that trembled, but she did not let herself look away from that razing gaze.

The silence seemed to stretch between them and tension knotted her stomach.

'Keep you until your father gives me what I want. He has something belonging to me. Now I have something belonging to him. It is a fair exchange.'

'And what is it that you want?' The words were little more than a whisper. She remembered too clearly her father's reaction when he had read the highwayman's demand and the shock and worry she had felt to see it.

'Too many questions, my lady. We can delay no longer.' Not once did his gaze shift from hers and she quivered from the intensity of it. She knew what he was and, despite his reassurance, what he could do to her.

'You shall not get away with this.'

'Indeed?' And there was such arrogant certainty in that one word.

'You are despicable, sir.'

'I am what your father has made me, Lady Marianne. Pray to God that you never find out the truth of it!' He opened the door and gestured her into the coach.

Marianne had no option but to hold her head high and climb inside.

She had her father's eyes. Black as midnight, wary, and watching him with that same contempt Misbourne used on those around him. Little wonder she was the apple of her father's eye. Little wonder he guarded her as if his pampered daughter were as precious as the crown jewels. In the rest of her face she favoured her mother. Her shapely lips pressed firm and her small

nostrils were flared. His gaze swept over the blonde tendrils that framed her face, so soft and pale beside the strong darkness of her eyes. But the eyes, it was said, were windows to the soul. He wondered whether Marianne Winslow's soul was as black as her father's. He pulled the curtains closed and the stiffening of the girl's body, the sudden fear in her face, spurred a twinge of irritation within him. As if he would ravish her, as if he would even touch her. Misbourne was the blackguard in this, not him.

'I have told you that you have nothing to fear from me,' he snapped. 'Given your propensity for escape, you will understand the need for preventative measures.' He produced a short length of rope.

'And if I refuse?' She raised her chin a notch.

'You have no choice in the matter, my lady.'

She stared at him as if he were the devil incarnate. 'You are a villain.' Her voice was high, her face pale.

'Yes, I am,' he said. 'And you had best not forget it, Lady Marianne, especially if you have any idea of resisting me.'

Her eyes widened, but she did not suffer an attack of the vapours or hysteria as he had expected of Misbourne's coddled daughter. Indeed, she did not cry or plead or scream. Everything about her was contained and careful. She just eyed him with a quiet defiance and more courage than many a man as he bound her wrists behind her back, checking that the rope was not too tight.

He turned his attention away from the woman and slid open the dark wooden panel beneath his seat to remove the small travelling bag from within. He took his time, yet his actions were slick and smooth, well practised. From the bag he took a pair of highly pol-

ished riding boots, a new hat and a pair of the finest black-leather gloves. Then he removed the pistols from his pockets, checked they were safe and laid them at the bottom of the bag. He shrugged out of his greatcoat, rolled it into a ball and thrust it on top of the pistols. The tricorn hat, his shabby gloves and the old boots followed, before the bag was stowed out of sight once more. He glanced up to find Marianne watching him. Their eyes met through the dim grey light and that same *frisson* of awareness rippled through him, just as it had before. And the thought that he could feel any measure of attraction towards Misbourne's daughter sent anger licking right through him.

She turned her face away, fixing her gaze on the dark curtains drawn across the window.

He kept his eyes on her as he slid his feet into the smart black boots, scraped his hair back into a low tidy queue at the back of his head and tied it in place with a black ribbon from the pocket of his tailcoat. But the woman was not stupid; she did not look at him again. Not once. Not through the little country towns of Brentford or Hammersmith or even the village of Kensington. He slipped his hat and gloves in place and the rest of the journey continued in silence, the tension between them seeming to wind tighter with every mile closer they travelled through London. Eventually, Callerton thumped the carriage body and Knight knew they were nearing St Giles Rookery. He looked at Misbourne's daughter.

'Time to move, Lady Marianne.'

She glanced round at him then. A small steady movement as controlled as everything else about her, yet he could sense the sudden escalation of distrust and see the flash of fear in those large dark eyes. He

felt his conscience stir at what he was doing, but her gaze flitted momentarily away and when she looked back at him it was as if she had drawn a veil across her eyes and the only expression on her face was one of contempt. She looked so like Misbourne that any doubts he might have harboured vanished instantly.

Knight reached for her arm and moved to execute the next stage of his plan.

In the study of his town house in Leicester Square, the Earl of Misbourne lay on a daybed covered by a cream woollen blanket and listened to the carriage sounds from the street outside.

'He is gone.' Francis Winslow—or Viscount Linwood, as he was otherwise known—Misbourne's son and heir, stood by the window and watched Pickering's carriage until it turned the corner and headed away from the square. 'Do you think he believed us?' Linwood's eyes were as dark and venomous as his father's as he came to stand by the daybed.

Misbourne gave a nod.

'It will be more difficult tomorrow when he returns and wishes to visit his betrothed. Although the story of our "carriage crash" being all over tomorrow's newspapers should help. I've ensured the news is already being whispered in the clubs.' His son was good at taking care of such details, but Misbourne offered no thanks; his mind was on other matters.

He slipped the crumpled sheet of paper from the pocket of his dressing gown and smoothed it out that he might stare at it again. The hand was bold, the words, few as they were, angular and angry. A place. A year. And the highwayman's demand.

1795, Hounslow Heath

*The document that was taken—in exchange for your
daughter.*

He was thinking, and thinking hard. There was
only one other person that knew of the document and
Misbourne had eyes and ears stationed in every main
port in the south watching for his return. It was possible that Rotherham had evaded detection, that he
was back in England already. Misbourne's blood ran
cold at the thought and he shivered as if someone had
walked over his grave.

'Father?' Linwood was staring down into his face
and he could see the concern and agitation in the eyes
that were so like his own.

'Let me think,' Misbourne snapped. It made no
sense. Whatever else Rotherham was, he was a man
of his word and one who liked everything done exactly
to the letter. There was still time left before he would
come. Time enough for the wedding between Marianne and Pickering.

Misbourne lounged back against the pillows of his
bed and read the words again. The criminal fraternity
had a way of talking even when they'd been sworn to
silence. A boast in the tap room of a public house, a
whisper in the ear of the buxom wench beneath them.
Thank God for illiteracy. He wondered how much the
highwayman could possibly know.

'You are not well, Father. Let me deal with this in
your stead,' said Linwood.

'Don't fuss so, boy, I tell you I'm fine.' An idea was
taking shape in Misbourne's mind.

'And I disagree,' said Linwood without a flicker
of emotion.

'You always were a stubborn little sod.'

'Chip off the old block, so they say.' Linwood held his gaze.

Misbourne gave a smile and shook his head. 'And they're not wrong.'

'Then let us go to the brotherhood,' said Linwood without returning the smile, speaking of the secret society of which both he and his father were members. 'Seek their assistance in this.'

'No!'

'It's different now that Hunter is the Master. He'll help us and—'

'I said, no, damn you, boy!' Misbourne felt a stirring of panic and knew he had to convince his son. 'We manage this ourselves. This is family business; it does not go outwith this room, no matter what else you might think.'

Linwood's face was angry and defiant.

'I will not risk Marianne's reputation. I will not risk your sister's safety. Do you understand?'

Linwood gave a sullen nod. 'What is this letter from fifteen years ago that he wants?' It was the question that Misbourne most dreaded to hear.

'None of your damned business.'

'Will you give it to him?'

There was a pause before Misbourne replied, 'Yes, I'll give it to him.' His scowl deepened and he pinched at the bridge of his nose, a sure sign that he was trying to control his temper. 'The day progresses and still we hear nothing.'

'We will.'

'What the hell is taking him so long?' Misbourne's upper lip curled in a snarl.

'He means to make sure we take him seriously—

and no doubt he wants to twist the knife a little. Whoever he is, he certainly does not like you.'

'And, by God, I'll give him good reason not to! By the time I've finished with him he won't know what he likes and what he doesn't.' Misbourne was only slightly mollified by the thought.

A knock sounded at the study door. The butler entered, holding a silver salver with a single letter laid upon it.

'Just delivered, m'lord, by an urchin.'

'Does the wretch wait for a reply?'

'No, m'lord. The boy ran off.'

Misbourne saw the servant's gaze take in his tender swollen cheekbone and felt a spurt of annoyance. He took the letter and dismissed the man with a flick of his fingers. The seal broke easily, but his hands were trembling with impatience and fear as he unfolded the letter and read its content before passing the note to his son.

'Aldgate High Street where it meets Fenchurch and Leadenhall,' said Linwood. 'He's chosen well. It's a busy junction at the best of times; it will be pandemonium there at three o'clock. And with its links to so many roads and alleys it will be difficult to cover the whole area.'

'Difficult, but not impossible,' said Misbourne. 'Once Marianne is safe…'

'Once Marianne is safe, we'll hunt him down like the villain that he is,' finished his son.

From the rooms above came the sound of a baby crying and a man and woman arguing, shouting and swearing at full volume. An old man was singing a drunken bawdy song and outside, in the street, a dog was barking. Marianne sat very still on the sin-

gle wooden chair and waited, just as she had waited
through all the previous hours. It was the sole piece
of furniture in the room. Her eyes ranged again over
the pile of filthy covers in the corner that served as a
bed. Mould grew on the walls and the floorboards were
bare. Two buckets sat behind the door—one held water,
and the other was so stained with filth that she did not
want to contemplate its use. There was no coal on the
fire, no pots or pans. Not so much as a cup to drink
from. The dirt encrusted upon the windows made the
light hazy and hid her view of the rookery beyond.

'Who lives here?' she asked. The filthy bed of rags
in the corner gave lie to her denial that anyone could
live in such squalor.

'A family with five children,' replied the highwayman's accomplice from behind his pale mask.

'All in this one room?'

'Aye, lass. But he'll pay them more than they get in
a year just for the use of this room for a few hours. He
helps where he can.'

'I did not know such poverty existed.' She had never
seen a place the like of this, with its maze of streets and
alleyways crowded with ramshackle houses. 'The children are so ragged and thin, with eyes that seem too old
for their faces, and their mothers…' She thought of the
women with their rotten teeth and low, revealing bod-
ices, and how they had fanned their skirts high when
they had seen the highwayman and his accomplice.

'For some, it is the only way they can feed their
bairns.'

She was horrified to learn it.

The light was a dull grey and the air was so ripe
with rotting rubbish—and worse—that she wondered
if she would ever clear the stench of it from her nose.

Something small and brown appeared from beneath the mound of blankets and scuttled across the floor.

'It'll not be much longer,' the accomplice assured her. 'He'll be here soon and then we'll have you back with your pa.'

'You seem to be a kind man. Why are you helping that villain?'

'He's not the villain in any of this, m'lady, for all that you think him. And I'm helping him because he's a good man and he fought his way across a battlefield to save my life. Don't judge him so harshly. He's only doing what he must, to set his demons to rest.'

The words were spoken with such sincerity that she could not doubt that the accomplice believed them. And she thought again of the tall dark masked man with amber eyes that made her shiver. 'Why does that involve my father?'

But the man shook his head. 'I've already said too much. Pardon me, my lady, but that is not my question to answer.'

When the clock struck three, Knight was nowhere near Aldgate High Street. He was drinking champagne in the bow window of White's Gentleman's Club with Bullford, Devlin, Razeby and Fallingham, and making sure the *ton* of London knew that he was there. He knew the boy he had paid would wait for Misbourne to arrive before passing him the note.

'What d'you make of the story of Misbourne's carriage crash?' Bullford was asking.

'Maybe Pickering's getting cold feet,' said Devlin. 'After all, she's hardly good *ton* at the minute. It will take a while longer before Misbourne lives down the

embarrassment over Arlesford. And it's not as if Pickering needs the money.'

'Lucky escape for little Lady Marianne, if you ask me.' Fallingham swigged at his champagne. 'Pickering's so old that he's in danger of dying on the job, if you know what I mean.'

All the men except Knight laughed.

'What do you think, Knight?' asked Bullford, draining his glass.

He should not give a damn about Marianne Winslow, but he did not wish to think about her lying beneath Pickering. 'I think it's time we opened another bottle of champagne,' he said. 'I've got better things to do with the rest of my day.' Callerton should have the girl well in place by now.

'Would that involve keeping a certain widow satisfied?' Devlin asked.

Knight smiled, but said nothing.

'Lucky bugger!' said Razeby. The rest of the men chortled in appreciation.

'Maybe you should be laying off the champers in preparation for tomorrow's four-in-hand race. Do you think you'll beat Hawick?' asked Bullford.

'Why? Are you thinking of wagering against me?' drawled Knight. His eyes slid across the room to the grandfather clock in the corner.

'Wouldn't dream of it, old man,' said Bullford.

'We like to make money, not lose it,' agreed Fallingham.

The champagne arrived. 'A monkey on it that no one can down the bottle in one,' said Devlin.

'Prepare to pay up,' said Fallingham, lifting the bottle and placing it to his lips. He began to drink while

his friends stamped their feet and chanted their support around him.

Knight waited until another two bottles of champagne had been opened before he slipped away.

'If this is a direction to yet another street...' warned Misbourne, grabbing the letter from beneath the apple cart in Cutler Street. 'This is the fourth note. He's had us on a wild goose chase all over London. The villain's intent on making fools of us.'

'He's intent on making it as hard as possible for us to track him...and Marianne,' corrected Linwood.

'Give the document to the boy by the organ grinder. Lady Marianne will be delivered to your home.' Misbourne read the words aloud. 'Are the men still following us?' he added beneath his breath to Linwood, who gave a subtle nod and lifted his wolf's-head walking cane from where it rested on the ground.

'Then let us hope the boy leads them straight to the villain's lair.'

'You should let me go,' said Linwood.

'Having you running through the streets will attract too much attention. No, it is better this way.' Misbourne slipped a folded and sealed document from his pocket and walked over to the fair-haired boy by the organ grinder. The boy saw him coming and Misbourne understood from the expression on his face that the boy knew what to expect. He took the document without a word and disappeared into the crowded street. And the two men lounging in the mouth of the alleyway behind Misbourne slipped into the crowd after him.

* * *

Knight took the document from the boy. 'You're sure you lost them?'

'Easy as pie. I passed it to Jim, who passed it to Dodger, who passed it to me. We led 'em a merry dance all the way down to the dockland just as you said and left 'em there.'

'Good.' Knight slipped the coins into the boy's grubby hand.

'Pleasure doing business with you, gov, as always.' And the boy disappeared again.

Knight's heart was thumping hard. The folded paper was fragile and yellowed with age. He could see the shadow of writing shining through its thinness. His mouth dried with anticipation. The question had haunted him every day of the last fifteen years—now he held the answer in his hands. He took a breath and carefully unfolded the document.

His eyes scanned the faded ink. The document was dated for June 1795 and was a letter from a senior government minister of the time to Misbourne. Several sensitive topics were discussed and it was clear, from both the tone and the detail revealed, that the two men were on friendly terms. It was a letter that many might have paid to read, the stuff of petty scandal, but Knight crushed it within his hand as a red mist descended before him.

Marianne heard the footsteps outside in the alleyway before the highwayman's accomplice did. The highwayman strode into the room wearing the same long dark coat he had worn upon Hounslow Heath, but his hat was the smart beaver she had watched him

don in the coach, and beneath the coat she caught a glimpse of the fine white shirt and dark waistcoat. The mask tied around his face had moulded to his features and his boots left a trail of footsteps through the dirt of the floor.

After all these hours of waiting, he had finally come to return her to her father. Her stomach tightened with anticipation. Then she met his eyes, and they were not golden and light but dark and dangerous and filled with such a cold hard rage that she knew, before he even spoke the words to his accomplice, that it had all gone wrong.

'Misbourne played us false.'

'He didn't deliver the document?' The accomplice sounded as shocked as Marianne felt.

'Not the right one. Does he think me so much a fool that I would not notice?'

'You said he was a blackguard but, even so, what manner of man risks his own daughter?' the accomplice whispered, but she heard him just the same.

'No!' Marianne leapt to her feet so suddenly that the chair tipped back and clattered on to the floor. 'You're lying! My father must be confused. You cannot have made it clear what you wanted.'

The highwayman walked right up to her and his eyes were dark and deadly. 'Your father knows exactly what I want, Lady Marianne.'

'No,' she whispered, shaking her head, knowing that what the highwayman was saying could not be true. 'He would not leave me here with you. He would do everything in his power to save me.' She knew it with all her heart.

Something of the rage diminished in the highwayman's eyes and the way he was looking at her made his

words ring true more than any angry assertions could have done. 'I am sorry, Lady Marianne.'

'There must be some mistake.'

The harshness of his whisper softened. 'There is no mistake.'

'You're lying,' she said again and her voice was very quiet and controlled, in such contrast to the terrible frenzied thud of her heart. Of course he was lying. He had to be lying.

He said nothing, just stood there and looked at her, and she could not bear to see the pity in his eyes.

'You're lying!' she shouted it this time. 'You just want more from him!'

'Lady Marianne.' Gently he tried to take her arm.

'No!' She flinched and pushed him away. 'Do not touch me!'

'We have to move,' she heard his accomplice say in the background. 'What do we do with the girl?'

The highwayman did not take his gaze from hers as he answered, 'We take her home with us.'

The accomplice gestured the highwayman aside. They talked in hushed tones, but Marianne could hear some of what they were saying.

'Maybe we should just let her go. If Misbourne isn't going to give up the document…' The accomplice was arguing to release her.

'We keep her until he does.' The highwayman was so adamant that she knew his accomplice would not persuade him. He meant to keep her and heaven only knew what he would do to her. He glanced round, saw she was listening and pulled his accomplice further away, turning his back so that she would not hear their words. They were so intent on their conversation that they did not hear the sound of feet and voices,

children's shouts and a man's growl. The door opened
and four children ran in, and behind them, a man and
a woman carrying a puppy wrapped in a filthy shawl.

The children did not seem fazed to find the highwayman, his accomplice and Marianne.

'All right, governor?' The oldest fair-haired boy
sauntered across the room and gave the highwayman
a nod.

'Tom,' the man snapped at the boy, but the boy was
not cowed in the slightest. 'Beggin' your pardon, sir,'
said the man to the highwayman. 'We thought you
would be gone. Excuse us and we'll leave you to your
business.' And then in roughened tones to the children, 'Out, the lot of you.' His head gestured to the
still-open door.

One of the boys emitted a harsh hacking cough
and the puppy began to whine. The family smelled of
dampness and dog and unwashed bodies.

'Our business is done for today,' replied the highwayman. 'Here…' He slipped his hand into his pocket
and she saw the glint of gold. The children gathered
around him like flies round a honeypot. Her gaze slid
to the open door and the woman standing beside it.
All eyes were on the highwayman's gold. Marianne
did not hesitate. She hitched up her skirts and she ran.

'Stop her!' She heard the highwayman's shout. 'Marianne, no! This place is danger—' But she slammed the
door shut behind her and did not look back.

She hurled herself down the close, through the gaping main door and out into the street. The clatter of
her shoes was loud against the stones, seeming to echo
against the crowding walls all around. Shabby clothing
hung on washing lines strung high between the houses,
flapping dark and grey and damp. Marianne dodged

beneath them and kept on running, ignoring the sharp press of the cobbles through her thin leather soles. A quick glance behind and she could see his dark figure further down the street, running so fast that the tails of his greatcoat were spread and billowing behind him like great black wings.

'God help me!' she whispered and, ignoring the stitch in her side, pushed herself to run faster, knowing that she could not afford to let him catch her. The paving was uneven and covered in filth. A dog snapped at her heels and a woman sitting in a doorway swigging from a bottle shouted something at her and laughed, but she kept on running. She stumbled, almost sprawling her length as she caught her foot in a hole in the road, but righted herself without slowing. Round the corner, she dived up a narrow alleyway to her right and the next one on her left, crisscrossing, desperate to find a way out, but every turn just seemed to take her deeper into the forest of houses.

The streets were growing narrower and darker, the buildings taller and more rickety; the people she passed were more sharp-faced and beady-eyed. Her breathing was so hard she could taste blood at the back of her throat, so loud that it masked the sounds around her. She knew she could not keep going, that she was spent. She dodged into another narrow street on her right and shrank back against the wall, closing her eyes and gasping air into her lungs. Her side ached like the stab of a knife blade with every breath.

There was no sound of the highwayman's footsteps. No sound of anything except the distant hum of everyday life and her own panting breath. She had lost him. She had escaped. She breathed her relief.

And then the scent of tobacco smoke drifted to her

nose and Marianne knew that she was not alone. She opened her eyes and looked around her. A little further up the street, three men lounged completely motionless against the fronts of the houses. Their clothing was all browns and greys, merging with the stonework of the buildings. Two sucked on long thin clay pipes. All three watched her with sharp hungry faces.

And for all that Marianne had sought to escape the highwayman, she knew these men were different. They would give her no assurances. Their fight was not with her father.

Her stomach dipped with dread. She made no sudden movement, even though every muscle was primed and tensed to flee. She glanced to her right towards the mouth of the street. Another two men were taking up the breadth of it, silent in their drab dirty clothes, and blocking her exit. There was a hollow sickness in her stomach and her heart was pounding in the base of her throat. She looked to her left, wondering if she stood a chance of running past the men, but a thinfaced man with a scar down his cheek was watching from the shelter of the close and another man, a great big bear of a man, was sitting on the step. And she was afraid, more desperately afraid than ever. Moving slowly, calmly, as if they were a pack of wolves, she edged away from the wall.

The thin-faced man stepped out of the close into the narrow street and it seemed to be a signal, for the other men moved to gather behind his lead.

She took her chance and whirled, trying to dodge past the two that guarded the exit of the street, but there was no way past them and she was forced back.

'Don't be in such a hurry to leave,' one of them said. 'There's plenty of fun to be had for a pretty lit-

tle thing like you.' She saw his eyes rake her body
before returning to rest upon her face. He licked his
lips slowly, meaningfully, with a fur-coated tongue.
Marianne glanced behind her at the advancing group
of men.

'No way out, darlin',' said the man who had spoken before. 'Smile at me and I'll be gentle with you.'
And he laughed.

She knew what they were going to do to her. She
knew, and there was nothing that she could do to stop
them. Nothing was going to stop them. She opened
her mouth to scream—and then she saw the tall dark
figure step into the mouth of the street.

Chapter Three

Marianne knew it was the highwayman, but he was alone and there were seven men around her. He walked forwards and the expression of darkness and ferocity on his face made her stomach flip. The ruffians began to close with eagerness upon him, but he did not hesitate, just kept on walking.

One of the villains gave a mocking laugh. 'You think we're scared because you're wearing a bleedin' mask?'

She did not hear the highwayman's answer. There was only the sickening sound of bone crunching against bone and the villain laughed no more. A hand closed tight around her upper arm and the thin-faced man looked down into her face.

'Unhand me!' She struggled to free herself, but the thin-faced man only smirked at her efforts.

She could not see the highwayman properly, but she could hear every fist that landed, could hear the grunts and the gasps and the curses from the ruffians. There was such menace about him that it made that of the villains pale to insignificance. The men before him seemed to crumple. One was thrown against a wall,

slithering down to lie in a limp and bloodied heap. Another turned tail and ran away. She had never seen such power, such strength, such utter ruthlessness. It shook her to the very core. And it shook the thin-faced man too. With a snarl of disgust he gestured the biggest, heaviest-set of his men towards the highwayman. The villain was a giant of a man, his fists huge and scarred, and as Marianne watched he slipped a wicked-looking hunting knife from his pocket.

'Come on, darlin', me and you've got some business together. Fitz'll take care of the distraction.' The thin-faced man manhandled her towards the mouth of the close.

'No!' She struggled against him, straining for release, and her eyes met the highwayman's across the carnage just for a moment. Something passed between them, something she did not understand. He was her enemy and yet he was also her only hope. He was different from the men in the rookery. He was different from any man that she had ever seen. His gaze shifted to focus on the men between them. She watched it harden, and darken, and she shivered just to see it. She stared in awe, wanting both to run to, and away from him. The thin-faced man's fingers bit all the harder into her arm as he wrenched her so roughly that she lost her footing and went down on her knees. He yanked her up and dragged her towards the building in which she had first seen him. And behind her she could hear the sounds of the fight intensify.

They were just inside the close when the scream pierced the air. A scream of pain and of terror. A scream that made her scalp prickle and her blood run cold. Then there was silence. She strained her neck and saw the big villain lying curled on the ground

sobbing like a baby. And the highwayman was still coming: relentless, unstoppable.

Knight saw Marianne Winslow being dragged towards a house by a thin-faced man. Her eyes were fixed on his and in that moment he saw her with all of her armour and pretence stripped away: her soul, bared in such honesty, and vulnerable. She was not Misbourne's daughter now, but a woman in her own right—one who was in grave danger because of him. He felt the extent of her fear, felt her unspoken plea reach in and touch him in a place he had thought lost long ago. Something inside him seemed to boil up and spill over. There were two men between him and Marianne. Knight knew that time was running out.

'Come on then, mate,' taunted the stockier of the two. 'Show us what you've got.' The black-toothed ruffian moved his fingers in a beckoning gesture. 'We don't fight with Queensbury rules he—'

Knight smashed his fist as hard as he could into the ruffian's nose. The man dropped and did not get up.

The sole remaining villain was backing away with his hands raised in surrender. 'You can 'ave 'er.' The man's face was pale beneath the grime. 'Just don't hit me, mate.' A telltale wet patch spread across the fall of the man's trousers as he spoke. Knight hit him anyway and kept on moving into the close.

From above came the sounds of the struggle. A door slammed, muffling the sounds. He took the stairs two at a time, up to the first floor, hearing the struggle grow louder as he ran. He kicked open the door and saw Marianne backed against the wall watching in terror while, in the middle of the room, the villain unfastened his trousers. Both faces shot round to him.

'What the hell…?' The villain scrabbled at the open fall of his trousers, his shifty grey eyes taking in Knight's highwayman clothes and the kerchief that still masked his face. 'Piss off and get your own.'

'She's mine,' said Knight.

'This is my territory—that makes her mine.' The thin-faced man pulled a razorblade from the pocket of his jacket and brandished it at Knight. 'Now piss off. Three's a crowd.'

'I agree.' But instead of retreating, Knight walked straight for the man. His left hand caught the wrist that swiped the razor at Knight's neck; his right grabbed the back of the half-mast breeches and, before the villain could react, ran him headlong out of the window.

When he turned back to Marianne she had not moved one inch; just stood there frozen, spine against the wall.

'You killed him,' she whispered.

He let the lethality fade from his face. 'I doubt it. We're only one floor up. Probably just broke a few bones.' He paused. 'Did he hurt you?'

Her gaze clung to his. 'No.'

Thank God!

Her voice was quiet and calm, but her face was pale as death and he could see the shock and fear that she had not yet masked in her eyes.

Someone outside started to scream.

'We have to leave here. Now.'

But she still made no move, just stared at him as if she could not believe what was happening.

'Lady Marianne,' he pressed, knowing the urgency of their predicament. He took hold of her arm and together they ran from the room.

* * *

The kitchen of Knight's house in Craven Street was warm and empty save for the two men that sat at the table. The stew that Callerton had prepared earlier was still cooking within the range, its aroma rich in the air. There was the steady slow tick from the clock fixed high on the wall between the windows. The daylight was subdued through the fine netting that Callerton had fitted across the window panes, lending the room an air of privacy.

'You were out of sight by the time I got out of there. And I knew you wouldn't go back to the room,' Callerton said. He unstoppered the bottle of brandy sitting on the scrubbed oak of the kitchen table between them and poured some into each of the two glasses.

Knight gave a nod. They both knew the arrangements if something went wrong.

'How is she?'

'She's resting.'

'You got to her in time?'

Knight gave another nod. 'Just.' Marianne Winslow's virtue had hung by a thread within that rookery. He wondered what he would have done had he not arrived in time. Killed the blackguard in the room with her. Blamed himself for all eternity.

'Thank God for that.' Callerton downed his brandy in one. 'You've got to give her back.'

He knew that. He also knew that he had come too far and could not give up Misbourne's daughter just yet. 'That's what Misbourne's banking on. We keep her…for now.' In his mind he could still see those dark eyes of hers, holding his with such brutal honesty, and the look in them that would not leave him.

Callerton rubbed at his forehead. His face was

creased with concern. 'The letter he sent is from the
right date. And it's definitely something that Misbourne would not want towncried. You're sure it's
not the right one?'

'Positive.' He did not let himself think of the woman.
This was about Misbourne. It had always been about
Misbourne.

Callerton grimaced and shook his head. 'It doesn't
make sense. Why give us something we could use
against him if it's the wrong document?'

'Maybe he's testing us to see if we know the right
document.'

'And once he knows there's no hoodwinking us he'll
give us the genuine article.'

'There's only one way to find out.'

'How do we send him the message?'

'Remember the night before Viemero?'

Callerton raised his brows. 'You're not serious?'

'Never more so.'

'It's too risky!'

'It will show him that we mean business.'

'Aye, it'll do that, all right.' Callerton played with
his empty glass. 'But I wouldn't want to be in your
boots tonight.'

Knight grinned. 'Liar.'

Callerton laughed.

Within the darkened bedchamber that was her
prison Marianne stood by the mantelpiece and stared
into the flame of her single candle. The shutters were
secured across the windows and despite the chill of
the early evening, no fire had been lit upon the hearth.

The thoughts were running through her head, con-
stant and whirring. Of the highwayman in the rookery.

Of their journey back to the shuttered room. It seemed like a daze, like something she had dreamt. She knew only that the highwayman's arm had been strong and protective around her and that the villains lurking in the shadows of the narrow streets had watched him with wary eyes and had not approached. No one had moved except to scuttle out of their way. Her family and her servants had always provided a barrier between her and anyone who did not move in her own small, vetted circle, but this was different. This was like nothing she had ever experienced. Men looked at the highwayman with a curious mix of hostility and deference, women with a specific interest they made no effort to hide. He had intruded into their world, snatched her right from their grasp. They had not liked it, but not one of them had moved to stop him.

He had kept her moving at a steady pace, twisting and turning through the dark maze of narrow lanes until, eventually, the lanes had widened to streets and light had started to penetrate the gloom. The streets had grown busier, but no one had entered the space around Marianne and the highwayman; everywhere they went a path had opened up through the crowd before them. Even in her dazed state she had known the reason: they were afraid of him, every last one of them.

And by his side, Marianne Winslow, who for the past three years had been scared of her own shadow, Marianne Winslow, who had more reason than any to be afraid, had walked through the most dangerous rookery in London, past villains and thieves, unscathed and unafraid. She was still reeling from it, still seeing the different way they looked at her because she was with him. And that sense of freedom, of power almost, obliterated the terror of the rookery.

She should have been shaking. She should have been sobbing and weeping with fear and with shock. She stared at the candle flame without even seeing it, knowing that the calm she felt was natural and not the result of counting her breaths and slowing them, or drinking a preparation of valerian. He was a man more dangerous than any other, yet with him she had felt safe. It made no sense.

The flame began to flicker wildly. Her attention shifted to the tiny stub of candle that remained and she knew it would not last much longer.

She lifted the candlestick and, holding it high, glanced around the bedchamber. It was a woman's room, but one that was not used, if the quiet, sad atmosphere was anything to judge by. The walls appeared a yellow colour and were hung with a few small paintings. A large still life, depicting an arrangement of exotic flowers, was positioned on the wall above the mantelpiece. She crossed the floor to search the dressing table. There was a vanity set, bottles of perfume, jars of cream and cosmetics, a box of hairpins, a casket of jewellery and two candelabra, both of which were empty. None of the drawers held any candles. She glanced towards the bed—large and four-postered, its covers and pillows a faded pale chintz, the colour of which was indefinable in the candlelight. At one side was a small chest of drawers and on the other a table. Neither held any candles. Nor did the small bookcase. There was nothing behind the gold-chinoiserie dressing screen in the corner. The candle stub guttered, making the flame dance all the wilder and the wick burn all the faster and the first snake of fear slithered into her blood.

Her fingers scrabbled at the shutters closed across

the window and found the catch, but no amount of prising would release it. It took her a few minutes to realise that they had been secured with nails.

There were two doors within the bedchamber: one in the wall against which the head of the bed rested, and the other to the left, opposite the window. She hurried to each one in turn, trying the locks, twisting and pulling at the handles. But both were locked, confirming what she feared—that she was trapped in here, with nothing to do save wait for the candle to extinguish. The knowledge made her stomach knot.

She had been safe in the rookery with him, but this was different. Now she was his prisoner. Alone in a bedchamber. And she knew how dangerous he was and how very angry he was with her father for not delivering the mysterious document. But her mind flickered back to what would happen when the candle burned out. He had said she had nothing to fear from him. She glanced again at the candle. It should have been the highwayman that terrified her, but it wasn't. She closed her eyes and counted her breaths, slowing them as she ever did when she was afraid, making them deeper to allay the mounting panic. And when she had calmed herself, she knew what she was going to have to do.

'All done.' Callerton finished brushing the last speck of dust from the shoulder of Knight's midnight-blue tailcoat.

'The boy should have delivered the note to Misbourne by now. We'll—' The banging started before Knight could finish the words. He raised an eyebrow. 'What the hell...?'

'It sounds like she's using a battering ram against the door,' said Callerton. 'Do you want me to tie her up?'

Knight shook his head. 'I'll deal with Lady Marianne.'

'You're due at Devlin's for dinner in five minutes.'

'Then I'll be late; Devlin will expect nothing else. It pays to cultivate a habit of unreliability. Besides, I've no stomach for the after-dinner entertainment.'

'More lightskirts?'

'He's hired Mrs Silver's girls for the night.'

'Again?'

'Again,' said Knight.

Callerton gave a whistle. 'You'll be late back, then.'

Knight scowled at the prospect. 'I'll have to make a show of it, but I'll be back in time.'

'Most men would love a chance to play the rake. Come to think of it, most men would be living the dream rather than faking it.'

'I'm not most men.'

'No, you're not,' agreed Callerton more quietly. 'Most men would have left me to die in Portugal.'

The two men looked at one another, feeling all of the past there in the room with them. The only sound was of something being thudded hard against wood, coming from above.

'We'll get him,' said Callerton.

'Damn right we'll get him. And in the meantime I'll silence his daughter.' Knight slipped the black silken mask from his pocket, tied it around his face, grabbed a branch of candles and strode up the stairs.

The ivory-and-tortoiseshell hairbrush splintered into three from the force of being hammered against the door. Marianne threw it aside and continued her assault with her fists and her feet, not caring about the pain.

The panic was escalating and she feared that she would not be able to keep a rein on it for much longer if he did not come soon. She banged at the door so hard that her blood pounded through her hands and she could feel bruises starting to form. She glanced round at the mantelpiece and the dying candle upon it. The light was already beginning to ebb. Soon it would be gone. Her stomach turned over at the thought. She bit her lip and banged all the harder.

She did not hear his footsteps amidst the noise. The lock clicked and then he was there in the bedchamber with her.

'Lady Marianne.' His half-whisper was harsher than ever. 'It seems you desire my company.' He stood there, holding the branched candlestick aloft, and the flickering light from the candles sent shadows darting and scuttling across the walls. His brows were drawn low in a stern frown and the shadows made him seem taller than she remembered, and his shoulders broader. He was dressed in expensive formal evening wear: a dark tailcoat, white shirt, cravat and waistcoat, and dark pantaloons. Beside all of which, the mask that hid his face looked incongruous. No ordinary highwayman.

'My candle is almost spent.' Her pride would let her say nothing more. She glanced across to the mantelpiece where the lone candle spluttered.

'It is.' He made no move, just looked at her. His gaze dropped to the broken hairbrush that lay on the floor between them. 'Not very ladylike behaviour.'

'Highway robbery, assaulting my father and abducting me on the way to my wedding are hardly gentlemanly.'

'They are not,' he admitted. 'But as I told you before, I am what your father made me.'

She stared at him. 'What has my father ever done to you? What is all of this about?'

He gave a hard laugh and shook his head. 'Have I not already told you?'

'Contrary to what you believe, my father is a good man.'

'No, Lady Marianne, he is not.' There was such ferocity in his eyes at the mention of her father that she took a step backwards and, as she did, her foot inadvertently kicked a large shard of the handle so that it slid across the floor, coming to a halt just before the toes of his shoes.

She saw him glance at it, before that steady gaze returned to hers once more. 'My mother's hairbrush.'

She looked down at the smashed brush, then back up at the highwayman and the fear made her stomach turn somersaults. She swallowed. 'Does she know that her son is a highwayman who has terrorised and robbed half of London?'

'The newspapers exaggerate, Lady Marianne. I have terrorised and robbed six people and six people only, your father amongst them.'

Her heart gave a stutter at his admission.

'And my mother is dead,' he added.

She glanced away, feeling suddenly wrong-footed, unsure of what to say.

He carried on regardless. 'Were you trying to beat the door down to escape or merely destroy my possessions?'

'Neither,' she said. 'I wished to…' she hesitated before forcing herself on '…to attract your attention.'

'You have it now. Complete and undivided.'

She dared a glance at him and saw that his eyes were implacable as ever.

'What is it that you wish to say?'

The smell of candle smoke hit her nose and she peered round at the mantelpiece to see only darkness where the candle had been. A part of her wanted to beg, to plead, to tell him the truth. But she would almost rather face the terror than that. Almost. She experienced the urge to grab the branch of candles from his hand, but she did not surrender to the panic. Instead, she held her head up and kept her voice calm.

'All of the candlesticks are empty.'

His gaze did not falter. She thought she saw something flicker in his eyes, but she did not understand what it was. He stepped forwards.

She took a step back.

He looked into her eyes with that too-seeing look that made her feel as if her soul was laid bare to him, as if he could see all of her secrets, maybe even the deepest and darkest one of all. She knew she should look away, but she did not dare, for she knew that all around them was darkness.

The silence hissed between them.

'I would be obliged if you would fill them. All of them.' She forced her chin up and pretended to herself that she was speaking to the footman in her father's house, even though her heart was thudding nineteen to the dozen and her legs were pressed tight together to keep from shaking.

His eyes held a cynical expression. He turned away and headed for the door, taking the branch of candles with him. She heard the darkness whisper behind her.

'No! Stop!' She grabbed at his arm with both hands to stop him, making the candles flicker wildly. 'You cannot…' She manoeuvred herself between him and

the door, trying to block his exit, keeping a tight hold of him all the while.

His gaze dropped to where her fingers clutched so tight to the superfine of his coat sleeve that her knuckles shone white, then back to her face.

She felt her cheeks warm and let her hands fall away. 'Where are you going, sir?' She was too embarrassed to meet his gaze. Her heart was racing hard enough to leap from her chest and she felt sick.

He raised his brows. 'I may be mistaken, but I thought you requested candles. I was going to have my man bring you some.'

Her eyes flickered to the branch of candles in his hand, then to the darkness that enclosed the room beyond. 'But…' The words stopped on her lips. She did not want to say them. She could not bear for him to know. Yet the darkness was waiting and she knew what it held. She felt the terror prickle at the nape of her neck and begin to creep across her scalp.

'Lady Marianne.'

Her gaze came back to his, to those rich warm amber eyes that glowed in the light of his candles. *Please*, she wanted to say, wanted to beg. Already she could feel the tremor running through her body. But still she did not yield to it, not in front of him. She shook her head.

'If I were to leave the candles here…'

'Yes,' she said, and the relief was so great that she felt like weeping. 'Yes,' she repeated and could think of nothing else. The highwayman passed her the branch of candles. Her hand was trembling as she took it; she hated the thought that he might see it, so she turned away. 'Thank you,' she added and sank back into the

room, clutching the candles tight to ward away the darkness.

There was silence for a moment, then the closing of the door and the sound of his footsteps receding.

She stared at the flicker of the candle flames and thought again that, in truth, he was no ordinary highwayman.

The clock in the corner on the mantelpiece chimed midnight. Misbourne left his son and his wife in the drawing room and made his way to his study. He needed time to think, needed space away from his wife's incessant weeping, because his heart was filled with dread and his stomach churning with fear over the gamble he had taken.

'Had he released her she would be here by now,' Linwood had whispered and Misbourne knew that his son was right. Yet he could not admit it, even to himself. He needed a brandy to calm his nerves. He needed time to gather his strength and hide his fears.

But everything changed when he opened the door to his study. For there, on the desk that he had left clear, lay two pieces of paper like pale islands floating on the vast sea of dark polished mahogany. One was a smooth-cut sheet of writing paper, and the other was a crushed paper ball. His heart faltered before rushing off at a gallop. He hurried across the room to the desk. The writing paper bore his own crest, but it was not his hand that had penned those three bold letters and single word.

IOU Misbourne.

The ink glistened in the candlelight. His hand was shaking as he touched a finger to it and saw its wetness smear. He whirled around, knowing that the words

had only just been written. Behind him the curtains swayed. He wrenched them open, but there was no one there. The window was up and the damp scent of night air filled his nose. He leaned his hands on the sill, craning his head out, searching the night for the man who had the audacity to walk right into his home to leave the message. But not a single one of the lamp posts that lined the road had been lit. The street was dark and deserted. Not a figure stirred. Not a dog barked. And of the highwayman there was no sign.

He knew what the crumpled ball of paper was before he opened it. The letter he had sent to the highwayman. A letter that could have been used against Misbourne. A letter that could cost him much in the wrong hands. Crumpled as if it were worthless. The villain knew what the document was. He knew, and there was only one man left alive with that knowledge. Misbourne felt sick at the thought. It was everything he had guarded against. Everything he had prayed so hard to prevent. He shut the window and closed the curtains, knowing it would do little good; the highwayman had been in his home, the one place that should have been safe.

He filled a glass with brandy, sat behind his desk and drank the strong warming liquid down. His eyes never left the words written upon the paper. Misbourne was more afraid than he had ever been, both for himself and for Marianne. He knew there was only one thing to do when the highwayman next made contact. *If* the highwayman next made contact.

Chapter Four

Marianne sat perched on the edge of the bed. The fire that the highwayman's accomplice had set last night had long since burned away to nothing and the air was cool. The early morning light seeped through the cracks of the window shutters, filtering into the bedchamber. The bed was only slightly rumpled where she had lain awake all night on top of the covers. She had not climbed within the sheets, nor had she worn the nightclothes that the accomplice had left neatly folded upon the dressing table. She had not even removed her shoes.

It had been the first night in almost three years that Marianne had spent alone. And she had barely slept a wink. All night she had waited. All night she had feared. But the highwayman had not come back to hurt her. Instead, he had filled the room with candles to light the darkness of the night. Eventually, as night had turned to dawn, her fear had diminished and all she could think of was the highwayman in the rookery and the look in his eyes as they had met hers. She thought of the villains quailing before him, of the wary respect in their eyes, of how he had kept her safe.

He was tougher, stronger, more dangerous than any
villain. And she remembered how, last night, she had
physically accosted him, clutching at him in her panic,
even barring the door so that he would not leave. She
closed her eyes and cringed at the memory. He knew.
She had seen it in his eyes. Yet he had not said one
word of her weakness, nor used it against her. She
slipped off her shoes and moved to sit on the rug in
the bright warmth of the narrow beam of sunshine.
And she thought again of the man with the hauntingly
beautiful amber eyes and the dark mask that hid his
face, and the strange conflict of emotion that was beating in her chest.

When Knight opened the door to the yellow bedchamber his heart skipped a beat. The words he had
come to say slipped from his mind. He stared and all
else was forgotten in that moment as he watched Marianne hurriedly rising from where she had been sitting
upon the floor. The room was dim, but small shafts
of sunlight were penetrating through the seams of the
closed shutters. She was standing directly in the line
of a thin ray of light so that it lit her in a soft white
light. There was an ethereal quality to her, so soft and
pale with such deep, dark, soulful eyes.

He realised he was staring and pulled himself together, entering the room and setting the breakfast tray
that he carried down on the nearby table. Her cheeks
were flushed and she looked embarrassed to have been
caught sitting in the sunbeam. His eyes dropped down
to the stockinged feet that peeped from beneath her
skirt, then travelled slowly up the wedding dress, all
crumpled and creased from sleep, to the smooth swell
of breasts that rose from the tight press of the bodice.

Her hair was a tumble of white-blonde waves over her shoulders, so long that it reached almost to her waist. She looked as beautiful and dishevelled as if she had just climbed from a lover's bed.

His gaze reached her face and he met the darkness of her eyes with all of their secrets and steadfast resilience. And that same ripple of desire he had experienced when he first looked at her whispered again. He closed his ears to it, denied its existence. Her blush intensified beneath his scrutiny and she stepped away, twitching at her rumpled skirts and shifting her feet to try to hide her stockinged toes.

He wanted to ask her why a twenty-year-old woman was so terrified of the dark. It seemed much more than a spoiled girl's foible. He knew how hard she had fought to hide her fear from him, and were he to ask the question she would, no doubt, deny all and tell him nothing.

'From Pickering?' He gestured towards the heavy ornate pearls around her neck.

She nodded. 'You knew that I was on my way to be married before my father told you, didn't you?' Her eyes looked different today. Lighter, a rich brown, and the contempt had gone from them. Something of her armour was back in place, but he had a feeling she had not pulled down her visor. Her manner was still guarded, but less hostile than it had been.

'It is a society wedding of interest throughout the *ton*.' He shrugged as if it were nothing of significance and did not tell her that he had made it his business to know all there was to know of Misbourne, or that he had been waiting and watching these two months past for an opportunity to take her from her father.

'And yet still you held us up.' He could sense both her curiosity and her condemnation.

'You think me ruthless. And when it comes to your father I cannot deny it.'

'You should not have hurt him,' she said and he saw her eyes darken with the memory of what had happened upon the heath.

Yet he could not apologise. He could not say he regretted it. Or that he would not have done the same, or more, again. 'I regret that you had to witness such violence.'

'But you do not regret what you did.'

He shook his head. 'Your father deserved much more.' It was a harsh truth, but he would not lie to her.

She swallowed and something of the defensiveness slotted back across her face. No matter what he knew of Misbourne, he admired her loyalty to her father— the courage with which she stood up to a highwayman to defend the bastard so determinedly. His eye traced the fine line of her cheek, the fullness of her lips. He caught what he was doing and felt the muscle clench in his jaw. With a stab of anger he averted his gaze and began to walk away. She was Misbourne's daughter, for pity's sake! He should not have to remind himself.

'There were seven men in that alleyway,' she said in a low careful voice, 'and you are but one man, yet you did not use a pistol.'

Her words stopped him, but he did not look round. 'A pistol shot would have brought more of the rats from their holes.'

'Why did you help me?'

The question, so softly uttered, cut through everything else.

He turned then, and looked at her, at the tempta-

tion she presented: those eyes, so soft and dark as to beguile a man from all sense.

'Why would I not?'

'You hate my father.'

Hate was too mild a word to describe what he felt for Misbourne. He paused before speaking, before looking into the eyes that were so similar and yet so different to her father's. 'Regardless of your father, while you are with me I will keep you safe.'

Safe. It had been such a long time since Marianne had felt safe. There had been times that she had thought she would never feel safe again, no matter how well guarded and protected she was by her family. She studied his face. In the shaft of morning light his eyes were golden as a flame. He was a highwayman. He had beaten her father and abducted her. He was holding her prisoner her against her will. She had watched the most brutal of London's lowlife cower before him. He could be anyone behind that dark silken mask. But whoever he was, he had not used her ill, as he could have. He had brought her candles to light the darkness. And he had saved her. He had saved her—and he had bested seven men to do it.

She met his gaze and held it, looking deep into those amber eyes, trying to glean a measure of the man behind the mask. He was not lying. A man like him had no need to lie.

The expression in his eyes gentled. His hand moved as if he meant to touch her arm, except that he stopped it before it reached her and let it drop away.

'Are you all right?' he asked.

She stared up into his face and could not look away. And the highwayman held her gaze.

'Yes,' she said at last and nodded. 'I am fine.' She

had said those words so many times in the past three years, but only this time, standing there in a shuttered bedchamber with a masked man who had abducted her, was she close to telling the truth. 'The letter that you think my father holds.'

He gave no response.

'I know you believe he understands…' She saw the flicker of something dangerous in his eyes, but it did not stop her. 'Will you ask him again and tell him exactly what it is that you seek?'

'I have already done so.'

She gave a nod and relaxed at his words. 'I heard you and your accomplice talking about a document… He will give it to you this time.' Her father would give whatever it took to redeem her. 'I will stake my life upon it.'

The highwayman said nothing. He just looked at her for a moment longer and then walked away, leaving her locked alone in the bedchamber.

Five minutes later Marianne heard the thud of the front door closing and the clatter of a horse's hooves trotting away from the house. She knew that it was the highwayman leaving. The accomplice's footsteps sounded on the stairs; she heard him come along the passageway and go into a nearby room. There was the noise of cupboards and drawers being opened and closed, then the accomplice unlocked her door, knocking before entering.

'If you will come this way, my lady, I am under instruction to show you to another room in which you might spend the day. One in which the shutters are not closed.'

He took her to the bedchamber on the opposite side

of the passageway. The daylight was light and bright and wonderful after the dimness of the yellow chamber. She blinked, her eyes taking an age to adjust. The walls were a cool blue, the bedding dark as midnight and the furniture mahogany and distinctly masculine in style. Over by the basin she could see a shaving brush, soap and razor blade, all set before a mirror, and she knew whose bedchamber this was without having to be told. Her heart began to pound and butterflies flocked in her stomach. She hesitated where she was, suddenly suspicious.

Something of the apprehension must have shown in her face for all she tried to hide it, for the accomplice smiled gently, reassuringly.

'He thought you would prefer the daylight. The sun hits the back of the house in the afternoon.' He paused for a moment. 'You need not have a fear, lass. I am to take you back to the yellow chamber before he returns.'

She looked round at the accomplice and the grey mask loosely tied to obscure his face. 'Could you not simply have removed the nails from the shutters?'

'No, Lady Marianne.' The accomplice glanced away uneasily.

'Because it is at the front of the house,' she guessed, 'and you fear that I would attract attention?'

'It is rather more complicated than that. The shutters must remain closed. Those in the master bedchamber too.'

'The yellow bedchamber...' She hesitated and thought of the hairbrush. 'It was his mother's room, was it not?'

The accomplice gave a hesitant nod.

'And this is his house.'

He looked uncomfortable but did not deny it. 'I must go,' he said and started to move away.

'You said he was a good man.'

The accomplice halted by the door. 'He is.'

'What he did to my father on Hounslow Heath was not the action of a good man.'

'Believe me, Lady Marianne, were he a lesser man, your father would be dead. Were I in his shoes, I don't know that I could have walked away and left Misbourne alive.' He turned away, then glanced back again to where she stood, slack-jawed and gaping in shock. 'For your own sake, please be discreet around the window. Being seen in a gentleman's bedchamber, whatever the circumstances, would not be in any young unmarried lady's favour.'

He gave a nod of his head and walked away, locking the door behind him.

What had her father ever done to deserve the hatred of these men? Her legs felt wobbly at the thought of such vehemence. She needed to sit down. She eyed the four-poster bed with its dark hangings and covers—the highwayman's bed—and a shiver rippled down her spine, spreading out to tingle across the whole of her skin. She stepped away, choosing the high-backed easy chair by the side of the fireplace, and perching upon the edge of its seat.

Marianne glanced at the window behind her and the brightness of the daylight. The accomplice was right. Especially given it had been little more than a year since the Duke of Arlesford had broken their betrothal. The scandal surrounding it still had not completely died away. One word of her abduction, one word that she had spent the night in a bachelor's house without a chaperon—no matter that she was being held alone

in a locked room—and her reputation would be ruined to such an extent that none of her father's influences could repair it. The irony almost made her laugh. Especially when she contemplated the darkness of the truth. Even so, she rose to her feet and walked to the window.

The view was the same as that of a hundred other houses in London—long, neatly kept back gardens separated by high stone walls, backing on to more gardens and the distant rear aspect of yet more town houses, all beneath the grey-white of an English autumn sky. There were no landmarks that she recognised. The catch moved easily enough, but the window was stiff and heavy and noisy to open. She did not slide it up far. There was little point, for there was no hope of escape through it. The drop below was sheer and at least twenty-five feet. She closed the window as quietly as she could and turned to survey the room around her.

It was much smaller than the yellow bedchamber and almost Spartan in its feel. Aside from the bed there was a bedside cabinet upon which was placed a candle in its holder. Against the other walls stood a dark mahogany wardrobe, a wash-stand and a chest of drawers with a small peering glass and shaving accoutrements sitting neatly on top. A dark Turkey rug covered the floor, but there were no pictures on the wall, no bolsters or cushions upon the bed. There was no lace, no frills, nothing pretty or pale. It was the very opposite of Marianne's bedchamber at home. It was dark and serious and exuded an air of strength and utter masculinity, just like the man who owned it.

His presence seemed strong in the room, so strong that it almost felt like he was here. And she had the strangest sensation of feeling both unsettled and safe at once. Her blood was flowing a little bit too fast.

She needed to search the bedchamber, to discover any clue to the highwayman's identity that she might tell her father when she got home. So she turned the key within the tall polished wardrobe and the door swung open. Sandalwood touched to her nose, a faint scent but instantly recognisable as the highwayman. Goosebumps prickled her skin and a shiver passed all the way through her body. There was something attractive, something almost stimulating about his scent. The rails were heavy with expensive tailored coats and breeches, undoubtedly the clothing of a gentleman, and a wealthy one at that if the cut and quality of material were anything to judge by. It did not surprise her for, despite his disguise, she had known almost from the first that he was no ruffian.

Check the pockets, she heard the voice of common sense whisper in her ear. She reached out her hand, then hesitated, holding her breath, suddenly very aware of where she was and what she was doing. Slowly she touched her fingers to the shoulder of the nearest tail-coat.

The midnight-blue wool felt as smooth and expensive as it looked. Her eyes scanned the breadth of the shoulders. She let her fingers trace all the way down one lapel and it felt as daring as if she were stroking a tiger, as daring as if the highwayman was still wearing the coat. That thought made her heart skip a beat. She slid her hands within, checking the inside for hidden pockets, skimming down the tail to the pocket that was there, but nothing was to be found in any of them. She checked each coat in turn; the feel of his clothing beneath her fingers and the scent of him in her nose made her heart thud all the harder and her blood rush all the faster as she remembered the strength and hardness of

the arm she had gripped so frantically last night and the weight of his hand around her arm in the rookery. And she wondered if this was what it would feel like to lay her hand against his shoulder, his lapel, his chest…

She gave a shaky laugh at the absurdity of her own thoughts. She did not like men, especially those who were dangerous. She closed the wardrobe door and, quietly and systematically, began to search the rest of the room.

The soap in the dish held the scent of sandalwood. She touched his badger-hair shaving brush and the handle of his razorblade, wondering that he had left such a weapon at her disposal. But then she remembered him in the rookery and knew that he had nothing to be afraid of. And another shiver rippled all the way from the top of her head down to the tips of her toes.

Everything was neat and tidy, everything in its place. Waistcoats, shirts, a pile of pressed linen cravats…and a black-silk kerchief. She hesitated, feeling strange to see it folded and pressed so neatly within the drawer. It seemed so harmless, so inconsequential, unlike the man who wore it.

There were two pairs of riding boots and three pairs of black slippers—all large. She did not look through his unmentionables, only closed the drawer so quickly that she wondered if his accomplice had heard the noise. Then she sat herself down in the easy chair by the fireplace, properly this time, and considered what she had gleaned of the highwayman from his room and possessions.

He was a gentleman, tall and broad-shouldered and strong. A man who wore a black-silk kerchief across his face. A man from whom one glance made her shiver, and of whom his scent alone made her heart beat too

fast. A man for whom she felt both wariness and fascination. Nothing in the room had told her anything more than she already knew.

Knight did not return to his town house until dinnertime that night.

'Did you win?' Callerton asked, serving up the stew he had prepared.

'Your money's safe,' replied Knight.

'Nice to know I made a bob or two without leaving the house.' Callerton grinned. 'Shouldn't Rafe Knight, gentleman and rake, be out celebrating his victory?'

'They have arranged an outing to a gaming hell tonight.'

Callerton screwed his face up.

'If I don't go there'll be questions. And we don't want questions.'

Callerton shook his head. 'Especially not this night.'

'Is Lady Marianne in the yellow bedchamber?'

'Took her back through at four just to be on the safe side. Thought I heard her having a rummage earlier in the day, but there was nought for her to find. I made sure of that before I put her in there.'

Knight gave a nod of gratitude. She had not succumbed to tears or tantrums. With a calm logic, of which he himself would have been proud, she had undertaken a search of his room.

'Been a long time since you had a woman in that bedchamber.'

A vision of Marianne sprawled naked in his bed popped into his mind, her blonde hair splayed across his pillows, her bare breasts peeping from between the rumpled sheets to tease and torture him. He pushed

the image away and clenched his jaw, knowing that he could not afford to think of her in that way.

'Maybe too long.' Definitely too long if he was having inappropriate thoughts about Misbourne's daughter. He forced his mind to think of tomorrow and all that lay ahead. Once Misbourne gave him the document he would not see her again. And that could only be a good thing. He would not allow his thoughts to stray to her again.

'Let us run through the plan again. We'll not have another chance. And then we'll send the boy with the meeting place and time to Misbourne so that he has not enough time to think up anything clever.'

Callerton gave a nod. 'Even Misbourne isn't bastard enough to risk his daughter a second time.'

'I hope you're right,' Knight replied, unrolling the crudely drawn map. For his own sake, and for Marianne Winslow's. He did not wish to consider what he would do if they were wrong.

The two men bent over the map and began to talk in earnest.

The morning was still dark when the highwayman's accomplice led Marianne out of the back door and across a few streets. They travelled on foot, keeping to the mews and alleyways, so that she did not recognise where they were or the direction they took. In a narrow alley that ran down the side of what looked to be a hospital building, a black coach was waiting. They hurried over to it and she thought they meant to climb inside, but the coachman jumped down and she saw that it was the highwayman in his greatcoat and hat. His accomplice climbed up to take his place.

'God keep you safe, friend,' he said to the high-wayman.

'And you,' replied the highwayman and glanced to the sky. 'Dawn is breaking. It should be light enough by the time I am seen being trundled home three sheets to the wind.'

The accomplice nodded and with a flick of the reins was gone, leaving Marianne standing alone with the highwayman.

'Are you ready, Lady Marianne?' he asked.

She nodded, and he took her arm and guided her out on to the street. There was the smell of a dye house in the air. The houses were small and a little shabby, but this was not some rookery, and even if it had been she felt safe with the highwayman by her side. Ironic, she thought, but true.

They did not speak, just walked in silence. Even though the hour was early, the air stirred; London was awakening. A cart rattled by and two dodgy-looking characters passed from whom she averted her gaze. She was glad of the highwayman's proprietorial grip on her arm.

They kept a steady pace heading onwards. It was only when they passed the great church that she re-alised they were going to the burying ground.

He led her through the gate and wove a path through the stones that marked the graves of the dead. The wind that howled across the ground was sharp, nipping at her cheeks and catching her hair, blowing strands of it across her eyes. Overhead, the sky was grey and dis-mal and the air ripe with dampness and the promise of rain. They walked on, their pace so brisk that she found herself slightly out of breath, walked on until they reached the larger stones and monuments erected

by the wealthy. And then, quite suddenly, he led her behind a tiny mausoleum built in the style of a classical temple, the stonework of which was blackened by age and the smoke from London's chimneys.

'This is the place,' he murmured, sliding a hand inside his greatcoat to produce a pocket watch. He flipped open the casing and checked the time. 'Ten minutes,' he said and the watch disappeared from sight once more.

Ten minutes and then she would be free. Ten minutes and all of this would be over. She would be back with her father and she would never see the highwayman again. Never know who he was behind that mask. She leaned back against the wall of the mausoleum and watched him.

'For what it is worth, I am sorry that you had to be a part of this, Lady Marianne. But you were the only way I could reach your father.' His eyes held a sincerity she had not expected to see.

'This document that you seek must be very important to you.'

'More important than you can imagine.'

'What is it?' She asked the question with little expectation of a reply.

He was silent for so long that she thought she had been right, but then he spoke. 'It is the answer to a question I have asked myself for these past fifteen years.'

'Fifteen years?' Such a long time. Yet his eyes, his voice, his body, the way he moved—none were those of an old man.

'June 1795,' he said.

'What happened on that date?' She saw the flicker of pain in his eyes, there, then gone so quickly and

replaced by such hard and utter ruthlessness that she felt shocked to see it.

'Ask your father the answer to that question, Lady Marianne, and see what he says.' That same half-whisper, harsher and angrier than ever.

'You are wrong about him,' she said. She did not know what lies the highwayman had been spun or why he had her father so wrong. All she knew was that she had to try, in these last few minutes they had together, to let him know the truth. 'He is the best of fathers. I know you will not believe me, but he is a good man.' She thought desperately of what she could say to convince him. 'He is a governor of the Foundling Hospital and, although he took great pains to see that it was kept secret, he contributed much of the money for its chapel to be built. He gives freely to the poor, to widows and orphans especially, yet he makes no show of his charity, and he—'

The highwayman gave a hard, harsh laugh of amusement and shook his head. 'The irony is not lost on me, Lady Marianne.'

'There is nothing of irony in what he has done.'

'Indeed? Foundlings and orphans!' In the space of a moment his eyes had darkened with the shadows that moved within them. 'He is your father. Defend him all you will, but not to my ears.'

She could feel the darkness that emanated from him, the barely suppressed anger tinged with bitterness. 'What is this hatred that drives you?'

'It is the desire for justice,' he whispered.

'More like vengeance for some imagined injustice.'

'There was nothing imagined about it.'

'What did he do to you?'

'He took from me that which was most precious.'

And she remembered the words he had spoken to her father upon the heath, before he had taken her.

'I don't understand,' she said.

'Neither do I.'

Their gazes held, locked, trapped in the moment. She could not have looked away, even had she wanted to. She stared at the tall dark highwayman with his great black coat flapping in the wind and the dark mask that hid his face, the very symbol of the villain he was. He was a man like none she had known. Strong, hard, ruthless. And yet…

The wind howled through the gravestones and the first drops of rain began to fall. Still they looked into each other's eyes, and the air was thick with a strange tension, like the unnatural calm before the storm, waiting for something she did not understand. She should have been more afraid of this man than any other. She felt that she was clinging to a great precipice, that her grip was slipping and she was beginning to slide inch by agonising inch towards the edge. And she knew what lay over that edge. She should have been grappling to regain her hold, but the edge was beckoning her closer and there was a part of her that found it dangerously alluring.

'Who are you behind that mask?' she whispered.

'Do you really want to know?' His voice was as quiet as hers as he stepped closer. She was surprised that she felt no compulsion to back away, even though her heart was pounding and every nerve in her body shivered. Her throat went dry, her mouth too. She wetted her lips and saw his gaze drop to them, before coming back to her eyes.

The tension wound tighter.

Another step forwards and they were standing so

close that, were she to inhale deeply, she would feel the graze of her chest against his. He did not touch her, yet her body tingled as if caressed by his very proximity.

'Marianne,' he whispered softly.

She looked up into his eyes and could see each golden striation within them, every dark lash that outlined them.

His face lowered towards hers and she knew that he was going to kiss her. And for one absurd moment she wanted him to do it. She wanted more than anything to feel his mouth against hers, even through the silk. And then she remembered, and stepped away.

Her breath was ragged as if she had been running and she was trembling so badly that she had to clutch her hands together so that he would not see it.

He did not come after her. He did not grab her or force his mouth upon hers. He just stood there and watched her. The wind blew and all was silent and cool aside from the thump of her heart and the scald of her cheeks. Her eyes met his once more.

A noise sounded from the other side of the mausoleum, making her start and breaking the tension between them. Part of her was relieved and another part dismayed.

Someone was making their way over the grass of the burying ground. With a tiny nod of acknowledgement to her, the highwayman turned away and went to meet whoever it was he was waiting for.

Marianne sagged back against the wall of the mausoleum. She did not understand what had just passed between her and the highwayman. But it did not matter, for the person on the other side of the tomb was bringing the document from her father. In a few moments she would be free and walking away from this.

A shot rang out, shattering the peace and silence of the place. She moved to peep round the side of the mausoleum and watched all hell break loose.

Chapter Five

'Run, governor!' the little lad yelled and began to run towards him. 'It's a trap!'

Knight saw three figures loom from behind the nearby gravestones and reacted even before he saw the first man take aim at the boy. He launched himself forwards, firing his pistol at the man as he scooped the boy up and ran for the nearest gravestone. The shot thudded into the other side of the stone as he dived behind.

'I'm sorry.' Smithy was white-faced, without a trace of his usual cocky bravado. 'They caught me. Held a pistol to my head and made me bring 'em here.'

'I understand,' Knight replied to the boy in a low voice. He knew the men would be creeping closer, knew, too, that it was him, not the boy, they were after. He reloaded his pistol and risked a brief glance round the edge. Another shot rang out and some fragments of stone crumbled to the grass on his left. 'Stay hidden,' he whispered, then dodged away through the gravestones towards the tall obelisk stone far enough away from the lad and the mausoleum. He could only hope that Marianne had the sense to remain out of sight.

The bullets rained in force, the shots deafening in the silence of the burying ground, the stench of the powder like rotten eggs all around. The wind of a bullet whistled close to his right ear as he ducked behind the obelisk.

'Don't just stand there! Get after him!' a rough voice yelled.

Knight reloaded the pistol again, smoothly and quickly, counting the seconds as the tread of boots crept closer. The first flicker of dark shadow to his right and Knight grabbed at the villain, wrenching the man in close and compressing the vulnerable area of his neck until he passed out. The body slid noiselessly to the grass.

'Where the hell did he go?' The villain's whisper told him where they were.

The bullets ceased. There was silence, and in the waiting he heard the howl of the wind and the beat of his own heart. He ran to his left, aiming for the next gravestone, firing as he went, and heard the yelp and the slump of a body as his bullet went home. He made it behind the stone before the pistol shot cracked against it, then moved again, crouching low through the stones, working his way round towards the last of the three villains.

A bullet thudded into grass before him, tearing up the turf. One villain remained, with two pistols. Two shots had been fired. Knight didn't give the blackguard time to reload, but broke cover and ran full tilt at him, slamming hard into him, taking him down. The man struggled, but Knight's fist stilled that; then he grabbed hold of the villain's throat and hoisted him up, pinning him against the nearest gravestone.

And then he saw Marianne.

'Get back!' he yelled but, as if oblivious to the danger, she ignored him and carried on walking until she had reached his side.

'Where is the document?' she asked the man.

'Marianne, do as I say.'

She glanced up at him and he saw, before she turned back to the man, that she did not yet understand what her father had done. 'I asked you a question, sir,' she said to the man.

'I don't know what you're talking about, lady.'

She shook her head. 'But…'

'Misbourne sent you,' Knight said to the man.

'Yes.'

'With the document,' said Marianne.

'To bring me in,' corrected Knight.

'No.' The man strained to shake his head.

Knight saw Marianne look pointedly up at him. 'You see,' she said, almost triumphantly.

'To kill you,' the villain said.

She paled.

'Then you had better run back and tell him that you failed.' Knight threw the man on to the grass, allowing him to scramble to his feet and back away.

From the corner of his eye Knight saw other dark shadows slinking between the gravestones. 'There are more of them. Take shelter behind the mausoleum, Marianne.'

'So that you may keep me prisoner?' She shook her head. 'I will not do that.' She edged away from him. 'They are from my father. They have come to free me.' And then she turned to run towards them just as the closest villain took aim.

It all happened so quickly. Marianne saw the man point the pistol straight at her. 'Do not shoot! I am

coming!' She saw the disregard on his face, saw the plume of blue smoke and heard the roar of the pistol, but the air was already being knocked from her lungs as something big and fast and dark threw her to the ground. A second pistol shot exploded, so close that it made her jump, but she could not see anything because the highwayman was on top of her, shielding her from the danger. In a heartbeat he had dragged her up and hauled her behind the nearest gravestone.

'Do not dare move from here,' he whispered with a ferocity no one in their right mind would ignore, then he was gone.

She stayed where he had left her, hugging her legs to her body, trying to calm the raggedness of her breathing while her mind reeled with the shock of what was happening and the knowledge that her father had not done the one simple thing that would have secured her release. He had sent men to kill the highwayman and they had almost killed her. None of it seemed real. Even though she had seen the man fire the pistol at her, there was a part of her mind that refused to believe it. It was all some horrible imagining. Yet the wind was cold in her face and she could feel the dampness from the rain seeping through the thinness of her shawl as she clutched it tight around her shoulders. She really was here, alive and unharmed—and there was only one reason for that: the highwayman.

She heard the sound of feet running and then a shout. Then the sound of fists, fighting, grunts of pain. Another pistol shot and she could smell the gunpowder in the wind and see the drift of smoke even through the rain. A man began screaming in agony and she prayed, *Please, God, don't let it be him.*

'You bast—!' someone shouted, but the words were

cut off and there came a thud of something hitting the ground hard.

Another shot. Then there was silence. A silence in which her breathing sounded too loud.

'Marianne.'

Suddenly he was there, reaching for her, helping her up, and she did not even think of drawing away.

'Are you all right?'

She nodded, not trusting herself to speak. Her gaze moved over the gravestone to the men that lay beyond. One was rolling around groaning and clutching at his lower trouser leg, which was soaked in blood. Three lay unmoving upon the ground. And another was slumped bleeding and lifeless on the steps that led down into the mausoleum. *Dead*, she thought and could not seem to move her eyes away from the grotesque sight.

'Marianne,' he said again, more softly this time.

She looked up into his eyes, at the fierceness and the urgency there. He was supposed to be the villain in all of this.

'Give me your hand.'

There was nothing she could say, no words that would come. She put her hand in his and followed him through the gravestones.

And as they left, Marianne glanced back to the ruffians that her father had sent, and the mausoleum beyond with the name of its occupant carved into the stone lintel above the door: EDMUND KNIGHT.

Knight headed towards the warehouses and timber yards, keeping to the shadows and the alleyways, alert and watchful. He kept a pistol in one hand, hiding it within the folds of his coat, and the other hand was

around Marianne's waist, both securing and supporting her. To avoid attracting attention he wrenched the
mask down from his face, letting it dangle around his
neck as if it were a neckerchief, but Marianne did not
seem to notice. Her eyes were dazed, her gaze fixed
ahead, although Knight doubted she was registering
much of her surroundings. Her face was so pale he
wondered if she was going to faint. He could not blame
her. He doubted most women, let alone one as indulged
and protected as Marianne, could have remained unaffected after being shot at and witnessing a fight so
brutal as to leave four men unconscious.

He glanced down at her dress, the dress that had
been intended for her wedding. Several of the bows
on the bodice were hanging by a thread. It was grubby
around the hem and the rain had dampened the skirt so
that it clung indecently to her legs. The fine lace shawl
wrapped around her had a rip in it and the ribbon with
which she had bound her hair was lost, leaving it long
and damp around her shoulders. Her appearance was
not so dissimilar to the women who surrounded them
in this part of town. She looked beautiful, abandoned,
wanton almost, except for her innocence and the vulnerability that she was no longer trying to hide. He held
her a little closer and knew that, whatever Misbourne
had done, his daughter did not deserve this.

Knight knew he could not risk heading home in
the daylight. There was a chance that Misbourne had
more men in the vicinity, that they were searching
for him even now. The last thing he wanted to do was
lead them to his house and his true identity. That, and
expose Marianne to more gunfire and violence. He
knew of an empty warehouse, which seemed the closest point of safety. And if Misbourne's ruffians were

on their tail they needed to get there fast. He guided her steadily towards it, unnoticed by those they passed as anything other than a man and his woman.

She had no idea where they were, other than that it was a dubious area of the city and that they were not so very far away from the church of St Luke's. The warehouse was large and almost derelict, but it provided shelter from the rain and from what they had left behind at the burying ground. The highwayman barricaded the door shut behind them and led her across the dust and rubble to lean her against a bare brick wall. She could see that the windows were small and almost as high as the roof, letting in light but showing nothing of the outside world other than the gunmetal-grey sky. Several of the panes had been broken or were missing. Pigeons nested in the exposed rafters, making soft cooing noises. One flew overhead, the flutter of its wings loud against the quiet drizzle of the rain against the roof, and sat watching them from a nearby ledge.

She did not look at him because she knew he was no longer wearing the mask. And she was afraid of what that meant…for her and for him. His hat dropped sodden to the floor and the rustle of his clothing sounded; from the corner of her eye she saw that he was taking off his greatcoat. He moved away to shake the water from it and then wrapped it around her shoulders.

She stood very still and focused on the buckskin of his breeches, the scuffed leather of his boots…anything rather than look at his face, even though it was the one place she really wanted to look. She felt suffocated by the tension. The knot in her stomach tightened. *He was unmasked.* And she knew more than anything in the world that she must not yield to the overriding tempta-

tion, swore to herself that she would not. Yet standing there alone with him in that warehouse, with his coat warm around her shoulders and the scent of sandalwood in her nose, she could not help herself. Despite every sensible thought screaming at her to resist, she slowly raised her head and looked up into the face of the highwayman.

However Marianne had imagined him to look, the reality stole the beat from her heart and the breath from her lungs. He was a man like none she had ever seen, a vision incomparable. Such dark masculinity that made her stomach flutter and tumble and her blood race so fast she thought she might faint. She stared and could not look away, her eyes ranging over the straight manly nose, the rugged angular jawline and square chin. Over the mouth that, even hidden, had tempted her to taste it and, now exposed, made her legs feel weak and her head dizzy. Desire seemed to whisper in the warehouse all around her. Attraction pounded through her veins with such explosive force that she felt herself tremble. She met those searing eyes that were so branded upon her memory and saw the amber in them darken. Her mouth went dry. She dropped her gaze, shocked at her response.

Her heart was beating faster than a horse at full gallop. She kept her gaze low, praying he had realised nothing of her reaction, hoping he did not see the heat that was glowing in her cheeks.

Her focus fixed on the dirty hem of her gown. But the deed had already been done. She had looked upon his face. She could identify him. Both of them knew it. Her fingers gripped tight against the sides of her skirt as she waited for him to react.

And then she saw the single crimson drop land upon

the pale silk of her skirt. There was a horrible sinking sensation in her stomach, for she knew what it was even before she raised her eyes to see the blood dripping from the fingers of his left hand, and the bright red stain that soaked the sleeve of his shirt. In that terrible moment everything else fell from her head.

'You are bleeding!' Her eyes shot to his.

'The bullet skimmed my arm.'

The bullet that had been meant for her. She stared at him, understanding fully for the first time what he had done.

He moved away to sit down, leaning his back against the red dusty bricks of the wall, and with his good hand began to unfasten his neckcloth.

'Let me help you,' she said and, shrugging off the greatcoat, she knelt by his side.

His gaze met hers. Then he let his hand drop away from the half-loosened knot of his neckcloth.

She leaned closer and, pushing aside the black-silk kerchief that still hung around his neck, her fingers finished what he had started. She unfastened the knot and unwound the linen strip from around his neck. In his highwayman's guise he was not wearing the fine dress shirts she had seen in his bedchamber, but something much cheaper and thinner through which she could see a hint of the flesh of his chest and the dark smattering of hair that covered it.

He made to take the neckcloth from her and their fingers collided, but she did not release the linen.

'I must bind the wound to stop it bleeding.' His voice was low, that same half-whisper even though the mask was no longer tied around his face. 'It is no sight for you, Marianne.' The linen was taut between their hands.

'Do you think I cannot face a little blood to help you?' In the rookery he had saved her from… She could not even think the word. And not half an hour ago, in the burying ground, he had saved her life.

'Most young women in your position would not offer to help me.'

'Then you should be glad that I am not like most young women,' she replied and thought of the terrible dark secret she was hiding.

'No, you are not, Marianne.' His gaze held hers and as she looked deep into his eyes she felt something shift between them. In her hand he yielded her the linen. Then he pulled a knife from within his boot and offered it, handle first, to her. 'You need to cut away the sleeve of my shirt.'

She looked at the blade and then up into his eyes. 'With such a weapon I could do a better job than the bullet.'

'You could,' he agreed, but the knife still lay upon his palm and she knew it was more than the knife he was offering her. Trust. It was such a fragile word. Power. It was not something she had ever known.

She looked at him a moment longer, then her fingers closed around the handle. The blade was sharp and wicked, and she wielded it with great care to cut away the thin linen sleeve of his shirt. With the skin exposed she could see the wound that gaped in the flesh of his upper arm and the glisten of the blood that leaked from it.

'Lay the sleeve flat upon the ground and check that where the bullet entered none of the material is missing.'

She did not understand the reason, but did as he instructed, smoothing out the blood-soaked linen, find-

ing the small gaping hole the bullet had made and
showing it to him. To her shock he pulled his injured
arm across his chest and began to poke his fingers
into the wound. She could see the way he gritted his
teeth against the pain; the blood flowed all the harder.

'What on earth are you doing?'

'The missing piece of shirt is within the wound. It
will fester if left there.'

'Allow me.'

'Marianne,' he growled.

'Are you afraid that I will hurt you?' she goaded.

'Perhaps.'

'I do not believe you. You do not fear anything.'

'We all have fears, Marianne.'

She felt the shadow of her past fall upon her. 'And
they always find us no matter how fast we run, or how
well we hide,' she muttered beneath her breath. But he
had heard her.

'Running from fear only makes it chase you. Hiding
from it only makes it seek you. You have to face fear.'

Their gazes locked and held just for a moment. Then
she took his injured arm within both her hands and
examined the red pulp of the groove the bullet's path
had cut through his skin. It was, as he had warned, not
a pleasant sight, but she did not allow herself to balk
from it. The metallic scent of blood was so heavy in the
air that she could taste it at the back of her throat. She
did not see the single scrap of bloodied linen at first.
Indeed, it no longer looked like linen, being dark red
and wet; only the edge of uneven threads made her realise what it was. She knew that it would hurt him. She
glanced up at his face and saw he was watching her.

He gave her a nod of encouragement.

She reached into the wound, feeling the muscles

tense slightly, and found the end of the linen scrap. She carefully picked it out, placing it on her palm and showing it to him.

'Open it out, fit it against the hole within the sleeve.'

And when she did, they could both see that it completed the sleeve—there was no more of the material within the wound.

Using the knife, she cut the neckcloth into strips, then took a clean pad of handkerchief from the pocket of her dress, pressed it gently to the wound and bound it in place with the strips, tying off the last of them so that it would not unravel.

'Thank you,' he said.

'You are welcome.'

The silence seemed suddenly loud within the damp chill of the warehouse.

Her father had not sent the document. The knowledge hung between them, although neither of them spoke it.

'What happens now?'

'We wait until nightfall so that we can cross the streets unseen.'

'And then?'

'And then you may go home to your father.'

Her eyes scanned his, searching for lies and trickery and finding none.

'There is much time to wait, Marianne. You might as well make yourself comfortable.' He gestured to the ground by his side. He was right. She sat down on the side of his good arm, leaning her back against the wall as he did.

'The day is chilled,' he said, and when he repositioned the coat so that it covered both their legs she did not stop him. Her dress was damp with rain and

when she breathed she could see the faint mist of her breath, yet she did not feel cold. Indeed, the side of her closest to him seemed to burn.

They sat in silence, their bodies so close, yet not touching.

She looked down at where their hands lay on top of his greatcoat. His, so very large, a man's hand, strong and capable, the fingers long and blunt, the knuckles grazed. Hers, so very small and pale in comparison. Both were stained with blood. His blood.

'You don't have to be afraid any more, Marianne.' He turned his right hand, the hand that was closest to her, over so that it was lying open and palm up.

And it seemed the most natural thing in the world to lay her hand upon his and feel the gentle close of his fingers.

They sat against the wall. Side by side, neither looking at the other.

They sat in silence, listening to the rain and the occasional distant sound of a bell tolling, and the howl of the wind through the roof. And the clouds moved across the sky, all the shades of grey and charcoal, racing so fast as to give her the illusion that she and the highwayman, not the clouds, were moving. And the rain drummed all the heavier before finally ceasing its attack. Even when it stopped they could still hear the run of water from the guttering. And all that time his hand was warm and strong and reassuring around hers.

'Hell, Knight! I thought he had you. I went to the burying ground, but it was empty and there was blood all over the place.' Within the kitchen of the house in Craven Street, Callerton was unwrapping the bandage from Knight's arm.

'I had to lie low until I was sure they would be gone.'

Callerton removed the dressing from Knight's arm and peered at the wound. 'The lass did a good job.'

'She did,' agreed Knight, thinking of how Marianne had helped him. Nothing about her was as he had expected. She was not over-confident, spoiled and demanding. He found her quiet dignity, her courage, the secrets in her dark eyes, intriguing. Too intriguing for a woman he had abducted. And definitely too intriguing for the woman who was the daughter of the man he had spent a lifetime hunting.

'This is going to hurt like the devil.' Callerton lifted the clean boiled rag and dipped it in the cooling boiled water.

'Do your worst,' said Knight and grimaced as Callerton began to cleanse the wound.

'Misbourne is an utter bastard. I can't believe he would risk his daughter's life for the sake of a piece of paper.'

'Believe it.' Knight's hatred of the man intensified at the thought of how he had endangered Marianne's life.

'If his men were sent in to free her, how could they make the mistake of shooting at her? You said it was point-blank range. They must have seen her.'

Knight frowned slightly as Callerton pressed harder on the wound. 'Because they weren't sent to free her. They were sent to kill me. None of the men made any attempt to retrieve Marianne. I doubt he even told them that I was holding his daughter.'

Callerton blew out a sigh and shook his head. 'So Misbourne's keeping quiet about Marianne's abduction, even to the ruffians that he's hired.' He paused and looked at Knight. 'But why try to kill you when,

to his knowledge, you're the only one who knows the location of his daughter?'

'Because he thinks I know what's in the document. Whatever is written on that piece of paper, Misbourne is willing to do anything to keep its secret safe. Even if it means risking his own daughter.'

'Hell,' said Callerton. He finished cleansing the wound and started to bind it with a fresh dressing and strips of linen. 'What is in that document?'

'The explanation for what played out on Hounslow Heath fifteen years ago. And the more Misbourne tries to hide it, the more determined I am to find it.'

'And Lady Marianne?'

'We let her go,' said Knight. Her father might risk her life, but he would not.

Callerton paused in his binding. 'She's seen your face. She can identify you.'

'Only if she sees me again. She does not know my name.'

'It's risky, especially with you having to play the rake around town.'

'It's a risk I'm going to have to take.' He remembered the look on Marianne's face when she realised that her father had not sent the document to free her: shock, disbelief, confusion, hurt. Misbourne was a villain, but seeing Marianne realise it gave him nothing of gladness or victory, only a sick feeling deep in his stomach. 'I never meant for her to be endangered or hurt. I thought Misbourne would give up the document, to save her from me, at the first opportunity.' He thought of her standing before him in that burying ground, prior to the arrival of Smithy and Misbourne's ruffians. And the urge he had felt to kiss her. And his palm upon which hers had lain in the warehouse tin-

gled, and the same desire he had felt then whispered through his body. He had to be losing his mind.

'Misbourne will think he's won.' Callerton tied off the bandage.

'He'll soon realise otherwise,' said Knight. He gritted his teeth and hardened his voice. 'The sooner she is gone from here, the better.'

Within the yellow bedchamber Marianne watched as the accomplice, still masked, poured the last of the hot water into the copper bath positioned before the fire and left. The highwayman lifted his own empty bucket and moved towards the door.

'The bath is warm to soak in and there are clothes in the wardrobe and drawers, old fashioned in style, but clean and dry. When you are ready, ring the bell and your dinner will be delivered to you. When you have eaten I will take you home to your father.'

She gave a small nod of acknowledgement. 'I have been thinking,' she began. She had done nothing else but think since the warehouse. 'The document cannot be in my father's possession. It is the only explanation.'

He said nothing, but she could see from his eyes that he thought otherwise.

'Believe me, if my father had the document he would have given it to you. I am certain of it.'

Still he said nothing. It was not as if he were arguing against her. She did not know why she felt the compulsion to explain to him. 'It is more than the fact he is my father.' She hesitated before rushing on. 'There are other reasons…very good reasons…' Of which she could make no mention. 'I know he would not have left me in such a situation if, by the production of a single

document in his possession, whatever that document might detail, he could free me.'

She saw the look in his eyes and understood what it was. She faced right up to him, suddenly reckless and angry. 'Do not dare pity me!'

He did not argue, did not move, just looked at her with those eyes of his.

'You think you know my father so well. You think you have it all worked out with your plans and your machinations. But my father has not delivered you the document and there can only be two possible explanations. The first is that...' she swallowed and was proud that she did not hesitate to say the words '...is that I am not the most precious thing to him. And the second is that the document is not in his possession. Either way, you were wrong in your estimation, sir.'

There was a dark flare of fury in his eyes. The air seemed to tingle between them, making her suddenly very aware of him as a man and of all of his power. She wondered if she had gone too far, yet she could not back down.

The seconds seemed to stretch. They stared at one another across the small distance.

'Your bath is growing cold, Lady Marianne,' he said, his use of her title erecting the barrier of formality, as if nothing had happened between them in the burying ground or the warehouse. And with a small inclination of his head he left.

The hour was late by the time they travelled the first part of the way through the lamp-lit streets, in the same carriage in which he had brought her to his house. Fog drifted in patches, slowing their progress. Eventually the carriage came to a halt in an alleyway and they

continued the rest of the journey on foot. There was nothing securing her wrists. He did not hold her, not her arm or her hand or her waist. He told himself that it was because she had no reason to escape, not now that he was taking her home to Misbourne. But that was not the only reason. The truth was that he liked the feel of her too much.

They did not speak, just walked side by side through the quiet streets that glistened with dampness and puddles. He did not wear the black-silk kerchief around his face, but the collar of his greatcoat was turned up and his hat pulled low on his head. Beside him, Marianne was wrapped in a long fawn cloak that brought back memories of his childhood. His mother had been taller and bigger in build than Marianne, so the bodice of the deep-blue silk beneath it had been pinned to keep it decent and the hem of the dress touched to the ground. The cloak's hood was pulled up over her head, but he knew that beneath it her hair was plaited neatly and tied with a silk ribbon that matched the dress.

They continued walking, keeping to the alleyways and mews through the occasional mist that swirled and hid them. Always in the shadows, that the few people they passed would not know either Marianne or him. Until at last he stopped at the end of the alleyway that would lead out near to Leicester Square.

He looked down at her and she looked up at him, and he was seized by the sensation that had things been different, had she not been Misbourne's daughter, had she not been the woman he had abducted, had she not been promised to another man…

But she was all of those things, and what lay between him and Misbourne was only just beginning. When it finished there would be a noose around Mis-

bourne's neck. And he could not afford to let himself think of what that would do to the woman before him; he did not need that complication.

She was Misbourne's daughter, he told himself, and nothing more.

'We are very close to the square in which you live. All you need do is walk straight along this street until you come to your father's house. Go home to where you are safe.' His half-whispered words sounded harsh in the soft quietness of the night.

Go home to where you are safe. She shuddered at the memory his words elicited.

He saw it, but misunderstood the reason. 'You need not fear to walk alone through the darkness. You will be safe. I will be watching you until you enter through the front door.'

'I am not afraid,' she replied. *Not with you.* It was absurd and ironic, and true. 'Not of the darkness here, outside, in the open…only indoors, in chambers, when all the candles have been extinguished.' She had never spoken even this small part of it to anyone before. Indeed, she did not know why she was telling him.

'Sometimes the worst monsters are those whom we allow to play in our imagination.' He glanced away into the distance, a hard look upon his face, as if he were remembering monsters of his own.

'Not always. Sometimes the worst monsters really are those that wait in the darkness.' She bit her lip, suddenly afraid that she had revealed too much.

His eyes came back to rest on her and the look in them was one of guilt.

'I should go.' But she did not move.

'You should. I…' he hesitated as if he did not want

to speak the rest of the words '...wish you happy in your marriage to Pickering.'

She felt only dread at the prospect of the marriage. She did not want to think of Mr Pickering or anything else, not at this moment, not while she was standing here with the highwayman.

'I hope that your arm heals quickly.' She looked up at him through the moonlight and the moment seemed to stretch between them. These were the last moments they would be together. The last time she would see him.

They stared at one another and the tension that was between them, that had always been between them, seemed to tighten and strain. She could hear the sound of her breath in the quietness of the alleyway and the pound of her heart against her chest. There seemed so much unsaid. She knew she should walk away, but she couldn't.

'I...' She bit at her lip, not understanding why she did not want to go.

'Marianne.' He leaned his face ever so slightly towards her, his gaze holding hers with such intensity, as if he might kiss her. She wanted him to do it. She wanted to feel his mouth against hers, wanted him to take her in his arms. But he did neither. Instead, he touched a hand gently to her face, stroking away some strands of hair that fallen against her cheek. 'You really should go home now.'

'Yes,' she whispered. Home. And this moment and this man would be gone for ever and everything would go back to the way it had been before. To holding candles to ward off the darkness, and being guarded so carefully by her father, and being afraid of every man that looked at her. If only she could capture this mo-

ment, capture this man who was taller and darker and more dangerous than any other and who used his strength not against her, but to protect her. This man who had saved her when all those who loved her had failed. In his very danger and strength was the safety she sought.

She had forgotten what it felt like to be without fear. Just as she had forgotten what it felt like to be attracted to a man. And the attraction she felt for him dwarfed any childish fancies she might have imagined she felt for her brother's friends. She knew what she wanted to do. Time was running out. Before she could think better of it she stepped towards him, stood on her tiptoes and with bare-faced, bold audacity touched her lips to his stubbled cheek.

He did not reach for her, did not even touch her for fear that it would make her disappear into the mist that swirled around them. Yet his lips found hers and they were the sweetest, most innocent lips he had ever tasted. She stilled, startled like a deer caught upwind of a hunter. He did not move for a moment, just let their lips rest together and share their breath, allowing her to grow used to the feel of him. He inhaled her: she smelled of violets and mist and moonlight, and all that was temptation. And when she did not bolt, he kissed her. A soft kiss. A gentle kiss. A kiss that said everything he could not say in words. That he was sorry. That he had never meant to frighten her. How it might have been, had their situations been different. And when he broke away she was still standing there, the expression on her upturned face serene and blissful, her eyes closed, her lips full and parted, as if he kissed her still. Then she opened her eyes and

looked at him, and he thought she was everything he had ever wanted. A woman of moonlight and mist, of innocence and mystery. Fragile, yet possessing a power she did not realise. All fine-spun glass and shimmering silver. The counterbalance to himself. And for one tiny moment of madness he was tempted to give it all up for her. And then cold hard reality crushed the foolishness of his thoughts.

'Go home, Marianne,' he said.

But she had already pulled the hood to cover her hair and shroud her face and was stepping away, beyond his reach in every respect.

They looked at one another across that small distance and then she turned and walked into the street and out of his life.

All the way down the empty street, all the way through the glow of the faint lamp-lit mist that hung in the darkness, not once did she look back at him. Not even when she reached the steps that led up to her father's house. And there was a part of him that wanted her to look. A part that wanted to know he had affected her as much as she had him.

He watched her lift the brass knocker and strike it against its plate, the clatter of it muffled by distance. Then she glanced back at him, as if she could see through the mist and the darkness to where he stood watching. And he felt a stab of primal satisfaction. The front door opened and a shaft of light flooded out into the street and she no longer looked at him, but only ahead to the butler and to Misbourne as her father pulled her inside.

Chapter Six

The house was in uproar. Marianne could not doubt
that her father was pleased to see her. She had never
seen him cry, but there was a sheen of tears in his eyes
as he held her close, hugging her to him as if she had
come back from the dead. Her mother's cheeks, normally never anything but perfectly powdered and pale,
were flushed and pink. There was so much excitement and joy as her parents embraced her; her mother
clucked over her and even her brother standing by the
side watched with a mixture of relief and unspoken
questions in his eyes. And she *was* glad to be back
with those she loved. She *was* relieved. But even as
she felt these things she could feel too that her family were slotting her back into the place she had left,
sliding the guard closed around her, imprisoning her
within that illusion of safety. She glanced at the blinds
in the drawing room, already drawn low to shut out
the night and the highwayman. And she smiled at her
father and she hugged her mother, and she thought of
the highwayman out there in the darkness and her lips
burned and throbbed from his kiss.

Marianne had changed. Something had shifted in the

world. And she knew with an absolute certainty that nothing would ever be the same again. Behind her back she slipped Mr Pickering's betrothal ring from her finger and hid it within the pocket of the blue-silk dress.

It was close to lunchtime the next day when Marianne's father came into the drawing room and sat down on the sofa opposite her and her mother. She could see her brother, Francis, waiting in the background and knew, before her mother spoke, that they had come to question her about the highwayman.

'Your papa wishes to speak with you, Marianne. Be sure to do as he asks.' Then with a nod of her head Lady Misbourne slipped from the room, leaving Marianne alone with her father and brother. Francis did not move from where he leaned against the wall.

'You are well enough this morning to be out of bed, Marianne?' her father asked.

'I am very well, Papa, thank you.'

'There are some questions that I must ask you about these last few days. Questions that, although I have no wish to distress you, must be asked.'

She felt a ripple of nervousness run through her.

Her father cleared his throat and looked awkward. 'Your mama tells me that…that the villain did not…' He cleared his throat again and did not meet her eye. Marianne glanced round at Francis, but her brother's face was a mask that showed nothing. 'Did not force himself upon you,' finished her father.

'He did not,' said Marianne. 'He did nothing like that. Indeed, he treated me with kindness.'

'Kindness?' Her father's gaze riveted to hers and she saw the sudden shrewd sharpness within them and was afraid, not for herself but for the highwayman.

'He did not hurt me,' she said. 'He brought me candles to light the darkness. And when I escaped and found myself lost in St Giles Rookery he saved me from a group of ruffians who would have…' She looked away in embarrassment. 'They meant to…' And then her eyes met her father's once more. 'The high-wayman saved me from them.'

She saw the look her father exchanged with her brother.

'I want to know everything about him, Marianne, where he took you, what he did. Everything.'

She swallowed and then slowly sketched a very rough outline of the past few days.

At the end of her story she saw her father close his eyes as if garnering strength or control over some strong emotion. 'At any point did you see his face, Marianne?'

A fleeting second to make a momentous decision. Her heart beat, and the seconds seemed to slow down. A pause that was so tiny, yet felt so vast. She should tell the truth, reveal a description of that so-handsome face. Especially given what he had done to her father.

'Whatever that villain may have threatened, pay no heed, Marianne, for I swear on my life that I will see the scoundrel caught.'

She knew what they did to highwaymen that they caught. The magistrates would not be lenient. Her father would see to that.

'He was masked. I saw nothing.' Marianne could not meet her father's eyes to tell the lie. Her heart tripped all the faster.

There was silence in the room and she expected them to say that they knew that she was lying. But they did not.

Her hands lay folded on her lap. She gripped them a little tighter together. 'He said he had taken me to force you to yield a particular document.' She hesitated. 'Why did you not give it to him, Papa?'

'Such a foolish question, Marianne!' Her father's face stained burgundy. 'Do you honestly think I would not have given it to him, were it that easily done?' he demanded.

'You do not have the document he seeks.' It was not a question, only an assertion of what she already knew.

'I have not the slightest notion of what he speaks. The man belongs in Bedlam. Demanding old documents of which I have not the slightest knowledge. He is both dangerous and delusional.'

'I told him you did not have it.'

Her father paled. His eyes opened wider and she saw in them a fleeting look of panic. 'He spoke to you of the document…of its nature?'

She saw her brother watching her father.

'Only that it was a document he believed you to own, that it was the reason he had taken me. He said he meant me no harm.'

'That is what villains say, Marianne.' He shook his head as if exasperated at her naïvety. 'Thank God he took fright at the strength of the men that I sent.'

'He took no fright whatsoever. And those men you sent were indiscriminate with their guns.'

'He had you with him?' Her father's face was aghast.

She nodded. 'They shot at me and he saved me, Papa, using himself as a shield that the bullet would not hit me.'

Again that exchange of looks between her father and brother.

'Marianne, are you telling me the highwayman was shot?'

'He was shot.' She glanced down at her hands, remembering that terrible moment when she realised he had been hurt.

'Are you about to suffer an attack of the vapours?' Her father was peering at her as if she were a fragile piece of porcelain that might crack at any moment. Before the highwayman she had been just that. And after the highwayman… What should have made her weaker seemed only to have had the opposite effect.

'I am quite well.' She stared at her hands, wondering what her family would say if she told them she had picked pieces of shirt out of the wound before binding it for him…or how it had been between them in the warehouse afterwards…and in the alleyway not a hundred yards from where they now sat.

And when she looked up again she could see her father was stroking his beard. 'So the villain is wounded.' His eyes were narrow and filled with such hatred that a chill ran through Marianne. He looked up at her and smiled a grim smile, then he took her hand between his and patted it. 'Have no fear, Marianne, I will see the villain caught, I swear it. He will pay for what he did and there will be an end to him. Now go and rest, my dear.'

'I am perfectly well, Papa, I assure you. I do not need to rest.'

'But you will do as I say just the same, Marianne. Your papa knows what is best for you.'

It was difficult to maintain a low profile when one was pretending to be a rake around town, but somewhat easier to stay away from the places that a respect-

able young lady might visit. Yet even so, Rafe found himself thinking about Marianne Winslow and subsequently keeping an ear to the ground regarding not just Misbourne, but his daughter too.

He knew that Misbourne had hired a thief-taker to find him and that he had not gone to the Order of the Wolf. He also knew that there was a considerable price on the head of the 'mysterious' highwayman. Misbourne's own newspaper carried word of it, saying that a group of London's best citizens had put the money together, but Rafe doubted there was anyone other than Misbourne himself involved. Five thousand guineas was a king's ransom—more money than some men might earn in a hundred lifetimes. Enough to tempt someone to break the underworld's code of conduct. But of Marianne there had been nothing at all, not even a whisper of a wedding to Pickering.

An image of her filled his mind: all pale and mysterious with her secrets and sensitivity that she strove to hide. He remembered the feel of her lips beneath his and the untapped passion beneath the innocence and wariness, and he felt his blood quicken, just as it did every time he thought of her. He wondered how long it would be before she was married to Pickering. Perhaps then he would have some peace from this torment.

'What do you say, Knight? Would you bed her?' Devlin asked as they made their way down the steps of their club in St James's.

Bed Marianne Winslow? He wanted her, he admitted it; wanted her with a force of lust that shocked him. He closed his eyes and pushed the thoughts away.

'Knight? You all right, old man?' asked Bullford. 'Seem a bit distracted.'

'I am distracted,' said Rafe. He gestured to the two

carts blocking the street, one of which had spilled its
load of coal over half the street, and across which several children were darting, collecting up pieces of coal
and running off with them.

'Not by that,' said Fallingham with a grin. 'More
likely a certain little lady.'

'You are not wrong,' admitted Rafe.

'The Widow White?'

'I could not possibly comment,' said Rafe, watching
the queue of carriages begin to build up in the street
while they waited for the accident to be cleared.

'I was asking about Miss Fox. She's at Covent Garden Theatre tonight, playing the part of Lady Mac-
beth,' said Devlin. The day was bright, but cool. No
sign of yesterday's rain. They walked on, leaving the
mayhem unfolding behind them.

'I didn't know you like Shakespeare,' Bullford piped
up.

'He doesn't. He likes well-shaped actresses with
large assets,' said Fallingham. 'And I hear that she's
already in negotiations with Hawick to be his mistress.'

'Not a done deal yet,' declared Devlin. 'I've got
m'father's box. Are you up for a night of it?'

Everyone gave grunted answers save for Rafe.

'Knight?' Devlin prompted.

But Rafe barely heard him. He was staring at a certain stationary dark town coach with a grey-bearded
and moustached man jumping down to investigate the
nature of the hold up. But he was not looking at the
fading bruise around the man's eye or the healing cut
upon his cheek. Rather, he was looking at the young
fair-haired woman still seated in the carriage.

Marianne's eyes met his. And everything else in
the world faded. He could feel the steady hard beat of

his heart. All that he had worked for, all that he had
planned for Misbourne, could be lost in this moment.
Any second now she would call out to her father and
reveal the identity of the highwayman who had abducted her. Yet he could not take his eyes from hers
and even across the distance of the pavement and the
road that separated them he could sense the tumult of
her emotion. She looked at him and he looked right
back. The seconds stretched too long so that the moment seemed frozen, as if he could have walked across
there and taken her for a second time.

Misbourne turned back and the movement caught
his eye, breaking the intensity between him and Marianne. Misbourne's gaze slid to his and their eyes met—
and it was as if Misbourne knew exactly who he was.
Rafe's world became quite still; his senses sharpened
and every nerve tensed. Then Misbourne turned away
as if he did not know him at all and the moment was
over.

'Good Lord!' said Devlin. 'Look at the mess of Misbourne's face. Coaching accident, my arse! I know
the marks of a fist when I see them. The rumours are
true, then.'

Fallingham and Razeby sniggered.

Rafe saw Lady Misbourne lean forwards from inside the carriage, throwing them a disapproving look.

Rafe kept on walking and did not look back, but
he was poised, with every step that he took and every
breath that he inhaled, for the shout of Misbourne's
voice and the sound of pursuing footsteps. Every muscle in his body was tensed. Every nerve stretched tight.
He felt as he had on the countless battlefields upon
which he'd fought across the years. Primed and ready,
sickened almost, with the wait for the fight to begin.

But the enemy did not give chase. All he heard were his own footsteps and those of his friends, and the irate voices of the passengers of the escalating coach jam. And when he glanced back, Misbourne was still hovering near the door of his coach, staring in the opposite direction at the accident, and Marianne was hidden from sight.

'Louts,' pronounced Lady Misbourne to her husband. 'Come in, sir, and close the door that we are not subject to their ill manners.' Then to her daughter, 'Avert your eyes this instant, Marianne.'

Marianne's heart was thudding so hard she wondered that her parents did not hear it. The skin on the nape of her neck tingled as if the highwayman's fingers stroked against it.

'Yes, Mama,' she replied out of habit, but she could not tear her eyes away.

He was dressed in a smart, dark, fitted tailcoat, probably one of the Weston's she had seen in his wardrobe, and dark pantaloons, just like the other men he was with. But that was where the similarity stopped. He was taller, more manly, his dark hair tied back in its queue. And so breathtakingly handsome that she could have looked at him for a lifetime and never tired of it. Even across the distance that separated them she could see the warm golden glow of his eyes and feel the intensity of his gaze. The highwayman. It seemed like everything else in the world dimmed and faded to nothing. She was aware only of him…and the strange connection between them. Her awareness of him was so intense that in that moment she smelled again the scent of him, heard again that harsh half-whisper against her ear and felt the touch of his lips upon hers.

Outside the carriage her father moved and Marianne saw the highwayman's gaze shift to him—and her father's to the highwayman's. She remembered her father's vow to bring an end to the man who had abducted her and the look of utter malice in his eyes. Her heart gave a stutter. She caught back her breath. And for a terrible moment she thought that her father had recognised him. But then he turned back to the carriage, to her and her mother, and she knew she must have been mistaken.

She did not look at the highwayman then, only at her father, lest he follow the direction of her gaze and fathom something of the truth.

Her mother scowled. 'Look at them, insolent young bucks! Out all the night long and only now, at this late hour of the morning, crawling home. It is a disgraceful way to behave.'

'Young men will be young men,' her father said with a tolerance that was at odds with everything that he was always saying about the society of the day. 'Once they are married with a nursery to raise they will soon settle down.'

Marianne blinked with surprise and saw the slight widening of her mother's eyes. Lady Misbourne gave a sniff of disapproval, pressed her lips tight shut and folded her hands together upon her lap. 'And what seems to be the hold-up on the road ahead?'

Her father explained about the accident and went back to looking at it. Marianne relaxed a little, touching a hand to the centre of her palm that *he* had held with such gentleness. She began to breathe again. And then she saw her father glance back at the small group of men, watching them for a second or two with the strangest expression upon his face.

'Papa,' she called to distract his attention. 'Perhaps we would be quicker to walk. The day is fine and—'

'Stay in the carriage, Marianne,' he snapped, cutting her off. His eyes narrowed and he cast a suspicious, almost frightened glance all around them before climbing into the carriage and shutting the door.

Rafe had reached the steps to his own house. Only Devlin remained by his side—the home of the viscount's latest conquest lay a few streets on and it seemed he was planning a visit. All the way back, Rafe had placidly followed the viscount's example, dawdling at the slow pace, smiling at the jokes, showing nothing of the turmoil within him. He had punched her father, abducted her at gunpoint, held her captive and exposed her to the seamier side of life and more danger in three days than she would have seen in a lifetime. She was Misbourne's daughter, for pity's sake. She had to have pointed him out to her father. But there had been no hue and cry, no covert shadow following him. And he knew that Marianne had not told her father.

What the hell had Marianne been doing in St James's at that time in the morning anyway?

Rafe discovered the answer to his question later that week. The gossip was all over town. Everywhere he went they were talking of it.

Rafe came home from the theatre that night and leaned against the jamb of the door, watching Callerton blackening their boots in the kitchen.

'Thought you would be back late.' Callerton glanced up. 'Told them you're tupping some woman again?'

Rafe nodded.

'You know you might actually have to bed a few or

they might start getting suspicious,' Callerton joked, but Rafe could not bring himself to laugh and Callerton stopped polishing the boots and looked at him, his expression suddenly serious.

'What's wrong? Has Misbourne come after you? Maybe the girl pointed you out to him after all.'

'She did not.' Rafe shook his head. 'Misbourne does not know me.'

'But something's wrong.'

'It's all over town that there was no accident on the way to Marianne Winslow's wedding,' Rafe said.

'They know it was the highwayman?'

Rafe shook his head. 'They think it was an excuse dreamt up by Misbourne to buy time.'

'For what?' Callerton resumed his polishing.

'It seems that Pickering has pulled out of the betrothal. They are saying that he told Misbourne on the day of the wedding and that Misbourne and Pickering came to fisticuffs over it.'

'Well, we know that's rubbish,' said Callerton. 'There was only one fist that smacked Misbourne's face and it wasn't Pickering's.'

Rafe moved into the kitchen and sat down at the table. 'Misbourne is threatening to sue for breach of promise if Pickering does not marry Marianne.'

'Again?' Callerton raised an eyebrow. 'You'd have thought he'd have learned his lesson with Arlesford the first time round.'

'It serves only to embroil Marianne in yet another marriage scandal.'

'Why do you care? There will be a damn sight more scandal by the time you've finished with her father.'

'Because had I not abducted her she would already be married to Pickering.'

'That's not the reason,' said Callerton.

Rafe met his friend's eyes.

'You're soft on the lass,' said Callerton quietly.

'Don't be ridiculous. She's Misbourne's daughter,' retorted Rafe as if that was a denial. He did not know what it was that he felt for Marianne, only that he felt it very strongly indeed.

'Aye,' said Callerton, 'she is that. And if you're set on destroying the father, you best not have a care for the daughter.' And he went back to polishing the boot.

Marianne saw him the moment that she walked into the room of the circulating library. He was standing amongst the shelves of novels, seemingly engaged within the pages of a book, but then his eyes glanced up and momentarily met hers before sliding back down to the page. Her heart skipped a beat before racing off at a gallop.

The library was quiet; only two other people were in the room and one of those was the elderly librarian seated in the corner. The other was Caroline Edingham, Lady Willaston, who immediately spotted them and headed straight for Marianne's mother, her eyes lighting up at the thought of scooping some gossip straight from the horse's mouth.

'Keep quiet over Pickering and let me deal with this, Marianne,' Lady Misbourne whispered beneath her breath.

'If you do not mind, Mama, I will have a look within the poetry room.'

'Go quickly before she is upon us. And do not return. I will come and fetch you.' Marianne made her escape, but not before she saw the false smile that her mother plastered upon her face to greet Lady Wil-

laston. 'My dear Caroline. It has been an age.' The two women were kissing one another's cheeks as if they were the best of friends before Marianne was halfway across the room.

She was careful not to look at the highwayman, but she thought she caught the faint scent of sandalwood as she passed him and it made her heart beat all the faster.

The poetry room was empty. Marianne made her way over to the shelves of the classical poems, took the first book down from the shelf and opened it. She stood with her back to the door, her eyes scanning the open pages without seeing a single line that was written upon them. Her mind was whirring. She did not know what to think of his presence here. She was afraid he would follow her—and even more afraid that he would not. When she heard the quiet tread of a man's footsteps she did not need to look round to know it was him.

He came and stood beside her, looking at the same shelf of classical books.

She could not help herself. Her gaze flew to his, to those clear amber eyes that were fixed upon hers, and that stern handsome face.

'Why are you here?' she whispered.

'To see you.'

Her stomach gave a somersault and her heart began to thunder in earnest. 'Don't you know that there is a very large price upon your head? My father has men searching for you even as we speak.'

'I know.'

There was a small silence.

'The other day in St James's… You did not tell your father.'

'No.'

'Why not, Marianne?' he asked.

'Because there is every likelihood that they will hang you if they catch you.'

The silence hissed between them.

She felt her cheeks warm. 'How is your arm?' He wore no sling. Neither had he done so that day in St James's.

'It did not fester.'

And with those words she was back in the warehouse and the air was thick with all that had happened between them.

'I am sorry about Pickering,' he said.

'I am not. In truth, I am relieved. I never wanted to marry him. It was my father who…' She had said too much. She turned away and laid the book down open upon the table as if she meant to read it.

'My father does not have the document that you seek. I asked him,' she said, trying to change the subject.

He was standing behind her, but she heard him step closer.

Her body was in uproar, but she did not edge away. Nor did she look round.

He said nothing. He did not need to. She knew by his silence what he thought.

'You think he is lying,' she said.

Still he did not speak, and she turned on him, feeling angry and confused. 'Why won't you admit it?'

She could see the determined set of his jaw, the resolve in his eyes, and, remembering his talk of justice and vengeance, she felt suddenly afraid for her father.

'You are intent on wreaking revenge upon the wrong man.'

'I do not think so,' he said softly. 'And it is not revenge, but justice.'

'And what is this justice you seek from him?'

'I have never lied to you, Marianne. I would see him dance upon the end of a gibbet.'

'My God, my father is right. You *are* delusional and dangerous.'

'Delusional and dangerous?' The breath of his whisper tickled her ear.

She jumped. 'If I scream, you are undone, sir.'

'I am more than undone. My life is in your hands. You can claim the reward your father has set upon my head.'

She closed her eyes at that.

'What are you waiting for? If you really you think me delusional and dangerous, go ahead and scream.'

He did not crowd her with his body, did not touch her to coerce, yet she could sense him and the attraction that hummed between them stronger than ever. The thud of her heart was so loud she wondered that it did not echo in the room around them. She should scream, but she knew that she wouldn't. Was he delusional? No. Was he dangerous? Very. To the men who would hurt her, to her father. But not to her. Never to her.

Slowly she raised her gaze to meet his. 'I will not let you harm him. You do know that, do you not?'

'I would expect nothing other.'

The very air seemed to vibrate between them.

'Marianne,' he whispered and stepped closer.

She knew that he was going to kiss her. She should have turned away. She should have run. Instead, she shivered with anticipation, with need, and raised her mouth to meet his.

He kissed her. And it was everything she remembered from the alleyway and more. A meeting of two mouths that were made to be together. He kissed her and it felt right. Safe and dangerous both at once, and utterly wonderful. Such gentleness, yet within it she had never been more aware of his masculinity and his strength. And she kissed him back, only a little at first, but then as her confidence grew, bolder, more fully.

Beneath her hands she could feel the hard muscle of his chest and the steady strong beat of his heart, though she did not remember placing her palms there. She felt his arms encircling her, enclosing her, yet she felt no panic at being held, only need and desire. She slid her hands up over his chest, higher, to wind around his neck, pressing herself closer until she could feel the brush of his chest against her bodice and the sensitivity of her nipples beneath her stays. The scent of him filled her nose; the feel of him overwhelmed her senses. She thought she could kiss him for all eternity and it would never be enough.

He drew back, breaking off the kiss, and she did not know why he had stopped. She felt dazed, weak, breathless. His breath was almost as ragged as hers. He eased her away so that the backs of her thighs were leaning against the table.

His eyes stared down into hers and they were dark and filled with the same torment that was fast rushing in to fill the place where all her wonder and joy had been. He stared for a moment longer and then released her.

'I should not have done that.' Still staring at her, he shook his head as if to deny what had just passed between them, then turned and walked away.

She stood where she was, her whole body tingling and aflame. Unable to think straight. Her heart still fluttering like a caged bird desperate to be free. Reeling from his kiss. Reeling from all that coursed through her body. Reeling from the thought of what she had just done. She touched trembling fingers to her lips. She had kissed him with all her heart and all her soul. Marianne Winslow, who had not thought she could tolerate the touch of a man ever again, had kissed him. A highwayman with a five-thousand-guinea price on his head, a man whose name she did not know, a man her father was paying half of London to capture. And a man who had sworn vengeance on her father.

She was still staring at the same page when her mother came into the room.

'She has gone at last, thank the lord. So many questions. Caroline Edingham could do with a few lessons in subtlety. And she's hardly one to be gossiping about anyone else. Not with the stories I've heard of her husband.' Her mother glanced at her. 'Have you made your selection?'

'I think I will take this one,' she managed to say and closed the book.

Her mother peered more closely. 'Are you quite well? You look rather flushed.'

'I am perfectly well, Mama. It is rather warm in here, do you not think?'

'Hurry along, Marianne. I told your papa we would not be long and you know how he worries about you. He will not be happy if we are late home.'

'Yes, Mama.' Marianne picked up the book and followed her mother.

* * *

Rafe Knight stood alone in his study, leaning against the mantelpiece and staring into the flicker of flames upon the hearth. Outside, across the heath, dusk was darkening the sky, yet he had not drawn the curtains or pulled down the blind. The day's newspapers lay unread upon his desk. The paperwork due with his man of business in the morning had not been touched. There was only one thing on his mind, and that was what had happened in the circulating library with Marianne.

She was Misbourne's daughter, he told himself again and again. A woman in whose veins flowed the blood of the man he despised. A woman who bore the same dark eyes as the devil. The last woman in the world he should want. Yet he did want her. He had wanted her almost from the very start. Maybe it was just physical need driving him. Maybe Callerton was right and he should be out there tupping women as frequently as he pretended. Maybe then he would be rid of the need that gnawed at him. But the thought of bedding another woman left him cold. The desire that burned in him was for Marianne Winslow alone. *Misbourne's daughter*, he thought again. Yet had it not been for her eyes, he would not have believed it. Eyes that, on first glance, looked so like Misbourne's, but when he looked deep into them there was nothing of Misbourne there. She was nothing like Misbourne. Nothing like that monster. But she *was* Misbourne's daughter and nothing he could do would ever change that.

A knock sounded at the door and Callerton came in, bringing with him the damp smell of the night. Cal-

lerton's eyes went to the bottle of brandy that sat on the table and the half-full glass beside it.

'Misbourne?' he asked.

Rafe gave no answer. He moved to the table and filled a clean glass with brandy before passing it to Callerton.

The two men sat in silence for a few minutes before Callerton said, 'It's Marianne Winslow, isn't it?'

'I had to see her.'

'Hell, why?'

He shook his head, not understanding the answer to that himself, knowing only that the compulsion gave him no peace. Nor had he revealed to Callerton what had happened in the warehouse or the alleyway. He drank down his brandy.

'She's his daughter, Rafe. And if you're going after him, then you can't dally with her.'

'I'm not dallying with her.'

'Aren't you?' Callerton demanded and topped up both their glasses. 'Are you denying that you want her?'

'I don't deny it. But that doesn't mean I'm going to act on it.'

'Christ, you could have your pick of the women in London. Why does it have to be her?'

It was the same question that Rafe had been asking himself.

'She could ruin all of this for you. One word in her father's ear, one point of her finger, and it will be you, not Misbourne, hanging from a scaffold. You have to stay away from her.' Callerton drank his brandy down in one go. 'Unless you've changed your mind over Misbourne.'

'I cannot do that,' said Rafe. 'I've dedicated my whole life to finding that bastard.'

He wanted Marianne. And he wanted her father's head on a plate. And he knew he could not have both.

Callerton was right. He needed to stay away from her.

Chapter Seven

Marianne sat in the corner of the drawing room of her father's town house that evening, the library book lying open but unread upon her lap. At the other side of the room Lady Misbourne was playing patience, the cards making a soft slapping sound as she placed them down upon the green baize of the card table. That, and the slow steady ticking of the clock upon the mantelpiece were the only sounds within the room.

Marianne was thinking of the highwayman and his kiss. She was also thinking of what he had said about the justice he meant to deliver to her father. She closed her eyes and saw again her father kneeling in the dirt on the heath with a bloodied lip and cut cheek. *Her own father.* She bit her lip and felt her cheeks burn with shame and guilt and confusion that she could be attracted to any man who had done such a thing. Now that her blood had cooled and that amber gaze was not upon her, the scent of sandalwood not in her nose, she felt a little sick at her behaviour. She had seen how the highwayman had dealt with the men in the rookery, and those in the graveyard. He would not hurt her. But he had already hurt her father, and promised

much more, and nothing that she said seemed to convince him of reason.

It was true that he had saved her, in the alleyway and in the burying ground, but he was the one who had abducted her in the first place. And it wasn't as if he had not been honest from the very outset over his hatred of Misbourne. Perhaps the document was just an excuse to torture her father. Maybe it didn't even exist at all.

Or maybe her father was right and he was delusional. He was certainly dangerous to her father. She realised now too late that she had been wrong in the answer she had given within the room of the circulating library. He made her forget her fear; he made her reckless and emboldened with this madness of attraction she felt for him. A man who could have such influence over her, making her forget who she was, making her behave in ways that she had never thought possible, was definitely dangerous to her too. Betrayal. For that's what it was, she thought miserably, whatever she chose to do. She was betraying her father. But if she revealed the highwayman, it would be a different kind of betrayal. She'd be betraying the one man who had saved her.

No matter what else she imagined, the cold hard truth was he was a highwayman, a stranger, a man who was threatening her father. There was no real choice to make when she thought of it like that, not if she had any semblance of a care for her father. And once she had told her father the truth… Maybe they would not hang him. Especially if she were to speak up and tell them how he had saved her. She closed her eyes and could not bear to think of what they would do to him. She could not afford to let herself think of him at all.

Her duty was to her father. She felt sick to the pit of her stomach, but she knew what she had to do. Closing the book on her lap and setting it down on the small table by her side, she rose to her feet.

Her mother glanced up from the cards laid out before her.

'Is Papa still in his study?' Marianne asked in a carefully controlled voice.

'I believe that your brother is with him, my dear.'

'If you will excuse me, Mama.'

Lady Misbourne gave a nod and looked down once more to her cards.

Marianne made her way slowly towards her father's study. She was doing the right thing, the thing that any dutiful daughter should do, but her heart felt heavy and there was a lump in her throat that she could not swallow down.

Her slippers were silent against the marble tiles. She paused outside the study, taking a deep breath, steeling herself to the task. The door was slightly ajar, and her mother was right about Francis, for she could hear the murmur of both his and her father's voices from within. Marianne reached her hand to the doorknob and heard the words her brother was speaking.

'I told you that a bullet would not keep him from his pursuit of the document for long. He says he's coming for you and it seems to me that this highwayman is a man very much of his word.'

She froze where she was, her ears sharpening, and listened.

'Not if I find him first,' her father said in an angry tone.

'Is a document really worth your life?' Francis asked.

'Yes,' replied her father more quietly, the anger replaced by sadness. 'I would give my very life that it never existed.'

The shock of it hit Marianne hard. The blood in her veins seemed to turn to ice. She stared at the dark-mahogany panels of the door and could not believe what she was hearing. There was a cold prickle across her skin and a terrible sinking feeling in her stomach. *Betrayal.* The word whispered again in her head.

'What is in it?' Francis asked softly. 'Why will you not trust me enough to tell me?'

'It is not a question of trust.' There was the slightest pause. And when her father spoke again there was such a hard horrible quality to his voice that she barely recognised it. 'Do not ask me of it ever again. I will not be questioned. In this house, my word is law. Do you understand, boy?'

'I understand,' said Francis. 'For your sake I hope your precious document is stored somewhere safe. Because whoever that highwayman is, he's coming for *it*, as well as *you*.'

She heard the chink of an empty glass and then her father's irate voice. 'Well, do not just stand there. Ring for another bottle of brandy.'

She slipped away, hurrying to the staircase. She was halfway up when she heard the bell ring, but she did not stop, just walked briskly until she reached her bedchamber. And when she got inside she turned the key in the lock and stood with her back against the door, her hand clutched around her stomach.

Her father had the document, just as the highwayman had said. And he had not been prepared to ransom

it for her. Even though he knew the dark secret that she hid from the world. Had she not heard it with her own ears, she would not have believed it. Even now, she could barely take it in. After all that had happened. After all he had promised. He had said that he loved her. He had said that he would only ever have her best interests at heart. He was her *father.* The one person she trusted over all others. And he had lied...just as the highwayman had known.

It was on the night of the new moon, two nights after he had kissed Marianne Winslow in the circulating library, that Rafe stood within the shrubbery of the garden facing Misbourne's town house. The night was clear and cold enough for him to see his breath before him, as if he breathed smoke into the night. There was no moon to relieve the stark blackness of the sky, only a scattering of small twinkling stars. He watched the house, just as he had watched these three hours past. Biding his time. Waiting for the right moment.

Every window was in darkness, each one shrouded by a blind. Rafe knew exactly what time Misbourne had gone to bed. He knew that Lady Misbourne had retired half an hour earlier and that they kept to their own rooms. Callerton, positioned in his watching place in the mews to the rear of the building, had told him that the only light still burning was that in Marianne's bedchamber at the top of the house. He knew that the candles in her room would burn long after she fell asleep. And he thought of her, despite all his best intentions not to. A woman that feared the darkness of a room, but not that of the night. A woman of mystery and secrets. A woman who he could not seem to get out of his head. He closed his eyes and turned his

thoughts to a still summer's night fifteen years ago. The pain of it made him wince, but when he opened his eyes there was nothing in him but the cold hard rage of determination.

He moved his fingers to check the leather scabbard strapped beneath his coat and the hunter's knife that was in it. The pistol was ready and loaded within his pocket and against his ankle, on the inside of his boot, he could feel the cold press of the narrow metal strip that would slide beneath the window jamb. With one sleek vault he was over the metal fencing that enclosed Leicester Square's garden and moving through the shadows of the night towards Misbourne's town house.

Marianne could not sleep. So she did what she always did when she was too restless and uneasy for sleep. The maid snored softly in the truckle bed beside her own, oblivious to the flicker of the candles as Marianne stole quietly across the bedchamber. She knew exactly which floorboards to avoid. She knew just how to open and close the door without a single sound. Silent as a ghost, she made her way down the back staircase to a world below that was so close and yet so distant from her own. The kitchen.

It was a place that an earl's daughter should never inhabit. The least likely place a monster from the night would ever seek her. The only place she could be truly alone, just for the shortest of times, to think. And Marianne desperately needed to think.

She sat at the kitchen table, barely noticing the cold stone beneath her bare feet or the goosepimple of her skin beneath the cotton of her nightdress. In the days since her eavesdropping she had hardly seen her father. Hardly spoken to him. She could not look him in the eye, for fear he would see the truth in her own.

She stared at the scrubbed wooden surface before her, knowing that she could not avoid him for ever. She was going to have to face him sooner or later. And although she was angry with him, there was also sadness and a nagging need to understand.

Lifting the branch of candles, she rose to return to bed.

Her feet were silent on the stairs, the flames of the candles flickering and sending her shadow dancing against the wall. The darkness of the main hallway was broken by the slim band of light beneath the door to her father's study. All of London slept, but not Marianne and not her father. There was no Mama to interfere and fuss. And there was no Francis. She took her hand from the banister and walked across the hallway to her father's study.

The quiet knock sounded at the door and Rafe tensed, his eyes shifting to the clock that sat beside his candle on Misbourne's desk. Two o'clock. Callerton had not given the signal to warn of Linwood's return and he knew that Misbourne would not knock at his own door. There was no time to clear away the piles of papers or to even slide the drawers closed. No time to react before the door opened.

'Papa,' a familiar voice murmured. And Marianne stepped into the room.

Her gaze raised and she saw who was standing behind her father's desk and the clear evidence of what he had been about. Her eyes widened, but she did not scream.

Rafe's heart was beating too fast. She had not pointed him out to her father before. But this was different. This was an invasion of her father's castle. He

waited for her to call out, or to snatch up the bell and ring it. He should have turned and climbed back out of the window. He should have run and disappeared into the darkness of the night while there was still time. But he just stood there, his gaze locked on hers.

Her eyes were black, her face as pale and beautiful as the vision that haunted his dreams. They stared at one another and those few seconds seemed to stretch to an eternity of torture and uncertainty and the attraction that was between them rippled and roared. And then she lowered her gaze, quietly closed the door behind her, and Rafe released the breath he had been holding.

She stood where she was, keeping the distance of the room between them. Her hair was long and loose and glinting silver in the candlelight. Beneath the long-sleeved shroud of a nightgown he could see the peep of her bare toes. Her gaze moved to take in the papers scattered across the desk and the drawers that hung open before meeting his own once more.

'I would ask you what you are doing here searching my father's study in the middle of the night, but I already know the answer.'

'He will not give the document to me, so I must take it.'

'Steal it, you mean.'

'No.' He shook his head and looked her directly in the eye. 'It is your father who is the thief. I seek to take back that which he stole.'

There was an uneasy expression on her face. He waited for her usual assertion that he was wrong, that Misbourne was the best of men and would not do such a thing. But she said nothing.

The silence seemed to hiss between them.

'You make no defence of him?' He raised his brows.

He saw her bite at her lip before she glanced away. And when she looked at him again she said, 'Have you found it?'

'No.' His eyes held hers as he moved from behind the desk and walked slowly towards her. He did not stop until he was standing directly before her, so close that his boots were almost touching her bare toes. So close that he could smell the scent of her, so sweet and enticing.

'What is written on that paper that, if my father did have it, he would go to such lengths to hide it, and that you will risk so much to find it?'

But he could not tell her what was written upon it, even had he wanted to. 'What has changed that you suddenly believe me?'

'Nothing has changed,' she said, but she would not meet his gaze and he knew that she was lying.

'If the document were in your possession, what, then, would you do with it?'

'The document is the evidence I need to see him hanged.'

The candles within her hand flickered wildly as if a tremor ran through her.

'Whatever my father might have done…' she bit her lip and her eyes held a haunted expression '…he does not deserve to die.'

'On the contrary, Marianne, for what your father did he should burn in hell.'

She closed her eyes at the brutality of his words and he felt the sting of his conscience.

'You would understand if it was your father,' she said.

'It *was* my father.' His voice crackled with the anger and bitterness that came whenever he thought of what

Misbourne had done. 'And my mother too,' he added, and the anger rolled away to expose the ache of grief in his soul.

'What do you mean?' She stared up at him, as if she could see the truth in his eyes.

'I should go. Your brother will be home soon.' But he made no move to leave. The air was thick with tension, with desire and attraction and everything that was forbidden between them. His gaze lowered to the nightdress that skimmed against her body, knowing that she was naked beneath it. And despite the situation and who her father was, he felt his body respond. He reached out, taking the branch of candles from her, and set it down upon the occasional table by their side. Then he took her hand and felt her cool slender fingers in his.

They stood hand in hand and he slid his thumb against the soft skin of her palm. He could see the rise and fall of her breasts beneath the embroidered bodice, see the way the cotton caught against their hardened tips. And he felt his mouth go dry and an ache within his breeches. He swallowed hard and knew there were a thousand reasons he should not be doing this, that this was madness.

'If you were not Misbourne's daughter...' But at this moment it made no difference whether she was Misbourne's daughter or not.

'What would you do?' she whispered.

'I would take you in my arms.' He slid his arms around her and felt the slight tremble go through her body. 'Like this,' he whispered against the top of her head and inhaled the scent of her hair. 'And then I would tip your face up to mine.' He touched his fingers to her chin and gently angled her head up.

'Yes,' she whispered.

'And then I would kiss you.' His mouth lowered inch by inch towards her, until their lips touched and he took her mouth with his own. He kissed her as he had dreamt of doing since the circulating library, tasting her this time, teasing her until her tongue met his, shyly at first, then more boldly. One hand rested against the swell of her hip, the other on the small of her back. He slid a hand higher to the narrowness of her waist and higher still to cup one breast, feeling her nipple pebbled beneath his palm, sliding his fingers to capture the bud through the thick cotton of her nightdress. She gasped, broke off the kiss, staring up at him with startled eyes, her breath suddenly ragged. He could feel the rise and fall of her breast beneath his hand, feel the harried thud of her heart. He stilled his fingers, but left his hand where it rested.

'I…' she whispered, and her eyes scanned his. 'We should not be doing this.'

'We should not,' he agreed. He could feel the way she trembled, standing poised as if about to flee.

Her teeth nipped at her lower lip. He kissed the hurt away with a single gentle kiss. 'I would that any other woman in the world but you were his daughter.' One last kiss and then he released her and stepped back. Then he turned and disappeared through the open window.

Marianne watched him go and did not know what to think. Her heart was racing and her lips throbbed and tingled where he had kissed. Her breasts were heavy and so sensitive that they ached for his touch. Where his hand had lain her breast seemed to burn and even just the memory of his fingers playing upon its tip

made her catch her breath with the sudden sharpness of yearning that shot through her. She wanted him to touch her there, she thought with amazement. She wondered what it would be like were he to touch her without the barrier of her nightdress. Touch her, skin to skin. The imagining made her heart beat ever more wildly. Imagining was safe. And with it the darkness of past remembering seemed to fade.

She stared across at the desk with its open drawers and piles of papers emptied upon its surface. Her father's documents. His private papers. And she thought again of the document that was so important to her father that he had refused to relinquish it even for her life. The highwayman said he had not found it. She moved to the window and quietly closed the sash, the blinds and the curtains—just as her father did every night. Then she began a calm and methodical search where the highwayman had left off.

She did not know what she was looking for. But she looked through all of the papers anyway, convinced that she would know the document when she saw it. She read, looked, searched, every drawer, every cupboard and shelf. And she found many things that her father would not have wanted her to find. Things that shocked her to learn of him. A small portrait of a woman who was not her mother, a great roll of crisp white bank notes tied with a ribbon, and the most scandalous playing cards on which had been painted naked women in provocative poses. But nothing that might qualify as 'the document'.

She heard the opening of the front door and the deliberate quietness of its closing. Francis, she thought, remembering the highwayman's warning. But she did not attempt to tidy away the evidence of her search

or even to extinguish her candle. She did not hear his footsteps. He opened the door with surprising speed and without knocking, stilling when he saw her, before entering and closing the door behind him as quietly as all the rest.

'I know Papa has the document, Francis.'

He made no effort to deny it.

'I need to know what it is.'

'Whatever the answer to your question, Marianne, you are mistaken if you think he will have it so casually stored with his other papers.' There was something about the expression in his eyes that made her realise.

'You have already searched for it.'

'It is not here. Nor within the safe.'

'Francis, what is this document, that a man would abduct me for it and Papa would risk my life to keep it?'

'That is what I mean to discover.' Her brother produced a piece of paper from his pocket, all wrinkled as if it had been screwed to a ball, then smoothed flat again. He opened it out and let her read the words of the highwayman's demand.

'Something happened on Hounslow Heath in 1795,' he said. 'I am going through the archives of *The London Messenger* for the whole of that year.'

'Have you found anything?'

'Not yet.'

'Will you tell me if you do?'

'You would do better to leave this to me. Our father has men searching for the villain. If they do not find him, I will.'

'You do not understand.' She shook her head. 'He could have killed Papa so very easily had he wanted to. And he could have…' she glanced away uneasily

before looking at him once again '…taken advantage of me. But he did neither, even when Papa twice failed to pay the ransom and sent men to kill him. He holds Papa responsible for some heinous crime of which he does not speak.'

'Marianne, he abducted you on the way to your wedding, held a pistol to our father's head and cost you Pickering as a bridegroom. And you defend him?'

'All of that is true. Yet, even so, he is not what you think him. It is true that he is a hard man, a ruthless man. A man who does not flinch or hesitate from anything, and one in which there is undoubtedly something dark and tortured. Yet I cannot rid myself of the sense that he is, beneath it all…a man of integrity. He believes in what he is doing, that it is just and right.'

'Integrity? Marianne, have you taken leave of your senses?' Her brother peered at her in a too-knowing way. 'Do not fancy that he is some Claude Duval, a gentleman highwayman who will dance with you and quote you words of love poetry.' Her brother's gaze sharpened. 'Or perhaps that is precisely what he did and you have developed a *tendre* for the rogue?'

'Do not be foolish,' Marianne snapped, fearing her brother was coming too close to the truth. 'Given my past, I am unlikely to develop a *tendre* for any man.'

Her brother looked away, a look of discomfort in his eyes. 'Forgive me, Marianne, I should not have said that.'

'I should tidy away Papa's papers. It would not go well if he knew what I have been doing in here this night.' She thought of how the highwayman had held her in his arms, of his kiss and the feel of his hand upon her breast. And her cheeks grew warm. No, it would not go well at all, if her father knew.

'I will help you, Marianne.' And together she and Francis began to put the papers away.

'So it was not in his desk?'

'Nor anywhere obvious within his study.'

'It could be anywhere. You haven't a hope in hell of finding it.'

'I have if I rattle him enough.' Rafe looked at Callerton. 'If he thinks I'm getting close, he'll move it.'

'And how exactly are you going to convince him of such a thing?'

'A few little scares here and there. He seems to be growing more nervous by the day. I need to keep a closer eye on him.'

Definitely nervous, thought Rafe as he watched Misbourne mop his brow and glance furtively around the glasshouse in the botanic gardens later that week. Misbourne's glance lingered on him for a moment, making his heart notch a little faster with the realisation of what he was risking by being here. But then the earl's gaze moved on, scanning the crowd. Rafe had not the slightest interest in the exotic plants on display and neither, he was prepared to bet, had Misbourne. Yet the earl, his wife and Marianne were here at the event, facing down the murmur of gossip over Pickering.

Rafe's gaze shifted to Marianne standing in front of her father. By her side Lady Misbourne was engaged in conversation with a woman of the *ton*. Marianne's eyes met his across the distance. Their gazes held and the moment seemed to stretch between them. She looked away, feigning interest in some plant, nodding and listening to something her father was saying. She glanced up again, her gaze again meeting his, a

small half-smile upon her face, her eyes a rich brown in the sunlight that flooded the glasshouse—shy and filled with a pleasure that mirrored what he felt filling his chest at the sight of her. Rafe knew he should look away, but he could not, even though Misbourne was standing right there and he knew he was risking too much. And then her eyes shifted to something behind him and everything in her changed.

The blood appeared to drain from her face, leaving her powder-white, her eyes widened and he could see shock, horror and abject fear in them. She stared as if the very devil had appeared before her, frozen in terror. He followed her gaze, glancing behind him at what she was seeing, but there was only the crowd that had been there before, and a neat tailored back disappearing through it.

And when he looked at Marianne again he saw what her father, standing behind her and busy in finding a fresh handkerchief within his pocket, could not, and what her mother, still engaged in conversation, did not notice. He saw her bloodless pallor and her eyes beginning to roll up in her head and he was already moving across the glasshouse towards her.

Lady Misbourne let out an exclamation as Marianne crumpled. Misbourne reacted, realising what was happening, but not fast enough. Rafe caught her before she hit the ground, scooping her up in his arms.

'Your coat, sir,' Rafe directed Misbourne, who shrugged out of his coat and spread the garment upon the ground. He laid Marianne gently down upon it. She was pale as death and limp, her long fair lashes feathering against the ivory of her cheeks. Her eyes flickered open wide, suddenly filled with the same terror he had seen in them before. And then she saw him

and the terror faded. And there was in its stead such vulnerability, such raw honesty, as if she were letting him see some the private hidden depths of her soul just as she had done that day within the rookery, and in response he felt something squeeze tight within his chest. He was seized with the urge to take her in his arms and protect her from whatever had frightened her, to save her from the darkness that the world could inflict. But Misbourne was leaning over her, his face pinched with concern.

'Marianne?'

'He was here, Papa,' she whispered.

'The highwayman?' Misbourne's words were so quiet Rafe had to strain to hear them.

'Not him,' she said. 'Ro…' But it was as if she could not bring herself to say the name.

Misbourne's face seemed to sharpen and pale. Rafe thought he saw the dart of fear in those devil eyes of his before he raised them to the small crowd gathered around. He snapped at his footman, 'Have the carriage brought round at once, James. Lady Marianne is unwell.'

She tried to sit up, but Misbourne pushed her back down. 'Stay where you are, girl.'

'I am feeling better,' she said, her gaze fluttering over the surrounding crowd. 'Please, let us leave now.'

Marianne was small and slender, but Misbourne was in his sixties and run to fat. Already his face was ruddy from the exertion of crouching down. He glanced up at where Rafe still stood, his eyes meeting Rafe's directly.

'Thank you, sir. Your prompt action saved my daughter injury.'

Rafe gave a nod of acknowledgement, his expres-

sion a mask that hid the emotion beneath. 'My carriage is outside and ready, if you do not wish to wait to transport your daughter from this place.'

Lady Misbourne was flushed with embarrassment, but Marianne was scanning the faces of the crowd and he knew she was looking for the one that had frightened her.

Misbourne's gaze held his with a strange intensity. 'If it would be of no inconvenience to you, sir…'

'None at all,' replied Rafe. He did not ask Misbourne's permission, just scooped Marianne up from where she lay and carried her out to where Callerton waited with the carriage. Lady Misbourne climbed inside beside her daughter. Misbourne hesitated by the open door.

'I am in your debt, sir,' he said with a sincerity of which Rafe had not thought the man capable. Only two feet separated them. He looked the murderer directly in the eye, knowing what Misbourne had done to his parents. He felt his gall rise at the knowledge and wondered if anything of the hatred showed in his eyes. Then Misbourne climbed inside and Rafe shut the door behind him and watched while Callerton drove away.

The crowd was dissipating now that Marianne had gone. He headed home at a steady pace. It was only when he was halfway there that he realised that he had not introduced himself and neither had Misbourne asked his name.

Chapter Eight

The nightmare, which had subsided since Marianne had met the highwayman, returned that night. It started, as it always did, with Marianne blowing out the candles in her bedchamber. But this time when the villain came with his sweet scent of cigar smoke that so filled her with revulsion, she realised that they were not the only two in the darkness. The highwayman stepped out between her and the man whose name she could not bring herself to say.

'Not this time, Rotherham,' he said in her dream. 'Never again.' Then he punched the villain again and again until the limp body slithered to the floor, just like the men had fallen in the rookery and in the burying ground. She knew the villain was dead and she was glad of it. When the highwayman turned and reached his hand to her the darkness vanished and the daylight was bright. And the room in which they stood was no longer her own bedchamber, but that of the man who had saved her.

She took the hand that he offered, with its scraped and bleeding knuckles, and kissed it; then she reached up and held his face between her hands and kissed that,

too, his cheeks and then his mouth, with a passion she did not know was within her. And when she awoke she was not crying out in terror as she normally did when the nightmare came. She felt safe, and in her mind was not that pale-eyed gaunt face, but a pair of amber eyes. And her thighs burned hot and her heart glowed warm.

Within the drawing room of the Earl of Misbourne's town house the next day the clock ticked too loud.

'It is not possible,' Lady Misbourne said. 'He is gone to the Continent and would not dare show his face in London again.'

'I know what I saw, Mama.'

'You must be mistaken, Marianne. It will be the fiasco with the highwayman that has stirred up dark memories of the past. Do you not recall how you were seeing him at every turn for months after we knew he had left the country?' Her mother squeezed her hand and glanced across at her father.

'Maybe you are right, Mama.' Maybe it was her carnal feelings for the highwayman that were making her remember. But she did not feel like she was remembering, she felt like she was finally beginning to forget.

'Maybe we should cancel my birthday party. I am in no spirit to celebrate.'

'I will not hear of it,' her father said. 'You need something to take your mind off all that has happened. Besides, now that Pickering is out of the picture, we need to think about arranging a new match for you. I have invited every eligible bachelor in London—including young Wilcox. That gentleman has long expressed an admiration and interest in you.'

Marianne felt a flare of panic in her stomach. She

began to count her breaths, her eyes seeking Francis's across the room.

Her brother pushed off from the wall against which he was lounging.

'Surely you jest, sir? Wilcox is a lawyer's clerk. He has neither money nor status. He is not good enough for Marianne. And after the mess with Pickering it smacks of desperation. The dust should be allowed to settle for a while before any new deals are struck.'

'You forget yourself, Francis. I know what is best for Marianne. The sooner she is married the better.' Her father spoke as if she were not even present.

'Even though the matter of the highwayman remains unresolved?' said Francis, refusing to back down.

'The highwayman is nothing in the greater scheme of things.' Her father waved a hand dismissively. 'My men will find him eventually.'

'They have found no trace of him so far. Nothing. No one is speaking, not for all the money you have offered. He is still out there. And all the while he remains free he is a threat, not just to you, but to Marianne.'

'I have two hundred men looking for him. What more can I do?'

'Bait a trap to catch him.'

'Lest you have forgotten, we have already tried that,' said her father. 'And it did not work.'

Francis betrayed not even the slightest flicker of response to his father's scorn. 'He knows our every move. He has to be watching us. Go to your safety deposit box at the bank, remove a few pages of paperwork and bring those home. They will lure him to us. And this time, we will be waiting.'

Her father looked at her brother. 'You may be on to something there.'

'No!' The word was out before Marianne could stop it.

Three faces stared at her.

'Do you not want him caught?' her father asked.

'If you catch him, then everyone will know that I was abducted. It would come out in the courtroom and not all of the court reporters work for your newspapers.' It was the only excuse she could think of. 'If it became known that I was gone from home overnight, unchaperoned and in the company of a man...' She did not need to finish it. They all knew the scandal would blight the whole family.

'You misunderstand, Marianne,' her father said. 'It is a private family matter of extreme sensitivity. It was never my intention that the matter go through the courts.'

She stared at him. 'But you said that you meant to bring an end to him.'

'And so I will, my dear,' he said as patiently as if he were explaining it to a child. 'I mean to deal with the highwayman personally.'

'Personally? I do not understand.'

'He is vermin, Marianne. And vermin must be exterminated. Once it is done you need never worry about him again.'

Her eyes widened with horror.

'Father, you distress Marianne with such details,' Francis said.

'Forgive me, my dear. My sole aim is your protection.'

Her protection. As he said the words she could not help herself thinking of the document he held more precious than her.

'Eleanor,' her father said to her mother, 'take Mari-

anne upstairs. I am sure you ladies have many arrangements for a certain twenty-first birthday party to busy yourselves with.'

'All finished, m'lady,' the maid said and stepped back that Marianne might see in the looking glass the hairstyle she had been creating for the past hour. 'You look so different, m'lady. It suits you well.'

'She's right. You do look different,' her brother said from the doorway.

Marianne felt her cheeks warm. 'I wish that Papa had cancelled this ball. I find I have no stomach for it.'

'And let the highwayman win?' her brother queried.

'This isn't about the highwayman,' she said. But in a way it was. She had not stopped thinking about him, not stopped worrying about what her father meant to do to him, or he to her father. She was deeply anxious about the plan her father and Francis were hatching. And at the back of her mind lurked the shadow of Rotherham.

'You and Papa spoke of a plan to catch him… What do you know of it?'

'I know that it is your twenty-first birthday next week and tonight is a ball to celebrate it, Marianne, and that our father will be here in a moment to lead you down the stairs and into the ballroom to greet your guests. I know that it is your duty to look beautiful and enjoy yourself and make our mother proud and our father glad that he spent his money throwing this ball for you. Tonight of all nights you should not be thinking of that villain.'

But she was thinking of him, more so tonight than any other.

Marianne looked at the coil of hair pinned high on

her head and the loose curls cascading down from it in the classical style that was so in fashion. She did look different, she thought. But it had nothing to do with her hairstyle or the fact that almost a hundred people were waiting for her in her father's ballroom. She was not even thinking of the waxen-faced Mr Wilcox. She was thinking of a pair of amber eyes and what it would mean if her father was to succeed in capturing the man to whom they belonged.

From his place lounging against the wall by the window, Rafe watched Misbourne lead Marianne into the ballroom.

A ripple of applause broke out and Marianne blushed and looked embarrassed. The dress was white, its bodice scattered with pink pearls and fixed with a single large ribboned bow, its skirt edged in a deep scallop of pink lace. Her pale curls teased artlessly against her face, making her look like some dark-eyed Aphrodite.

'Misbourne's looking for someone to fill the shoes that Pickering recently vacated,' said Devlin. 'I'd tumble her.'

'Ever the gentleman,' muttered Rafe, unable to hide his irritation.

'And you wouldn't, given half a chance?'

'I've no mind to be caught in parson's mousetrap,' said Rafe coolly.

'None of us have,' said Fallingham. 'We're hardly suitable fodder for a débutante. Makes you wonder why Misbourne invited us.'

'We're five of the *ton*'s most eligible bachelors,' said Bullford, 'and he's looking for a husband for his

daughter: that's why he invited us. He's rumoured to have spent three grand on this bash.'

'I heard Prinny's on the guest list, although quite how he managed that I don't know,' said Razeby.

'Also heard that he's lined up Frederick Wilcox as next in the betrothal line.'

Rafe had heard that too.

'Never heard of him. Who the hell is he?' asked Devlin.

'Apprentice lawyer. Works with Misbourne's man of business,' answered Rafe.

'Hardly a suitable match for the daughter of an earl,' said Bullford.

Fallingham smirked. 'Must be in a hurry to get her married off. Maybe little Lady Marianne isn't quite so pure as she looks.'

The others sniggered. Rafe knew the rake he was playing would have laughed, too, but when he looked at Fallingham he could barely smother the urge to punch his smirking mouth.

He walked away before temptation got the better of him.

'What's got into him?' he heard Fallingham asking after him, but he was out of earshot before the answer came.

Rafe kept to the background, but there was never a moment he was not aware of Marianne. He told himself that he was here because it was an excuse to make a foray into Misbourne's lair, that any extra knowledge he could glean of his enemy was of potential use. But it was not Misbourne that he watched. He knew the risk he was taking in being here, but when it came to Marianne he just could not seem to stay away.

Marianne seemed to sense him. She was dancing

with Wilcox when she saw him and he wondered if he had gone too far in coming here, to her birthday ball. Her gaze met his for those few seconds and held and he saw something flare in her eyes, but she gave no other sign that she had recognised him. And then Wilcox led her away and she did not look back until she could do so as part of the dance.

Wilcox's pate was gleaming with sweat, his hand possessive upon Marianne's at every opportunity. She seemed to withdraw, shudder almost at his touch, just as she had done with every man who danced with her. Rafe watched and knew that he should not care. But then her gaze touched his again, and he knew that he did care, more than he would have thought possible. And he knew, too, that no matter how dangerous, he could not stand here all night and watch her dance with men she did not care for. So he waited for the music to end and then made his way steadily through the crowd towards Misbourne and his family.

'Thank you, Papa, for going to so much trouble for me.' Marianne forced herself to smile at her father, knowing that he must have worked very hard to have so many of the *ton*'s best in their ballroom.

'It was no trouble, my sweet. I am glad that you are happy. You have your choice of young gentlemen as dance partners this evening.'

She bit her lip and could not help from stealing another glance towards the highwayman's group. His friends were still there, but he seemed to have disappeared. She felt her heart sink a little and something of her excitement waned. She smiled all the harder that her father would not see it.

'I have not been introduced to most of them.'

'That will not be a problem. I will ensure that the necessary introductions are made.'

'You know everyone here?' she asked.

'Of a form,' her father said.

'Even those gentlemen over by the windows, the ones who are reputed to be so very dangerous and wild and rakish?' And one of whom was more dangerous than he could imagine.

'The gossipmongers exaggerate. I see three viscounts and two wealthy gentlemen there—all young and all unmarried, each and every one of them.'

'Papa!' Marianne chided, turning away to find herself looking directly at the approach of the highwayman.

Her heart stopped. Her stomach turned a somersault. He could not actually mean to approach her before her papa, could he? But then those amber eyes met hers and she knew that was exactly what he was going to do.

'Lord Misbourne.' He gave the smallest of bows and she saw the warmth vanish from his eyes as he looked at her father.

Beside her she sensed her father stiffen.

'Lady Marianne.' Just as in the botanic gardens that day, his voice without the disguising whisper was rich and deep and delicious. Like a feather stroked from the bare skin at the nape of her neck all the way down, it made her spine tingle. Marianne felt the blush heat her cheeks. 'Would you grant me the honour of the next dance?' He had not asked her father, nor had he waited for an introduction.

'I would be pleased to partner you,' she said quickly before her father could disagree, then shot a look up at her father. 'Papa?'

Her father did not look angry or slighted, maybe because he saw only the man who had helped them at the botanic gardens. But she could not help noticing the strange expression upon his face as he held the highwayman's gaze. 'Marianne, may I introduce Mr Rafe Knight,' he said, his voice revealing nothing of his thoughts.

Rafe Knight. She had thought of him as 'the highwayman' for so long.

'Mr Knight,' she said and curtsied. Then he took her hand in his and, before her father and the best of London's *ton*, led her out on to the dance floor.

It was a Scotch reel, hardly conducive to conversation or any degree of intimacy.

'Rafe Knight,' she repeated, her eyes meeting his. She knew his name at last. And she knew, too, that the opportunity for which she prayed had just been delivered.

'Marianne Winslow,' he replied in that deep rich tone.

She couldn't help herself; she smiled and her heart felt overflowing with gladness, and then the music took them apart. When it brought them back together his hand was in hers and he was birling her around.

'I have to speak to you,' she whispered, breathless not only from the dance.

Then she was off and being birled by the next man in the line before being passed back to him. 'In private.'

The steps led them fast down the centre of the set. At the bottom, just before they peeled apart to travel back up the outside of the set on their own, she whispered, 'It is important.'

Her hand was small and cool within his. His lady

of silver and moonlight. The look in her eyes thawed the chill in his heart and her words fired his blood. He could not deny her, no matter the risk.

'Head for the ladies' withdrawing room after this dance.' Callerton would call him a fool if he knew, but then Callerton didn't need to know.

She nodded and smiled a secret smile that he knew was just for him; God help him, but he felt his heart warm and expand at the sight of it. And his thumb slid a stroke against the soft skin of her hand before he released it. They danced and he could not keep his eyes off her. They danced until finally the music stopped. Misbourne was watching him again as he returned her, watching him with something in those dark soulless eyes that made Rafe feel uneasy, as if the man knew much more than he was revealing. But he turned away from Misbourne and made his way from the ballroom to wait for Marianne.

Marianne walked slowly, her eyes scanning the bodies that crowded the hallway and staircase, looking for only one man: her highwayman—Rafe Knight.

His touch was gentle against her arm.

'The study,' she whispered and he followed her there. They slipped inside and closed the door behind them.

The desk was clear aside from a half-full glass of brandy that sat upon it and the candles in the wall sconces were alight, as if Misbourne had not long left the room. Rafe remembered the last time he had been in here: Marianne, in her nightdress, in his arms, her mouth sweet and eager beneath his, her breast and the thud of her heart beneath his hand.

'Mr Knight,' she said, and now that they were alone

she seemed shy, as if she, too, was remembering what had happened between them in this room.

'I think we know each other well enough, Marianne, that you should call me by my given name.'

'Rafe,' she said and he savoured the sound of it on her lips.

'That day in the botanic gardens…who did you see, Marianne?'

'No one,' she said hurriedly, glancing away—but not before he saw a shadow flit across her face.

He knew that she was lying. That look of terror on her face that day had haunted him ever since. He knew what he would do if he ever found the person responsible. His fingers touched her cheek in the gentlest of caresses. Her skin was so soft, so perfect, beneath his fingers.

Her eyes came to his, scanning them as if she could read the darkness that was in his soul. 'We do not have much time. My mother will notice if I take too long.'

'Your parents guard you well.' Her parents. And he was reminded again of why this was futile. There could be nothing between them save the torture of knowing what they could not have. Yet still he stayed, standing in Misbourne's study, looking at the woman who was Misbourne's daughter.

'They do,' she murmured, glancing away again with that strange uneasiness about her. But then she seemed to gather herself; when she looked at him again she was stronger and filled with an urgency of purpose. 'My father and brother are planning some means to draw you out of hiding. Whatever they might communicate to you, do not heed it; it is a trap to catch you.'

'I do not mind being caught as long as I take Misbourne with me.'

'You do not understand,' she said. 'My father has no intention of involving the courts.' She swallowed. 'He means to kill you.'

He gave a small hard laugh.

But she misunderstood his irony. 'You do not know my father, Rafe. Incredulous though it may sound, he is serious. He really does mean to kill you.'

'I do not doubt it for a minute, Marianne. I was never the one who doubted his capacity for murder.' He saw the hurt flash in her eyes before she turned away and he could have bitten out his own tongue at his carelessness.

'Marianne.' He caught her hands in his. 'Forgive me. I am wont to forget that he is your father. I did not mean to hurt you.'

She glanced up into his eyes. 'He *is* my father,' she said, 'and I am not unaware that I am betraying my family in warning you of his intent, that I seem to have done nothing other since we met. But I do not wish for him to hurt you.' She glanced down as if embarrassed by the admission. 'Nor do I wish for you to hurt him.'

Her words were soft against the silence that followed. He wished he could offer her reassurances, tell her that her father was safe. But he could not lie to her. False hope was crueller in the long term.

'I thank you for your warning…and I do understand something of your dilemma.'

'Do you?' She looked up at him.

'Of course. I am not unaffected by the situation in which we find ourselves.' She had no idea of the way she affected him, or what it did to him knowing that he could not stop until he watched her father dance upon the gibbet.

He saw the blush touch pink to her cheeks and

thought what a cruel game fate was playing with them both.

His thumbs slid against her small slender fingers and in return he felt them close around his.

'Did you come tonight that you might continue your search?' He could see that she was holding her breath.

'No, Marianne. I came to see you.' He pulled her closer. The air sparked between them, the tension was so tight that he felt his blood rush hot with it.

'It is dangerous for you to be here.'

'Very dangerous,' he agreed, lowering his mouth to hers.

He kissed her as he had been dreaming of kissing her all of these nights past. He kissed her until she was breathless and weak-legged. Her arms wound around his neck, her fingers threading through his hair, freeing it from its queue. He sensed the untapped passion in her that contrasted so starkly with her innocence and shyness. He could feel it in her kiss, feel it in the tremble of her slim body pressed to his.

Rafe forgot all about Misbourne. He forgot about the document and the quest that had spurred him through the last fifteen years. There was only Marianne Winslow and the depth of feeling and passion that was exploding between them.

His hands were on her breasts just as she had imagined every night as she lay in her bed. But this was real. He was touching her and his touch was gentle, not greedy or grabbing or hurtful. Her body was flush against his, fitting as if they had been made as two halves of the same mould. She let herself relax against him, revelling in his strength and his sheer size, and in the hardness of his muscles.

The scent of him and the faint undertone of san-

dalwood made her feel heady and safe and excited all at the same time, drunk as if on the bubbles of champagne that her brother had let her sip from his glass when she was sixteen. Her mouth was filled with the taste of him, her tongue meeting his in a dance that she did not want to stop. He caressed her, every part of him against every part of her. Tongue to tongue. Lips to lips. His hands on her breast and her hip. His heart against hers, and as he kissed her, as he touched her, she felt the barricades she had erected around herself begin to crumble.

Even through all the layers of her clothing she could feel the stroke of his hand against her nipples. His fingertips traced against the very tops of her breasts that only just showed over the neckline of her dress. She caught her breath at the sensation and felt her blood rush all the wilder and her nipples tighten unbearably as if they ached for his touch. She did not remember the darkness of the past. She did not remember her fears. She thought only of Rafe Knight, of the magic he was stoking within her body and how much she wanted this intimacy with him.

His breath caressed the crook of her neck and she angled her head, allowing his lips to tease where his breath had been. He touched his lips to the small tender hollow at the base of her throat, then kissed all the way along her collarbone, tasting her, making her thread her fingers through the length of his dark hair and hold on to him. And when he reached the small puff sleeve of her dress he eased it off her shoulder that he might kiss the skin beneath.

The sensation made her gasp so loud that he drew back a little and looked into her face. She did not release him, just kept her hands where they cradled on

either side of his head, her thumbs stroking tiny caresses. His eyes looked almost as dark as her own, and
there was a look in them that she knew was desire. She
knew it, yet she was not afraid. For she felt the same
hunger, the same need in herself.

'Marianne,' came his highwayman's whisper as he
placed a kiss in the middle of her *décolletage*. 'Marianne,' again as his lips slid lower.

'Rafe,' she replied and arched against him, desperate to feel him all the more.

Within his arms he bowed her gently, as if she
were a willow, as his mouth closed over the top of her
breast, as his fingers edged her bodice infinitesimally
lower. A moan escaped and she did not know it was
her own mouth that made the sound. She clutched his
head tighter to her breasts, holding him as if she would
never let him go. She was so lost in the moment that she
heard nothing save the beat of her own heart and of his.

She did not understand at first when Rafe stiffened
and glanced swiftly round at the door. Her mind was
dulled with passion. And then, when she looked again,
her father was standing in the doorway, grey-faced
with worry, eyes wide with shock. Her mother, standing behind him, gave a little shriek.

Her father pulled her mother inside the study and
closed the door behind them both. 'Good God, woman,
cease your hysterics unless you have a mind to broad-
cast this affair to every last one of our guests.'

Rafe had released Marianne and positioned himself to shield her from her parents' view, but he could
not hide the truth. Awareness of precisely of what she
had been doing hit her like a deluge of cold water.
She could not believe it. Even as she clutched an arm
around herself, her father's gaze swept over her and

Marianne felt that Rafe's every touch, every kiss was branded upon her for her father to see. Her cheeks scalded hot with shame. And then her father's gaze moved to Rafe and she saw it harden.

'Papa…' she started, but her father ignored her.

'I think we have something to discuss, Mr Knight,' he said.

'Indeed we do, sir.' She saw Rafe give a nod, but his eyes were anything but submissive.

'Take her upstairs,' her father hissed at her mother. 'And try to make her look as if she has not just been seduced.'

'Papa, it was not like that.'

'Do as I say, Marianne,' he snapped, his eyes so dark and clouded with anger that she feared what would unfold between him and Rafe.

'Papa, it was my fault. Mr Knight was—'

'Marianne,' Rafe said and only then did he shift the lethality of his gaze from her father. His eyes met hers and they were dark and meaningful, conveying a message that she should do as he asked. 'Go with your mother. Everything shall be well.'

Yet still she hesitated to leave the two men alone.

'Marianne,' Rafe said more softly and she realised that she had to trust him. She gave a nod and, with one last lingering look that spoke all that she could not say, she turned to her mother.

Chapter Nine

Misbourne waited until the door closed behind Marianne and her mother before he spoke. 'You have ruined my daughter, Mr Knight.'

'I am aware of the situation,' Rafe said. He knew that there was no way back for Marianne after this. Only one ending to this evening could save her.

The door burst open and Linwood appeared, a feral look in those black eyes of his. 'You abominable rake! By hell, I will call you out, sir, for what you've done to my sister.'

'Get out,' said Misbourne coldly. 'I am dealing with the matter.'

'You cannot seriously mean to—'

'I said get out.'

Linwood glowered at his father, then turned and walked away, closing the door behind him.

'Ignore him,' said Misbourne.

'Surely you mean to call me out too?' Rafe asked, part of him hoping that the bastard would, even though he knew it would never come to that. For no matter how much he hated Misbourne, he could not stand back and watch Marianne's reputation crumble to dust be-

fore all of London. The writing was on the wall; it had been ever since Misbourne had opened the study door.

'Do I need to?' asked Misbourne.

'Only if you have an objection to my marrying your daughter.'

'I shall organise the wedding for Wednesday,' said Misbourne. 'I think you will understand the need for a speedy and discreet affair.' He lifted the glass decanter from the occasional table and poured brandy into two glasses, one of which he passed to Rafe. Rafe ignored the proffered glass, his eyes holding Misbourne's.

'We should return to the ballroom.'

'You are right,' Misbourne conceded. 'We must keep up appearances.'

'But I cannot marry him!' Marianne exclaimed after her father finished his announcement to the family in the breakfast room the next morning.

'You seemed to like him well enough in my study last night.'

Marianne felt the heat glow in her cheeks. 'It was just a kiss. He did nothing more.' She was lying; it had been so much more than a kiss. It had been something that made her forget herself, the past, her fears. In those moments she had felt alive and vibrant and unafraid, a thousand miles removed from everything that was Marianne Winslow.

'Just a kiss, Marianne?' Her mother raised an eyebrow. 'Your father and I both saw exactly what was going on.'

'Merely being alone with Rafe Knight in my study was enough to compromise your reputation,' said her father more calmly. 'Knight is no green boy. He knew the risk he was taking.'

A risk far greater than her father understood.

'Honour decrees that he offer for you.'

'But you don't understand.' She glanced round at her family, at her mother's pursed lips and her brother's dark gaze, and the stubborn set of her father's jaw. Rafe was the highwayman her father had set half of London to kill. Her father was the man against whom Rafe had sworn a dark vengeance. The two men she loved, each sworn to destroy the other. And no matter what she felt for Rafe, no matter how much the idea of becoming his wife might entice her, she knew that it was far too dangerous.

'I understand very well.' But he didn't. He had no idea.

'It was my fault. I asked him to meet me in the study.'

'Good Lord!' she heard her mother mutter beneath her breath. She did not look at Francis, just kept her eyes on her father, on the angry disapproval in his eyes and the curling of his lip. She knew they were all disappointed in her.

'And why would you do that, Marianne?'

'Because I wanted to…' *Warn him of your plan.* She closed her eyes and swallowed down the guilt and warring emotions. 'Because I wanted him to kiss me,' she finished, and felt her face flame all the hotter.

'And he obliged.'

'Yes.' She glanced down. 'So you see, it was my fault.'

'He is hardly the innocent in this.'

'And neither am I,' said Marianne quietly.

The words hung in the room, all clumsy and uncomfortable.

'It makes no difference,' her father said, but the look in his eyes had softened.

'But, Papa—'

'No buts,' her father said. 'You will marry him on your birthday.'

'Wednesday!' she said. 'So soon?'

'Wednesday,' her father said. 'And that will be an end to it.' The strength and angry stubbornness was back in his eyes. No argument was going to sway him.

She turned to walk away without asking to be excused.

'Marianne!' her mother exclaimed, but Marianne ignored her and kept walking.

Her father's words made her hesitate halfway across the drawing room. 'Until you become Knight's wife you do not leave this house, Marianne. Knight is procuring the special licence. The ceremony shall take place in this very room so there is no need for travel. After the last attempt at a wedding day I'm not taking any chances. I want you kept safe from the highwayman.'

Marianne felt like laughing and crying both at once. If only her father knew that he had just betrothed his daughter to that same highwayman. She did not look back, just walked right out of the room.

'Treat her gently,' Misbourne said to his wife, then waited until the door closed behind her before turning to Linwood. 'Ensure that all windows and doors are kept locked. No one enters the house without being vetted by me, you or your mother. And I mean no one, not even the lowliest of tradesmen.

'He may not be the bridegroom I would have chosen...' Misbourne stared off into the distance and thought of the past '...nor this the means of their betrothal, but he will marry her and that is good enough.'

'He's a damnable rake, taken to running with Devlin and his crew of late. He seduced Marianne, despite what she says. She is young and her head filled with foolish notions of romance. She fancies herself in love with the rogue and seeks to protect him by taking the blame on herself. You never should have invited him and his cronies. I don't care what he did at the botanic gardens.'

'You are too hard on him. We all make mistakes when we are young.'

'It is unlike you to be so solicitous. Few people knew of their being in the study alone. We could hush this up. Knight does nothing save drink and game and womanise. Are you so desperate to see her married off that you would have her wed such a man?'

'I cannot deny that I will be happy to see her wed.' Misbourne felt the stain upon his soul grow heavy and dark as the shadows seemed to whisper in his ear, reminding him of what he had done, what he could never forget. 'I long for the day that she is settled...and safe.' And then he realised that he had revealed too much and that his son was watching him too carefully. He pulled himself together, closed his ears to the voices that whispered to him. 'So she will marry him, and there will be no more gossip. Now, I wish to hear no more about it.' When the door closed behind his son, a dark frown creased his face, and the darkness of the past rolled in to turn the dust-flecked sunlight of the breakfast room to cold grey shadow, and Misbourne longed for Wednesday.

'What the hell do you mean you are marrying Marianne Winslow on Wednesday?' Callerton stared at him aghast. 'Have you forgotten who she is?'

'You do not need to remind me of her relationship to Misbourne; it is ever in my mind. But I have compromised her and I will not leave her to face the shame of it alone.'

'I told you to stay away from her. You could have any woman in London and you have to go dallying after Misbourne's daughter. Hell's teeth, Rafe!'

'I do not want any other woman. I want her!' Rafe raked a hand through his hair.

'Enough to marry her?'

'Were Misbourne not the complicating factor, yes.'

'But Misbourne is in this as much as she. Are you are prepared to call Misbourne father for the sake of having her? For that is what it comes down to, Rafe.'

Rafe's hand flexed so hard that the brandy glass within it cracked. 'What else can I do? Walk away and leave her ruined?'

'Yes, if that is what it takes.' Callerton's face was pale. 'I would not see any woman's reputation hurt, but no good can come of this.'

'You know I cannot do that.'

'Your blood cries out for vengeance, Rafe. Do you think it to be so easily silenced to save his daughter's honour?'

'What is between Misbourne and I can never be silenced. It plays out to the end.'

'You will not stop until there is a noose around his neck.'

Rafe looked at him, the confirmation in his eyes.

'And yet you still mean to marry his daughter?'

'Marrying Marianne will not prevent me from bringing her father to justice.'

'Think of what that will do to her. If Misbourne

hangs for murder, his family will be destroyed. You will be a part of that family, Rafe.'

'I will never be a part of Misbourne's family. Marianne will take my name. She will be my wife. I will take care of her.'

'Do you think she will forgive you for destroying her father?'

'If I do not fulfil my oath, then I will not forgive myself. It is a matter of honour both to marry Marianne and to see her father executed. And I will do both.'

Callerton shook his head. 'You are making a mistake in marrying the girl, Rafe. There can be only trouble down this route. You can choose to save her honour or your own, but you cannot have both.'

'Mr Knight,' Marianne said politely and made her curtsy. And when she peeped up through her lashes, that steady amber gaze was on hers and she blushed at the sudden heady rush of anticipation and longing.

'Lady Marianne,' he replied and the sound of his voice seemed to stroke a caress all the way down her spine. He was dressed impeccably in a tailcoat of dark-blue, buff-coloured breeches and riding boots. In one hand was his hat, riding gloves and crop, and in the other a bouquet of flowers.

'For you.' He passed her the bouquet, not large and showy as Mr Wilcox's had been, but small and plain and made entirely of white rosebuds.

'Thank you, Mr Knight. They are beautiful.' Marianne inhaled their perfume.

'They reminded me of you.'

She felt herself blush and lowered her eyes. 'White roses are my favourite flower,' she murmured.

'How lovely, Mr Knight,' said her mother with a

false smile, whisking the bouquet into the hands of the footman to find a suitable vase.

'Indeed, Lady Misbourne,' he said, but his gaze did not move from Marianne's and the look in them was passionate and possessive and everything that was contrary to the pale innocence of the flowers.

The silence in the room was heavy and awkward. Her mother lifted her tambour and worked upon her embroidery. Marianne swallowed. There was so much she wanted to say to Rafe, none of which could be spoken in front of her mother.

'The weather is uncommonly fine for the time of year,' she said, trying to fill the silence.

His eyes looked golden in the sunlight that flooded the drawing room. His face, so handsome and serious that she longed to press her lips to his and tell him that she loved him. To tell him that she understood all that he had done for her and all that he was prepared to do to save her once again, even though she could not let him.

In the silence the knock at the front door was so sudden and loud that Marianne jumped. Then the butler appeared, whispering soft words in her mother's ear and her mother frowned. 'I shall come at once.'

She looked at her daughter, then at Rafe. 'Excuse me while I step out of the room for a few moments.' She left the drawing-room door wide open in her wake. Marianne glanced towards it and lowered her voice.

'I am grateful for your desire to save my honour, but I cannot let you do this, Rafe.' She looked up into his eyes. 'You cannot possibly marry me.'

'Marianne, we do not need to have this conversation.'

'Yes, we do. It is too dangerous. If my father were to discover who you are…'

'We will deal with that if it happens.'

'He has sworn to kill you!'

'I know what your father does to those who cross him.' There was an underlying bitterness to his tone that made her shiver.

'And you have sworn vengeance upon him.'

'Not vengeance,' he said, correcting her as he had done before. 'Justice.'

'Justice that involves you wishing him dead.'

'I cannot deny it.'

Her blood ran cold at how adamant he was about it. 'He is my father, Rafe. And I love him, even with his imperfections. I cannot bear that you should wish to hurt him…'

His expression remained hard.

'…or he, you.'

His hand closed around hers, his thumb stroking the centre of her palm.

'I will not marry you, Rafe. I cannot. Surely you see that?'

'I see that if you do not marry me you are ruined.'

'I will survive a little social embarrassment.' She glanced away. 'I have survived much worse.' And her mind flickered back to touch on a shadow from the past that was fading more with every day that passed.

'After Arlesford and Pickering you will not survive this.'

'I will not marry you,' she said again, even though he was the only man in the world she would willingly marry.

She saw something flicker in his eyes.

'What is between us, Marianne, cannot so easily be

extinguished. It will burn whether we marry or not, whether we will it or not.'

'You are mistaken,' she said, even though she knew he was not. Her heart was already lost and nothing she could do would reclaim it.

'Am I?' he asked, stepping closer.

She swallowed, feeling her heart begin to thump and that same fluttering in her stomach that she felt whenever he was close.

He raised her hand to his lips and kissed where his thumb had traced.

'Marry me, Marianne,' he said in the highwayman's harsh whisper. And when his arms came around her, she went into them willingly. When his mouth touched hers, she kissed him with all the love that was in her heart.

'Your mother has left you unchaperoned?' Her father's voice shattered the moment.

She jumped and felt a panic over whether he had heard Rafe's whisper and recognised it as the highwayman's. 'There was a caller at the front door; she went to deal with it.' She stood slightly in front of Rafe.

Her father's eyes slid to meet Rafe's.

She tensed, ready to protect her highwayman. But when her father spoke she knew he had heard nothing after all.

'Mr Knight.' He gave a small bow of the head.

'Lord Misbourne.' Rafe's bow was so slight as to be insulting and Marianne heard the anger and dislike that edged his words. They were like two dogs facing one another, hackles raised. She could sense the energy in Rafe, a barely contained snarl, ready to pounce and rip out her father's throat. Her father was less aggressive, but watchful and uneasy just the same.

'I will call for Marianne to take her for a drive in Hyde Park tomorrow afternoon.' He should be asking her father's permission, not telling him what he intended. She held her breath, waiting for her father to respond to the insult and remembering his decree that she was not to leave the house.

'I do not think so,' her father said carefully and there was nothing of the angry voice he would have used had anyone else uttered such a slight. 'Marianne has much to prepare for the wedding ceremony. We would not want her to over-exert herself.'

'Indeed not. But she is in good health and a carriage trip in the park is hardly likely to over-exert her. Do you doubt my ability to protect her?'

'Never that.' Her father smiled as if Rafe had just cracked some secret joke. 'Like myself, Mr Knight, you are not a man to be lightly crossed. I think you will make my daughter a very good protector.'

Like myself. The words seemed to hang in the air between them, offered by her father like an olive branch and unwittingly the very comparison that would inflame Rafe.

'Come Wednesday, Mr Knight, Marianne will be your wife and her care passes to you. Until then, she is under my protection.'

She felt Rafe stiffen.

'I do not need a protector,' she said. 'I am perfectly able to protect myself.' But both men ignored her. 'And as for a trip in the park, Mr Knight, it would be very pleasant, but I am afraid I am busy all of tomorrow afternoon.'

'Perhaps we should have a drink in my study, Mr Knight, and discuss the wedding plans.' Her father

smiled, but it was strained and there was something in his eyes that she did not recognise.

Her hand hung loosely at her side. She moved it surreptitiously so that the edge of her little finger touched ever so lightly against Rafe's hand. Her gaze slid to his, imploring him to be civil, telling him with her eyes what she could not tell him with her words.

'Another time, Misbourne,' Rafe said. 'I am already engaged to attend a meeting. I bid you good day.' The rejection was tempered by a bow of his head, a concession she knew was only for her sake. 'Lady Marianne.' He pulled her to him and kissed her mouth, his lips searing against hers. It was an action to claim her as his before her father—an action both of defiance and possession. Her father watched with dark eyes and to Marianne's surprise said not one word of disapproval. 'Until Wednesday,' Rafe said as he released her and disappeared through the door.

Her father looked at her and said nothing.

'If you will excuse me, Papa.'

He gave a nod. 'Of course, my dear,' he said as if nothing untoward had happened.

Misbourne watched his daughter leave. Three more days and she would be married. 'Every cloud has a silver lining.' He smiled grimly to himself. No matter who Rafe Knight was, no matter what he did, Misbourne could only be glad of the turn of events. 'Wednesday—only three more days,' he whispered, but he knew he would not sleep until Knight's ring was upon Marianne's finger and she was safe as his wife.

Without Rafe's presence Marianne's fears over the marriage seemed to take hold once more, to magnify out of all proportion. Her appetite waned so that she

did little more than pick at her food. At night she lay restless, tossing and turning on her bed, unable to sleep for the turmoil of thoughts tumbling in her head. Preparations of valerian did not help. Counting her breaths did not help. Nothing that she did in the longest hours of the night made any difference. And when she did sleep, out of sheer exhaustion, there was nothing of rest, only of the worst imaginings.

She was in the country, standing beneath a leaden sky, while the wind howled like a banshee and blew a chill cold enough to freeze the stoutest of hearts. Before her was a lonely hill at the top of which grew a solitary tree, tall, its branches gnarled and twisted as a demon from a hellish tale. The light was so grey and dismal she could not see clearly. She stared up the hill, at the tree and saw the movement of a shadow against it. Something about the sight gripped her heart with terror.

She began to run, desperate to prevent what was about to happen, clambering up the steepness of the hill. But the grass was wet and slippery beneath her feet and the wind was like a great hand forcing her back, stinging her face, roaring in her ears. She fought for all she was worth, but by the time she reached the summit, the night had come and she could no longer see. In the silence she heard the creak of a rope swinging heavy in the wind. *Rafe!* she cried in the dream. *Papa!* But in reply came only the crashing of thunder that rolled across the sky and the fork of white lightning that, in the transient moment of its flicker, lit the man's limp body swinging from the noose strung from the tree. And no matter how hard she tried, she could not see whether it was Rafe or her father. But it did not matter, because she was too late, and when

she woke her maid was peering down anxiously into her face and Marianne's cheeks were wet with tears.

The horror of the dream would not leave her, but grew only worse so that as the days crept by, hour by agonising hour, she could not dispel the sense of impending doom. She imagined persuading Rafe that she would not marry him a hundred times, even practised what she would say to him. She both longed and dreaded to see him. But Rafe did not visit again. Not on the first day, or the second or even the third. And all the while there were dressmakers and florists and menus, everything that went with the preparations for a normal wedding, except for the announcement of the betrothal in her father's newspaper. There was no mention of that.

Her mother fussed incessantly, and her father and Francis were always in the background, always guarding and watching. Marianne was not left alone even for a minute. And every night the door to her bedchamber was locked from the outside.

By Tuesday night Marianne could think of nothing other than Rafe and what the morning would bring: her twenty-first birthday and her marriage.

She heard her father go to bed a little after one o'clock. Her body was tired, but her mind was racing; she pushed back the covers and rose from the bed, moving to the window. She edged the curtains open and looked out into the night. The lamps were still burning and overhead the bright light of the moon was hidden behind the charcoal clouds of the night. She looked out over the houses and the dark foliage of the gardens opposite that stirred in the breeze. And as she watched she thought she saw the dark figure of a man standing there amidst the shrubbery. Rafe. And

despite everything her heart lifted and something of the worry diminished.

She pressed her palm to the window as if to touch him. But the figure made no similar gesture, only stood there watching. She stared all the harder and, as she did so, the clouds parted to reveal the moon. In the ethereal silver light she saw not Rafe, but Rotherham.

She jumped back, wrenching her hand from the window, her heart thudding so hard that she could scarcely breathe, her legs trembling violently. She took a deep breath, trying to calm the nausea that was roiling in her stomach. Then she stepped to the window once more, determined to see if it really was Rotherham. But the clouds had covered the moon once more and the figure had vanished, absorbed by the blackness of the night. *Had it been real, or simply her imagination?* She stood there a while and watched, but there was no movement and no sign that anyone had been there.

'My lady?' the maid whispered from the truckle bed behind her.

'Go back to sleep, Polly. I am all right.'

But she wasn't all right. She wasn't all right at all.

Chapter Ten

Wednesday came both too quickly and not quickly enough. Rafe declined the seat that Misbourne offered and stood at the front of the drawing room of the town house in Leicester Square. The room had been dressed with both white and pink flowers, and huge bows and swags of ribbons. The heavy perfumed scent of lilies tickled his nose. Although the day was overcast and the wind held the chill of autumn, the fire had not been lit and he was glad of it. The chairs had been set out in rows and the guests, who were only around ten in number, sat within them, the quiet hum of their chatter filling the room, speculation glinting in their eyes at a surprise wedding organised so close to the bride's betrothal to another, that had allowed no apparent time for a new courtship. It could not have escaped their attention that there had been no mention of a wedding at Marianne's birthday ball only a few days earlier.

Callerton glanced round at them again, easing his cravat a little looser as if it pressed too tight around his neck. Rafe could see the unease in his friend's eyes; so at home on a battlefield, but clearly uncomfortable in the drawing room of a high-society town house.

They watched a footman enter the room and whisper in Misbourne's ear. The earl slipped away.

'Look on the bright side,' Callerton whispered to Rafe as they turned to face the front. 'You'll be able to search to your heart's content. You'll find out where he's hiding it eventually.'

'That's not why I'm doing this.'

'I know.' Callerton touched his fingers to the pocket watch of his white-worked waistcoat. 'If I've forgotten the ring, do you still have to marry her?' He risked a smile.

Despite everything—the severity of the situation, what he was about to do—Rafe returned the smile.

Then the string quartet in the corner began to play and the guests rose to their feet and Rafe knew without looking round that Marianne had entered the room. Callerton had turned to watch her, but Rafe resisted the temptation. He knew what he was about to do. Marrying the daughter of the man he had spent a lifetime hating had not been part of the plan. But he was honour-bound to marry her and he would not let her face ruin at the hands of the *ton* simply because he hadn't been able to resist her. And if he was honest, there was a damn sight more to it than that.

She was inside his head, inside his heart. She flowed in his blood and was in the very air that he breathed. He could not get enough of her. He cared about her. And he wanted her as he had never wanted a woman in all of his life, for all that she had Misbourne's blood flowing in her veins, wanted her with a passion that seemed to simmer and nag and plague him night and day. There was the faint smell of violets and the rustle of silk. And inside, his heart leapt even at the same moment that the resentment began coursing through

him, the utter distaste that he was about to ally himself to Misbourne.

He remained facing forwards, refusing to turn while he reined in the disgust and hatred he felt for the man, knowing that at this moment, more than any other, he must mask his true feelings. And when he turned his head to the side at last, Misbourne had retreated to the first row of seats, leaving Marianne standing there alone.

The sight of her made Rafe's heart miss a beat. Every time he looked at her it was as if he was seeing her for the first time—yet simultaneously as if he had always known her. That feeling of familiarity and tenderness as if she were already his, and always had been. And protectiveness. His woman, he thought, with a fierceness.

Gone were the bows and swags and heavy layers of lace. The dress was a plain ivory silk, devoid of all decoration, yet cut to fit Marianne's slim figure perfectly. The neckline was square and low enough to expose the smooth perfect skin of her *décolletage*. Even her neck was bare, devoid of so much as a ribbon—a fact that reminded him of the outsized ugly pearls that Pickering had bought her. And he realised with a stab of shame that Marianne had probably expected him to bring a necklace as his gift to her. But Rafe had brought no gift, either for the wedding or for her birthday. His gaze swept up to her hair, simply styled and caught up in a chignon from which several curling silver-blonde tendrils escaped to tease against her neck. The simplicity suited Marianne. He had always thought her a beautiful woman, but today Rafe could not take his eyes from her.

Her gaze fluttered up to meet his and he saw the

uncertainty in her dark eyes. And without thinking he took her hand in his, and gave it a small reassuring squeeze. Her fingers felt cool beneath his, and he could feel the slight tremor that ran through them. He wanted to tell her that she had nothing to be afraid of, that all would be well, but then the priest opened his Book of Common Prayer and began to speak the words that would bind them together.

Marianne had seen the hard line of Rafe's jaw and the way he could not bear to look round at her. She knew that he was only doing this out of a sense of honour, that she was the last woman on earth he would have chosen to marry. And her heart ached because she loved him; she knew that whatever he felt for her, it was not love. How could it be when, every time he looked at her, he was reminded of the man he despised?

And then his fingers closed around hers. And the warmth of his skin seemed to spread throughout her, thawing the ice and the fear and dread that flowed in her veins. It was such a gentle gesture, small and surreptitious in nature, but the strength of the man seemed to seep into her from that one point of contact, calming her nerves and all of her fears, buoying her, rekindling that tiny spark of hope that in some way, against all the odds, all might be well between them.

Marianne felt that what was happening was unreal, as if it were part of some dream. The priest's words droned on and all Marianne could think of was that this could not really be happening. She was marrying the man who had abducted her *en route* to her wedding with Pickering. The man who had sworn to destroy her father, a man who was darker, stronger, more dangerous than any man she had known.

'I, Marianne Elizabeth Winslow, take thee, Rafe Knight, to be my lawfully wedded husband,' said the priest for the second time, peering at her with exasperation. And Marianne wondered if she could do it, if she could close the door of no return and bind him to her. She glanced around.

All the guests were staring with bated breath, almost gleeful at the prospect of her ruining yet another betrothal. Her mother's mouth was tight, her eyes signalling frenziedly that Marianne must say the words. Her brother was looking at her with his usual closed expression. She could see the sheen of the sweat upon her father's forehead, see the way he gripped his hands tightly together and the pallor beneath the grizzled grey of his beard, and, worst of all, the anger and fear that vied in his eyes. And finally her gaze moved to Rafe, to those clear warm amber eyes that seemed to reach through everything and touch her very soul, just as they had done that first day on Hounslow Heath.

His face was as if chiselled by the hand of a master sculptor from the marble of the gods—that strong manly nose, those perfect sculpted lips, the hard line of his jaw clean-shaven and strong. She remembered how he had saved her from being attacked in St Giles Rookery, how he had taken a bullet for her in the burying ground. And how he had not ridiculed her fear of the dark, but brought candles. He was the only man in the world she wanted to marry. The man that she loved. She did not think of anything else. All her fears were forgotten, all her worries were gone. She looked into his eyes and she said the words straight from her heart.

'I, Marianne Elizabeth Winslow, take thee…'

And when she had finished all that had to be said, Rafe slipped a gold wedding band on to the third fin-

ger of her left hand and the priest pronounced them man and wife.

'Let no man tear asunder what God has blessed and put together.'

Rafe lowered his face to hers and he kissed her, not some formal polite touching of lips, but a kiss in which all of the passion that was between them fired and blazed with a fury, so that she felt herself almost consumed by the fierceness of it. And when he drew back, the guests and even her mother were staring as if they could not believe it. Her brother's eyes were narrowed, dark as thunder, and her father looked... relieved.

The wedding breakfast was held within her father's dining room. They ate fine steak and drank the best of champagnes. And in the centre of the table was the elaborate sugar palace that had been sculpted for her wedding to Pickering and beside it a cake that had been iced for her birthday. Her father was the soul of the celebration. He laughed and joked, and, contrary to his usual demeanour, was the very best of hosts. And Marianne felt the squeeze of her conscience that he did not know the truth of the situation.

She glanced up to find Rafe's eyes on her, as if he could see every thought that was in her head, and beneath the table she felt him take her hand and rub his fingers against hers. He smiled, a smile that was all for her, and her heart glowed with the happiness that only he could light. She smiled back—and it was enough to get her through the rest of the breakfast, the conversations with the wedding guests and the string quartet renditions that her father had arranged for the celebrations.

* * *

By the time all was done and the hour had come for her to leave with Rafe, Marianne was aware of a new nervousness. Especially when her mother held her close, kissed her cheek and whispered a reminder that Marianne did not want to hear. Her father only looked into her face, and he nodded, as if everything had come right. Then he took her hand and kissed it, before giving it to Rafe.

'She is your wife now,' he said, and there was a catch of emotion in his voice. 'Look after her.'

She felt the slight underlying tension in Rafe directed at her father, but as his fingers closed around hers, he showed nothing of it.

He said not a word, only led her out to the waiting carriage and settled her inside before taking the opposite seat.

All of the wedding guests had assembled in the street to cheer them on their way. Her mother and father stood on the steps to the town house, smiling and proud. Behind them, leaning against the frame of the opened front door, stood her brother, his eyes dark and angry, his expression sullen. When she turned away, she heard the shadow of the past whisper in her ear.

Ahead lay the night, and a fresh breath of fear breathed upon Marianne.

Rafe could sense Marianne's nervousness and knew it must be difficult for her to return as his wife to a house where once she had been his captive. The clock ticked loudly in the silence of his drawing room.

'An eventful day for your birthday,' he said.

'Yes.'

The silence stretched between them.

'The day has been long, Marianne,' he said. 'We should retire for the night.' He wanted to make her his wife in truth, to make love to her.

She did not meet his gaze, just kept her eyes trained on the tea cup before her.

'I have not finished my tea,' she said and took another sip from the delicate bone-china cup. She had been so long in the drinking of it that any tea remaining in the cup must be stone cold by now.

'Then bring it with you.'

She glanced up at him, a shocked expression on her face.

'This is your home now, Marianne. There are no servants save for Callerton. We do not stand on ceremony. You are mistress here and may do as you please.'

A small shy smile fluttered briefly to her mouth, then it was gone again and she was gripping so tightly to the cup's handle that her knuckles shone white.

'Come,' he said, holding out his hand to her.

She set the cup down upon its saucer with very careful precision, keeping her eyes steadfast upon it. He saw the deep breath she took before rising to her feet with the air of a woman going to her execution. Her gaze moved to his hand and she hesitated before reaching out and placing her fingers within it. The room was warm, a fire blazing in the hearth to drive away the autumnal chill, yet her skin felt like ice to the touch. And still she would not look at him. He pulled her gently into his arms; her whole body was rigid, tense, chilled.

'Marianne,' he said gently.

She swallowed and stood stock still. He could feel her nervousness as if it were a living breathing thing in the room between them. He touched the point of her

chin and tipped her head up so that she could no longer hide her face from him. In her eyes, before she masked it, he thought he saw the ghost of fear.

'There is no need to be nervous. We will do nothing that you do not wish,' he assured her gently. 'I promise you.'

She looked at him then and reached up to stroke her hand to his cheek, cradling it with such tenderness. 'You are a good man, Rafe Knight.' Her touch was light and loving and tender.

'I am many things, Marianne, but good is not one of them.' There was a five-thousand-guinea price on his head. He had abducted her at gunpoint and sworn to destroy her father. They both knew the truth of what he was.

'Whatever you say, you have been good to me.'

She moved her hand and the new gold wedding band glinted in the firelight. He captured her fingers and touched them to his lips, kissing the ring he had placed there earlier, and felt a possessiveness surge through him. She was his wife, he thought, his woman. And he kissed the skin of her slender fingers. Trailed his kisses over the back of her hand and round to the tender white skin on the inside of her wrist where he flicked his tongue to taste her.

He heard the small breathy gasp she released and felt her body soften its resistance as she leaned into him, splaying her other hand flat against the lapel of the same black tailcoat in which he had married her.

'Marianne,' he whispered and took her mouth with his, kissing her gently, wooing her with his lips, tempting her with his tongue. She was so sweet and innocent, opening to him, her nervousness melting away as the passion that had always been within her kin-

dled and ignited. He felt the blossoming of her need as keenly as he felt his own. He scooped her up into his arms and carried her upstairs to his bedchamber.

The house was in complete silence. Callerton had left them in privacy for their wedding night.

He kicked the door shut behind him and set her down on the Turkey rug without releasing her from the circle of his arms. The room was warm. A fire still burned on the hearth, the coals glowing orange and red. She glanced over at the bed and again he felt that stiffening of her body.

'Rafe…' she whispered and there was such dread in her eyes that it shocked him. 'I…' She bit at her lip.

'There is nothing to be afraid of, Marianne. What happens between us will be pleasurable for us both. And I meant what I said: you need do nothing you do not want.'

She only smiled at him in grateful relief. But when he touched his hand to the buttons of her dress she shrank back.

'Marianne?'

She backed away further, increasing the distance between them. 'I…cannot…' Her eyes were wide and sparkling with tears as they flicked between him and the bed.

He stared at the panic escalating in her.

'Marianne.' He spoke the word as softly as he would to a skittish mare; stood stock still, keeping his hands low and open, as if he would soothe her, calm her. 'We do not have to do this tonight. If you wish to wait…'

'Yes,' she said as a drowning woman might clutch at a lifesaving hand. 'But we are supposed to…'

'No one need know, Marianne. Only you and I.' His gaze held hers.

She bit at her lip. 'You would not force me?'

'Of course not. I would never force you.'

'Even if it is your right as my husband?'

'It is never a man's right to force a woman, Marianne. No matter what you may have been told.'

She dropped her gaze.

'I shall not bed you, Marianne, until you ask me— maybe not even until you beg me. I give you my word.'

Her gaze came back to meet his. And the raw emotions in her eyes—relief and gratitude and love— reached right through his chest to touch his heart. He held out a hand to her. She hesitated only a moment and then placed her own in his. He closed his fingers around hers and felt the tension in her relax. She slipped her arms around him and buried her face in his chest, pressing her lips to his breast bone through the cotton of his shirt.

'Thank you,' she whispered.

He dropped a kiss to the top of her hair, then released her. 'I will leave you to change into your nightclothes. A man and woman might share a bed to sleep and nothing more. When I return, that is what we will do.'

They looked at one another and he could see the guilt in her eyes.

'I am sorry, Rafe.'

'You have nothing to be sorry for, Marianne.'

She closed her eyes as if she could not bear to hear the words.

He kissed her forehead and walked away, wondering just why the hell his wife was so afraid of the marriage bed. But he knew this was a matter of delicacy and could not be rushed. He needed to be patient and teach her gently of how it could be between them.

* * *

Marianne did not look. She kept her eyes fixed firmly on the wall while Rafe stripped off his clothing, her body tensing with the prospect of him climbing in next to her. But when she finally felt the bed dip and her heart thunder so hard that she thought it would leap from her chest, he did nothing more than kiss her eyebrow and bid her goodnight. They lay side by side, not touching. And yet they did not need to touch, for she could feel his warmth thawing her fear steadily with every hour that slipped by. She listened to the sound of his breathing. And when he slept she rolled on to her side and studied his profile in the candlelight.

In sleep he looked younger and the severity was gone. He was so handsome: those dark brows sitting low over his eyes, the strong masculine nose, the full firm lips and the line of his jaw. He was so strong, so irascible. He had no fear and could stand undaunted by the world. Yet his words from the warehouse whispered through her head. *We all have our fears, Marianne.* She could not imagine that he had ever felt afraid or powerless or small. Nothing frightened him. He was the one from whom others fled.

There was definitely darkness in him, and danger. And yet she had never known a man of such integrity. A man who did what he believed was right without a damn for the rules. A good man. The man that she loved. She did not understand why, when all of these things were true, she could not give herself to him. She feared that it might always be this way—she feared that Rotherham had ruined her for ever.

She woke in a dapple of autumn sunlight. For a moment she thought she was in her own bed in Leicester

Square, but then she remembered: her wedding and her new home in Craven Street. In her line of view she could see that the curtains framing the window were a deep dark blue, not pale-pink chintz. And the faint scent of sandalwood in the air made her shiver in a response over which she had no control. She was tired from too many hours spent awake, but the fear that had gripped her so intensely last night had gone this morning.

She heard the sound of toothbrushing from across the room and shifted her eyes, but nothing else, to the sound. Rafe was standing with his back to her at the wash cabinet. He was not wearing the breeches he had worn all night, only a towel tied around him so that from the waist up he was naked. Marianne felt her mouth go dry.

She knew that she should avert her eyes, but she found she could not tear them from him. Wearing his clothes he looked tall and strong and athletic, but without them he was…magnificent. Like one of the marbles in a book of the classics. She could see every line of muscle that rippled beneath the skin of his back and shoulders and upper arms as he moved. He was a pale-golden colour and damp with water droplets that glittered in the sunlight. His hair was dark with water and slick against his scalp and over the nape of his neck. She felt the breath catch in her throat and her nipples grow taut and more sensitive as she looked at him. Yet still she could not look away. Her eyes traced the breadth of his shoulders and the way his body narrowed at his waist and hips and she wondered what it would be like to trace her fingers down the length of his spine. Her heart began to beat faster.

He spat the toothpowder into the basin and rinsed his mouth with water from the glass. When he turned round it was too late to shift her gaze and pretend she was still sleeping.

'Good morning, Mrs Knight,' he said in his velvet voice.

His eyes were the colour of clear orange-blossom honey in the sunlight. The shadow of beard stubble had been scraped from his face and when he smiled at her, her heart skipped a beat and she felt pure unadulterated desire flash through her body.

'Good morning.' Her words sounded strangely husky. She didn't dare glance down to the towel wrapped around him like the kilt of a Scottish highlander, or stare at the sprinkle of dark hair across his naked chest. The blush burned on her cheeks.

'I have almost finished. Then I will bring you warm water and cook you breakfast.' He turned away and pulled on clean drawers beneath the towel while he spoke.

'Ham and eggs. And coffee. Or would you prefer hot chocolate?' The towel dropped away and she could see a hint of the firmness of his buttocks through the linen of his drawers before he pulled up a pair of dark pantaloons to cover them.

'Coffee would be very nice, thank you.' It came out high enough to be almost a squeak and the heat in her face intensified.

Rafe reached for a clean ironed shirt and turned to her once more before pulling it on over his head. She caught a glimpse of a flat abdomen ribbed with muscle and a line of dark hair that led into his breeches before the fine white cotton slid down to cover it and she felt the slither of desire low in her belly.

Oh, my! It was all she could do not to speak the words aloud.

'Callerton will not return until this afternoon. He wanted to give us some privacy.' He smiled again, but she felt guilty, knowing what Callerton thought they would have been doing last night. What they should have been doing. What she wanted to do…but could not.

He sat down in the easy chair by the fireplace. 'We need to hire some servants. I thought you might wish to take charge of that…as you are now mistress here.' And when he stood up he was wearing stockings and shoes.

'I…' She was not sure she knew how to do such a thing. At home her family allowed her to do nothing.

'Or Callerton could do it, if you prefer.' He fixed the collar of his shirt.

'I will do it.' She wanted to do something for him. If she could not fulfil her wifely duties in the bedroom, she would at least undertake them everywhere else.

He looked into the peering glass as he tied his cravat in place.

'How do you wish me to run the house?'

His eyes met hers in the glass. 'However you see fit.'

She watched in continued fascination as he donned his waistcoat and tailcoat, and when he came to stand by the bed again he was fully dressed. 'If you wish to discuss anything of it, Marianne, then we will discuss it.'

And she had the feeling that it was not only the housekeeping of which he was speaking.

She nodded.

He turned and went to fetch her water.

* * *

They breakfasted together in the dining room. Unlike when she had been here as his captive, she ate all that was on her plate, but there was a new awkwardness between them that had not been present before.

He took her with him on his morning ride over the Wenlock Barn fields, saddling up one of his horses for her. The hour was still early, the fields quiet save for a few other horsemen. They walked their horses for a while, breathing in the nip of morning air, fresh and invigorating and filled with the scent of autumn—dampness and brambles and dew-laden grass. The sky was white-grey, but the light bright. The russet leaves of the surrounding trees whispered even though there was no breeze. The quietness of a day just awakening. The calm that had been his respite on all of the days in the past months, the chance to breathe between playing the parts of the rake he was not and the highwayman he had forced himself to be. He glanced across at Marianne. She filled her lungs with the air and put her face up to the sky. He could see the pleasure in her eyes.

'It is wonderful,' she sighed.

'Do you see that great oak tree over there by the barn?' He gestured to the distance.

She nodded.

'I'll wager you a kiss that you cannot reach it before me.'

'We cannot race! What would everyone say?' But her eyes sparkled and her face shone with excitement.

'Do you care so very badly what everyone says?'

Marianne considered it for a moment. 'No, I suppose I do not.' She gave a laugh, as if the realisation astonished her, and then she spurred her horse and took off for the oak tree.

He laughed, too, to see such gladness, then galloped after her.

She was a good horsewoman and it was a race in earnest to the end. Afterwards they walked their horses to cool them and chattered and laughed some more. Only as more horsemen began to appear on the grounds did they leave and head home.

At the stables they dismounted and saw to their horses, removing saddles and tack and brushing them down. For a woman who had never done such things she learned quickly and with a relish that surprised him. Her fingers were quick and deft with the buckles and she was strong for her size. She dealt with all the low parts. He dealt with all the high parts. They were the perfect team.

'You are looking very happy for a woman who did not win the race,' he said, looking at the roses in her cheeks and the sparkle in her eyes and the windswept curls that had escaped from her pins to dangle enticingly around her face.

'I am feeling very happy.'

He laughed at that. 'I admit that you would have won were I not riding the stronger horse and were you not riding side-saddle.'

She smiled even more at that. 'Do you really think so?'

'I know so,' he said. And then they were looking intently at one another and sensual awareness rippled between them. All was quiet. They could hear the murmur of distant carriages and the cries of delivery men and hawkers, and, in the stable stalls, the soft whicker of a horse.

He reached over and lifted a stray curl from her cheek, tucking it behind her ear.

'And now I suppose you wish to claim your kiss,' she said quietly.

'I was under the impression that you liked my kisses.'

'I do.'

Her eyes held his.

He made no move.

'But someone might see us,' she said and knew she was just making excuses.

'There is no one to see us, Marianne. As I told you yesterday, Callerton will not return until much later and you know there are no other servants.'

The tension stretched tighter between them.

'Rafe,' she whispered, stepping closer and reaching her face up to his. When their lips touched, he took her in his arms and kissed her, fully, properly, as he had wanted to kiss her last night. He made love to her with his mouth, teasing her, nibbling her, tonguing her, until she was clinging to him, until she was kissing him hard, with passion, with want and desire.

'Rafe,' she said again, gently nipping his lower lip with her teeth.

He pulled the pins from her hat, removing it and setting it aside, before starting on her hair. Plucking the pins from it, mussing it, threading his fingers through the long silken waves, wrapping it around his fist, angling her head to kiss her neck and lick at the tender spot where her blood pulsed as strong and fast and hard as his. He sucked her, tasted her, grazed her. And the passion that flared between them was not gentle, but raged hot and urgent and dark with desire. She arched against him and he felt the press of her body, the tease

of her thighs. He was hard for her, his shaft straining as if it would burst through his breeches.

He slid his hand down to cover her breast and it seemed he could feel the hard nub of its peak even through the thickness of her deep-red riding habit, through the layers of her underwear that separated their skin.

She moaned as his fingers closed over her breast, massaging her there—and it was a sound of relief and of growing need. Her hands slipped beneath his coat, moving over his stomach, against his chest, over his throat, his jaw, pulling the ribbon from his queue.

He released her hair, stroked his hand down to find her other breast, teasing its bud through the layers of her clothes before sliding both hands to her hips. She groaned her dismay when he left her breasts, pressing herself closer to him as if she wanted him to touch her there again. But his hand stroked over her buttocks before lifting her up and perching her on the edge of the wooden tack table.

Her legs opened naturally and he stood within them feeling the graze of her riding boots against the outer edges of his calves. He kissed her harder, finding her breasts once more, closing his hands over them, flicking his thumbs against their peaks until her breathing was hard and her eyes were a dark-midnight black. He nudged her legs wider and pressed himself to her.

She gave a small breathy gasp and stilled before pulling back from his kiss.

'Marianne,' he said, never shifting his gaze from hers, his voice a whisper and husky with need. 'I gave you my word. I will not break it.'

'But…' She glanced down to where their bodies touched.

'We are fully clothed,' he said. 'And it will stay that way.'

Her eyes met his once more.

'Trust me,' he whispered.

She stared into his eyes as if peering into his very soul. 'Yes,' she said.

And he lowered his mouth to hers and began to kiss her all over again, kissing her until he felt the tension ease from her body, kissing her until she was pulling him to her and his hands were on her breasts, teasing and playing. Then he wrapped his arms around her and bowed her, arching her back to mouth at her breasts as he had done on the night of her birthday ball.

He longed to unfasten the thick high-necked riding habit, to peel it from her body. He knew how soft her skin was, had tasted a flavour of what her breasts would be like to suckle.

'Yes,' she whispered again, clutching his head tighter to her.

He slid a hand to her hip, then lower, stroking against the wool of her skirt, caressing her thigh, feeling the heat grow in it, sliding his fingers round to stroke the inner edge while his teeth scraped through her bodice to excite her nipples. And when his hand finally touched her core, finding it, feeling it, through all of the layers of clothes, she jerked and gasped, and he raised his eyes to look into hers, watching her as his fingers set up a rhythm between her thighs. Watching her until her breathing became louder and more ragged, until he felt her slight movement against his hand. Then his mouth closed over her breast and he bit her very gently: first one nipple, then the other. She let her head drop back, moaning aloud, glorious gasps and groans of utter pleasure, as she found her

orgasm. And it did not matter that he was hard and straining like a green boy. He took her in his arms and he kissed her mouth and her eyelids and the tip of her nose. And he held her close until the frenzied thump of her heart calmed.

And when the daze had gone from her eyes she looked at him and whispered, 'I don't understand what just happened. What was it?'

'It was the beginning, Marianne,' he said and took her hand in his to lead her from the stables and into the house. And that night when they went to bed he held her in his arms, just held her.

Chapter Eleven

Callerton sought him out the next day. Rafe left Marianne writing letters at the little desk in the drawing room while he spoke with his friend.

'Misbourne was out on the town celebrating last night,' Callerton said. 'Bought everyone in White's a glass of champagne and announced to all of London that his daughter was married to Mr Rafe Knight.'

Rafe said nothing. He was related by law to Misbourne. And he was married to Marianne Winslow. It was both his nightmare and his fantasy.

'What happens now in the Misbourne stakes?' asked Callerton, a deliberate blank look in his eyes.

'I do not know. We have to let things settle for a while.'

He thought of Marianne and what it would do to her to learn what her father had done. To see him dragged through the courts; to watch her family fall apart; to watch her father's execution—and know that it was her husband that had brought them to it. He winced at the thought.

Callerton said nothing, but the look in his eyes was too knowing.

'I cannot turn back from this,' Rafe said. 'I owe it to my father. To my mother too. They deserve justice. What would it make me if I were to turn back now? After all these years. After all that it has taken to get this far. That it was acceptable for Misbourne to kill them?' *Or that he loved his wife?*

Callerton poured them both a brandy and they drank it in silence.

Marianne watched her husband undress and slip beneath the sheets beside her. It was the third night she would sleep next to him in his bed. She felt the brush of his fingers against hers as they lay side by side. She turned her head on the pillow and looked at him in the candlelight. At the man she so loved. At the man who was risking his life to be her husband—the man who held such hatred in his heart for her father.

He smiled and gave her hand a squeeze. Despite everything, she felt something inside her blossom.

'Does the light disturb you?' she asked, knowing that many people found it difficult to sleep in the candlelight. And the candles had burned all through the past two nights.

He shook his head.

There was a small comfortable silence before he asked, 'Have you always been afraid of the dark?'

'No.' He didn't ask the natural next question, but she answered it anyway. 'Only for the past few years. And I suppose it is not so much the darkness of which I am afraid, but more what it hides. In corners and cupboards. Under beds and...behind curtains.'

'Monsters,' he said as if he understood.

'Of the worst kind.' She felt a chill prickle through her at the mere thought.

'Like highwaymen,' he said softly, with the strangest look in his eyes.

She shook her head. 'There are worse things than highwaymen.'

'Are there?' he asked. His focus shifted to the distance as if he were thinking, or remembering, before switching back to her. 'Will you tell me what frightens you, Marianne?'

'You would not understand,' she said. 'You are so strong, so invincible. How can you understand fear when you have known none? Or understand what is like to feel utterly powerless, when you are so powerful? To be dangled at the mercy of another? To feel terror? You know none of these things.'

'I understand more than you realise, Marianne. I have known all that you name.'

She could not imagine it. He seemed utterly fearless. 'Yet you are not afraid now.'

He shook his head. 'I faced my fear. I embraced it.'

'What was it that you feared?' she whispered, knowing it must have been something truly terrible.

He paused for so long that she thought he was not going to tell her, then he said, 'Highwaymen.'

'I do not understand.'

'I feared highwaymen. The fear paralysed me. Terrorised me.'

She understood how that felt.

'But you became a highwayman yourself.'

'Yes.'

'You robbed and you stole.'

'From six men only, Marianne. To conquer fear you must face it.'

She nodded.

'May I blow out the flame of one candle? There is still light enough from the remaining two.'

'No,' she replied.

He did not argue or try to persuade her. He just squeezed her hand in reassurance.

'Blow them all out,' she said, her heart beating very fast, the fear sliding through her blood just at the thought.

'You don't have to do it all at once,' he said.

'I know,' she replied. 'But I want to.'

He did as she asked. It seemed the darkness was sudden and complete. She shuddered with the terror of it, and struggled to harness the fear running out of control. Her eyes were wide and staring, but all she saw was the inky blackness. Then Rafe pulled her to him and held her, and she felt the beat of his heart against hers and the strength of his arms encircling her. His breath was steady and calm. She did not count her breaths, only matched them to his. After a while the panic subsided and she grew calm, noticing for the first time that the blackness was no longer black. The curtains were not drawn and faint silver moonlight spilled into their bedchamber. She turned her head to look at it.

'What do you see in the darkness now?' he asked.

'I see moonlight and starlight.' She returned her face to his. 'And I see you.' And she touched her lips to his.

A ball at the town house of Lord and Lady Chilcotte. It would be their first public occasion as a married couple. Marianne smoothed down the silk skirt of her silver-gauzed white evening dress and tried to calm her nerves. There was bound to be gossip. Over the speed of their marriage following the abandoned

wedding to Mr Pickering, over the seeming lack of a courtship. She just hoped that no one had heard the truth of what happened at her birthday ball. A knock sounded on the door of the bedchamber they shared. And then Rafe was standing there.

'I am ready,' she said.

'Not quite,' he replied and as he approached her she could see that he was holding a black-velvet box. He handed it to her.

'It is my wedding and birthday gift to you. I am sorry that it is late.'

She opened the box and there inside was a fine string of diamonds that sparkled in the candlelight, with a large single dark sapphire at the centre. It was the most exquisite necklace she had ever seen, beautiful enough to take her breath away.

'Starlight and moonlight...and darkness,' he said, taking the necklace from where it lay in the box and holding the sapphire up to the candlelight so she could see that the stone, which had appeared black, now glowed a deep rich blue. Their eyes met and she remembered lying safe and snug in his arms all through the night.

'Rafe...' she whispered. 'Thank you. It is beautiful.'

'Like you,' he said. 'I should have given it to you on the day of our wedding and your birthday.' He took the necklace from where it lay in the box and draped it around her neck. She felt the cold of the diamonds and the warmth of his fingers where they touched the nape of her neck to secure the catch of the necklace, and her skin tingled and a shiver rippled right through her body. His fingers seemed to stroke and tease and the sensation shimmered all the way down her spine. Her nipples prickled. Her stomach sucked in tight. Her

breath caught in her throat at the heady intoxicating sensations tingling through her. She could not move, just stood there transfixed by the depth of desire that the lightest brush of his fingers created.

She looked at herself in the peering glass and did not recognise the dark-eyed woman that looked back at her. Her cheeks were flushed pink. Her lips looked full and ached to be kissed. And her eyes glittered dark with such undisguised passion that even Marianne recognised it. She looked so different from the timid, nervous girl that was Marianne Winslow. The woman reflected in the mirror was beautiful, just as he had said, and confident and unafraid, just as she had always longed to be. And the tall, dark, handsome man standing behind her was looking at her with desire.

She lifted her hand to adjust the necklace, but Rafe was there first. She felt the heaviness of the stone shift to lie just above the cleavage of her bust. His fingers adjusted the sapphire so that it lay perfectly central, but the feel of his touch so close to her breasts, however transient, made her nipples tighten for him. In the peering glass it looked almost as if he were touching her there, and God help her but she wanted him to. Wanted it so much that it shocked her. But Rafe did not shift his fingers from the sapphire or his eyes from their joint reflection in the glass.

Yes, she wanted to say. *Please*, she wanted to beg. She had to bite her lip to prevent herself. His eyes had darkened to an intense smoulder. She willed him to touch her, willed it with all her might, never taking her eyes from his.

His fingers slid infinitesimally lower.

Her breath was as ragged as if she had been run-

ning. He must have felt the frenzied rise and fall of her chest beneath his fingers, but she did not care.

He moved lower still so that he was touching the tops of her breasts pressed full against the low neckline of the dress.

Her throat was dry with anticipation. She swallowed and wetted her lips. She wanted to groan. She wanted to reach her hand round to his and clasp his fingers tight to her breast, wanted them to slide beneath her bodice.

He traced a delicate teasing pattern over the upper globe of her breast, toying with her as he felt the hard fast thump of her heart and the need that quivered right through her body, yet his every move was light and sensuous and slow.

Yes, she wanted to scream.

He traced all the way across her other breast and back before dipping his finger into her cleavage. The sensation was so exquisite that she could not prevent the little breathy sigh escaping her. She watched his eyes darken at the sound. His hand slid over her dress to cover the whole of her breast. She gasped again and could not help herself from arching against him, driving herself all the harder into his hand. He moved his other hand so that both were cupping her breasts as he pulled her back flush against his chest and she could feel his warmth against the length of her. She watched their reflection in the peering glass—watched his hands moving over her breasts with a possession that felt so right. Her breasts were so sensitive that, where his fingers stroked and massaged, it was as if his touch passed through the layers of her clothing to brand her naked skin—just as it had done in the stables. And she remembered what he had done with his

mouth, with his teeth…with his hand, and her breath shook with anticipation.

His eyes looked as black and glittering as her own. He was as racked with this strange tension as she, a tension that hummed so loud the whole room seemed to vibrate with it. She should have been embarrassed to watch herself behaving so wantonly, but she felt nothing of that emotion, only impatient desire. His touch was a taste of heaven, and her breasts ached for release from the tight strictures of her corset. She arched again, driving herself into his hands, wanting to feel him all the more. And in response the fingers of one hand rubbed gently against the hard nub of her nipple while the other unfastened the upper buttons of her dress. She felt nothing of fear, only of relief that he was doing what she so desperately wanted. And impatience and a thrilling urgency.

The bodice gaped, but did not fall. She watched and could not look away, holding her breath with anticipation. A flash of white skin that strained for release from its imprisonment within the corset.

'Please, Rafe…' she gasped, unable to prevent it.

'Do you want me to stop?' the man in the peering glass asked, his voice thick with desire and need.

'No,' she said and her whisper was husky and breathless. 'Don't stop.'

His eyes never left hers in their reflection, watching her as he inched her bodice lower with agonising slowness. Teasing her with such sweet torture until at last her corset was revealed in full. Against the top of it the pale swell of her breasts was taut and longing for his touch. But he did not touch her. His left hand rested lightly against her stomach.

She reached her arms up so that her pale-pink nip-

ples peeped over the edge of her bodice, needing them
to be free, and higher still until they erupted over the
edge of the corset and its underlying shift. She stared
at the woman in the glass—a different woman from
the one Marianne had always believed herself to be.

'Tell me what you want me to do,' he murmured,
his voice deep and gravelly beside her ear, his breath
tickling the skin of her neck. She angled her head to
allow him greater access and where his breath had
scalded he traced a small trail of kisses. 'I am under
your control.'

She was trembling with need for him.

'Tell me, Marianne,' he repeated between kisses.
'Say the words.'

Her head felt dizzy with the force of the desire
surging through her body. Her breath was ragged and
strained, her breasts almost fully exposed, and all the
while the sapphire burned like a blue fire against the
pallor of her skin.

'I want you to touch me,' she whispered.

In the peering glass Rafe's gaze was dark and intense, simmering with something she did not understand. He moved his right hand so that it hovered over
her right breast, so close that the skin tingled and
seemed to burn, so close that it looked as if his hand
was already clutching her breast in the glass.

She held her breath and trembled with the strain of
the wanting and waiting. And still his eyes held hers,
unyielding, unrelenting, binding her to him in this
madness that held them both. She swallowed. 'Touch
me, Rafe.'

His hand edged closer so that she could feel the
very tip of her nipple brush against his palm. 'Here?'

'Yes,' she said.

And at last he closed the space and at last her naked breast was within his hand. She sighed her relief, feeling the ecstasy of his touch, feeling the magic of his fingers weaving a sensual pattern against her sensitised globe, feeling them pluck and tease the tight bud.

And when his other hand captured her left breast and played the same teasing pattern upon it she felt she was melting against him in a rich heady sensation of pleasure and need. This man who was her husband, this man whom she loved.

'Rafe,' she whispered, watching in the glass as her hands closed over his, pulling him to her, wanting him never to stop. She was trembling with the force of the need throbbing through her. She moaned and her legs began to crumple.

His arm fastened around her waist, holding her upright as he turned her in his arms. The passion in his eyes when he looked at her razed all else in its path.

'Marianne,' he said, his breath as ragged as hers. And then their lips found each other, and what exploded between them was so much more than a kiss. It was filled with need and heat and passion, while at the same time exposing something vulnerable and intimate that only two lovers could share. And then he pulled back to look into her face.

She felt dazed, unable to think straight, like there was no one else in the world but them, no world at all beyond this room. She wanted the moment to last for ever. 'Why have you stopped?'

He smiled and touched his thumb to her lips. 'So that we might finish the rest of it later.'

'Later?' She blinked, unable to think about anything

other than wanting his lips on her breasts and his hand between her legs.

'I will be yours to command,' he whispered against her neck. And then he helped her dress again and, wrapping the deep-blue cloak around her, he took her hand in his and led her down to the waiting carriage.

At the entrance to Lady Chilcotte's dining room, lit by the light of a thousand candles within the two massive crystal-tiered chandeliers, Marianne felt the sudden stiffening of Rafe by her side. She followed the line of his gaze and saw her father across the room, standing by the French windows. Despite the open windows the room was overly warm and airless. The whole of the *ton* seemed to be present and she knew that they were watching both Rafe and herself. She heard the whispers and saw the stares and speculation, reminding her of why she had not wished to come here tonight. Her grip upon Rafe's arm tightened ever so slightly. He must have felt it, for he slid a surreptitious thumb over her hand and his eyes met hers.

'I had Callerton start the rumour it was a love match,' he murmured for her ears only.

A love match. She looked up into the amber eyes of the man who did everything to defend her from the world. A man from whom even the toughest of criminals ran, a man who was much more fierce and powerful than anyone in this room could guess. Yet with her he had been only gentle. For Marianne this really was a love match. She wanted to tell him, but knew she could not. There were so many reasons why. What they had together, this strange connection, the overwhelming attraction—none of it could last. And were he to discover the truth…

'Thank you,' she whispered, her voice thick with emotion.

His hand closed over hers, so warm and reassuring, and she felt his strength filling her.

They shared a smile and she felt safe and confident and happy.

And then together they stepped into the Lady Chilcotte's dining room to face the whole of London's *ton*.

Rafe watched Marianne speaking to Lady Fothergill across the room as Devlin pressed a glass of champagne into his hand. He wanted the evening to be over. He wanted to be alone with Marianne. He wanted to pleasure her a thousand times over, to touch her, to taste her as she lay naked beneath him. He wanted to hear her cry out his name as she came again and again, all through the night. He wanted to slide into her body, to love her, to ride together and spill his seed as she climaxed. He wanted to consummate his marriage. But he knew he must not rush this. In his own single-minded selfish pursuit of Misbourne he had not considered how frightened Marianne must have been when he abducted her. He had taken away her power, her control, her freedom, subjected her to his will through his own greater might. Now he would give her all of that and more. If and when they consummated their marriage was her decision. And for every night, every hour, every minute of his torture, he had only himself to blame.

'Congratulations, old boy—or should I say commiserations? You have been well and truly caught in parson's mousetrap. Now I know why you were asking those questions over Misbourne's banking de-

tails.' Devlin tapped a finger on the side of his nose. 'Strictly hush-hush, of course.' Devlin swigged half of his champagne down in one gulp. 'Thought you would have waited for the answer before taking the plunge from bachelorhood.'

'The matter was too pressing to wait.' Rafe did not move his gaze from Marianne. The diamond chips sparkled around her neck. His eyes dropped lower to the sapphire that glinted dark against the smooth pale curve of her breasts.

'Judging by the way you are looking at her, I think I can imagine just how pressing.' Devlin smirked.

Rafe did not smile. Devlin had no idea of his feelings for Marianne, or of just how desperate his body was with the need for her. He turned his mind to other matters, shifting his gaze to meet Devlin's, and took a sip of champagne from the glass in his hand. 'So, were you able to access Misbourne's details?'

'No problem,' said Devlin. 'When one's father owns the bank, no one asks too many questions. Kept it quiet from the old man, of course.'

'Of course.' Rafe gave a small cold smile.

'You struck gold, quite literally, with Marianne Winslow, you sly dog,' said Devlin. 'Misbourne's loaded and no mistake. He has a substantial quantity of bullion. And his safety deposit box was full of jewellery, mainly diamonds and rubies, one of the stones the size of an egg. Plenty of investments. A broad spread of stocks and shares, ownership documents for coal mines in the north and tobacco plantations in the West Indies. He also has a whole pile of bonds worth over a hundred grand, and the deeds for several properties around the country.'

'Any gaming debts? Any vowels or secret letters?' Rafe asked nonchalantly and took a sip of his champagne.

'Nothing like that, you'll be glad to know,' said Devlin.

Rafe smiled at just how wrong Devlin was with that remark.

'Didn't think you cared much for Misbourne—or Linwood, for that matter.'

'I don't,' replied Rafe coolly.

Devlin raised an eyebrow. 'You're a cold-hearted bastard when you want something, Knight.'

Rafe smiled.

'Don't underestimate old Misbourne. He used to run with m'father when he was young.' Devlin threw him a significant look. 'I've heard some wild stories—of women and gaming tables. Doesn't gamble any more, but still likes the women. Got a temper on him like the devil himself. Not a man you should cross…especially over his daughter. So have a care and be discreet if you mean to dally.'

'I have no intention of dallying,' said Rafe. His eyes shifted to Marianne again. She seemed to sense his gaze and glanced round to meet it, holding his eyes for a few seconds across the floor and then looking away with a telling blush.

Devlin looked from Rafe to Marianne and back again. 'Good God, it's true what they're saying.' Rafe could feel the weight of Devlin's shocked stare on him. 'I thought it was about the money, but it isn't, is it? You *do* want her.'

'Oh, I want her, all right,' said Rafe, and set his barely touched champagne on the tray of a passing

footman. 'Thank you, Devlin.' He made his way across the room towards his wife.

At supper Marianne had only picked at her lobster and pushed the creamed potatoes around her plate. The butterflies fluttering in her stomach had quelled her appetite. And when they did settle she just had to glance in Rafe's direction for them to start all over again. She had fielded Lady Routledge's questions over the speed and secrecy of her courtship with Rafe, kept up a steady and polite conversation with Mr Dobson seated on her right, and felt her cheeks warm and a secret pride in her heart at the many looks levelled between her and her husband. She glanced over at him and saw that he was making his way towards her and the spirals of excitement low in her belly danced and burned at the sight of him. And she thought of what would happen later between them, when they returned home.

Chapter Twelve

She was sitting on the edge of the easy chair by the fireplace, still wearing her white-and-silver ball gown when he entered their bedchamber. He walked to where she sat and placed the branch of candles on the mantelpiece.

She rose to her feet, her eyes scanning his face. And he could see the desire in them and the slight nervousness as she wetted her lips. He reached to her and touched the silver-blonde tendrils that dangled against her cheek.

'Is it later?' he asked.

'Yes,' she whispered.

'What do you want me to do, Marianne?'

'Kiss me,' she said.

So he stepped closer and, sliding his palm to cup her cheek, he looked into her eyes and kissed her, as gently as he had kissed her that very first time.

Her whole body seemed to give a sigh of relief. She came into his arms.

He slid the pins from her hair and kissed her until her lips were swollen and pink and moist. He kissed her until her eyes were black with passion and her

breath was uneven and fast. He slid a caress over her shoulders, down the length of her spine, over her hips, against her stomach, but not once did he touch her breasts.

Her arms were wrapped around him, her hands splayed against his back, the pressure light at first, then harder as the desire began to pulse stronger through her body. He felt the glide of her hands over his hips, then up the front of his coat before they slid beneath the lapels. She hesitated for a moment, her hands resting lightly against his waistcoat.

'I am yours, Marianne,' he whispered against her ear, then grazed his teeth against the soft lobe before taking it into his mouth and flicking his tongue against it.

Her fingers slid within his waistcoat, palms against him, and her hands crept against his chest.

He touched her breasts then, feeling for her nipples through the layers of her clothing as she felt for his through the fine linen of his shirt, mirroring every press of her thumb, every slide of her fingers until she understood what he was doing.

She squeezed harder at his chest.

His hands closed more firmly around her breasts.

She scraped her nails against his nipples.

He licked along the delicate line of her jaw as his nails flicked against the silk of her bodice.

She opened his coat and pushed the lapels back as if she would wrench the coat from his shoulders.

'Take it off,' she whispered.

He released her long enough to do as she said, dropping the coat to the floor and never taking his eyes from her.

She watched him and he could see the pink flush

of excitement and desire in her cheeks, the sparkle in her black eyes and the rapid rise and fall of her breasts bound tight by the white-and-silver bodice.

'And your waistcoat too.'

He shrugged it off and saw her swallow. She bit at her lip, looked at him with both daring and hesitation. He kissed her again, a full rich kiss on her mouth. She hesitated no more, but pressed her mouth to his chest, kissing first one nipple, then the other, licking him through the thin linen of his shirt, scraping her teeth there. And when she was done she raised her mouth to his and kissed him. She broke the kiss to look into his face, searching his eyes for a moment before she stepped a little out of his arms and turned around, presenting him with her back. With one hand she swept up the curtain of silvery waves, holding them high, baring the nape of her neck, exposing the line of buttons that ran down the back of her dress.

He moved closer, let his breath stir the wisps of fine hair around the nape of her neck and saw the tiny shiver that rippled through her in response. Then he let his mouth follow his breath, touching his tongue to that tender skin. He felt her inhalation, watched as she dipped her head, allowing him great access to the sensitive spot. He teased his tongue there, kissed it.

'When you touch me there I can feel it right through me, all the way down to the soles of my feet,' she whispered.

He bit her lightly and she moaned in pleasure.

He kissed her neck, while his fingers traced slowly down the line of her spine until he found the first small silk button of her dress. Her head lolled to the side and he bit her again and slowly, one button at a time, began to unfasten the bodice of her dress. It gaped wide long

before he reached the final button. He kissed her ear and then helped ease the dress down. She slid her arms free from the small puff sleeves, and in a soft rush of silk the dress landed around her ankles. She wore only one petticoat—plain white cotton. He stroked it from her until it lay on top of the silver-and-white silk.

Breathing in the scent of her, he pulled the tape of her corset loose from its securing bow. As his fingers began to unlace it his mouth traced kisses along one shoulder to the edge of her shift, then the other, kissing the soft white skin until the corset fell away to land on the floor with a thud.

He stilled his lips where they were, feeling her breath, feeling the rush of her blood. She stood very still, then she slowly turned and looked at him.

The white shift was plain and loose, covering her all the way down to mid-shin. But through its fineness he could see a hint of the flesh and shadow of her body.

He took her in his arms, kissing her mouth, their tongues entwining, dancing, mating. And while his lips made love to hers, he placed one hand flat against the small of her back, arching her body towards him, tightening the shift against her breast as he slid his hand over it.

She moaned against his mouth as his hand found first one breast, then the other, feeling them fully freed from the confines of her corset for the first time. He trailed the kisses over her chin, down the centre line of her neck by the side of the sapphire-and-diamond necklace, over her *décolletage*, to the edge of the shift. His mouth paused there while his eyes sought hers.

'Yes,' she said. 'Oh, yes.'

He moved against her breast, kissing all round the small mound, teeth scraping lightly through the

linen, teasing round the nipple without touching it. She arched more, thrusting her breast to his mouth, her fingers winding in his hair, clutching him tighter. He touched his tongue to her nipple, feeling it bud hard against him. He licked it once and felt her heart leap beneath it. And then he closed his mouth over it, tasting it, suckling it, flicking his tongue again and again against the tip until he could see it pink and straining through the wet translucent linen.

Marianne could not think. She could only feel. And what she felt was Rafe and her need for him, and the wonder he was bestowing on her body. Her thighs were burning, the secret place between her legs slick and wet and filled with a strange dull ache.

He brought her upright again, one hand resting lightly against the small of her back, the other on her hip. His eyes were a rich dark mahogany in the candlelight; she stared into their depths, and touched her hand to his jawline, trailing her fingers along its edge, rubbing against the roughness of the faint shadow of beard stubble that had grown there since the morning. She felt the bob of Adam's apple as she touched it and could not help herself placing a kiss there, caressing it with the tip of her tongue before drawing back. Then her fingers touched the end of his cravat, touched the knot that was tied there and she remembered the warehouse: removing his neckcloth and cutting the sleeve from his shirt and all that had passed between them then and since.

I am yours, Marianne. The knowledge seeped through her like the soft streaming smoke of a candle extinguished in the darkness. She breathed it in, allowed it to permeate.

Her fingers struggled with the collar of his shirt;

he came to her assistance and the buttons opened. The lawn of his shirt was fine, soft, white. Through it she could see the darkness of the hair that grew across his chest. She laid her hand lightly against it, feeling the soft spring of hair and the hardness of the muscle beneath. And her eyes moved to his left arm, to the sleeve beneath which she knew the bullet had sloughed. Her gaze moved back to his.

'Take off your shirt,' she whispered.

He pulled it free of his breeches, peeled it off over his head and stood there before her. The candlelight flickered across the hard lines and muscle of his chest, his stomach, his shoulders and arms. She looked at the nakedness of his skin, at the size of him, at how very different his body was to hers, at the strength, the power, the potential. His arms were loose by his side, allowing her to do whatever she would.

I am yours.

Between the elbow and the shoulder of his left arm was a patch of pink puckered skin. When she looked at it her heart swelled to fill her chest and she felt the prickle of tears in her eyes. She leaned forwards and touched it with her lips, light as a feather, letting them rest there against the newly healed scar.

'I am yours, too, Rafe,' she said softly as she kissed the scar. Her hands slid slowly against the muscle of his chest, feeling the roughness of the hair and the warmth of his skin, feeling the beat of his heart.

And then she stood back. *She was his.* She stepped out of her shoes. Unfastened the tape of first one stocking to slide it from her foot, then the other. Her gaze met his and held it. She pulled the end of the bow in the ribbon that threaded through the neckline of her shift. The ribbon unfastened. She pulled the shift over

her head, letting it fall to the floor, and stood there naked before him.

'Marianne,' he whispered, the same whisper of a highwayman a lifetime ago. His gaze moved over her. She could see the bulge in the front of his breeches, the way it strained against the material. She knew what he could do. But she trusted him.

He slipped off his shoes and stockings and came to stand immediately before her. She glanced down at their bare feet, at his and at hers, and stepped closer so that the tips of their toes were touching. And then she looked up at him.

'Kiss me,' she said.

He kissed her mouth until she was breathless, kissed her breasts until she was panting. And when he laid her on the bed she pulled him down with her so that their mouths shared and tasted and breathed as one, so that his lips were hot and hard, teasing and stroking against her nipples until she was gasping and pulling his hair, until her thighs gaped open to him.

'Take me,' she said, needing him, wanting him. Her body tensed with the knowledge of what lay ahead, the sharp penetrating pain, the invasion, yet even knowing it, she needed him; she wanted him and whatever it encompassed.

'Not yet,' he said, then she felt the touch of his hand on her, the slide of his fingers against her moisture. He stroked her, his mouth kissing hers, keeping time. She opened her eyes and looked up into his. He stilled, his hand resting against her woman's place as if he would shield it, protect it from all intrusion. And his gaze on hers was dark and smouldering with passion and desire.

'Take me,' she said again.

But he shook his head and he kissed her again, a deep rich, thrusting kiss that matched what was in his eyes. Then he began to stroke again between her legs, massaging that same part of her that he had touched in the stables. A magical steady rhythm that made her gasp with the pleasure that was building, that made her blood rush and her heart thud harder and faster, and her body strain and chase something she did not understand. She opened her legs wider, exposing her vulnerability to him. But his fingers worked that same rhythm that was so tuned to everything her body strove for, teased until her hips bucked up off the bed and she was gasping aloud for need of him and everything exploded in shards of light and colour and a pleasure so immense that it took over all of her mind and body and soul. She could do nothing other than tumble headlong into the surge of it, to give herself up to the roaring of it all around her, sweeping her up, taking her out of the bedchamber, taking her out of her herself to another place she did not know, overwhelming her with its ecstasy. Gasping for breath, clutching at Rafe, pulling him to her, kissing him as the furore ebbed, and the crashing waves gentled until, like a receding tide, they washed over her, rhythmically, leaving only the echo of the pleasure pulsing through her.

He blew out the candles and lay down by her side. He stroked the long mess of her hair from her face and he kissed her, then he settled her in his arms and pulled the covers over them. And they lay together in the darkness and she wondered at how much he had given her and taken nothing himself, wondered at how much she loved him, until at last, safe in his arms, she slept.

* * *

Rafe sat at his desk the next night, his cravat hanging loose around his neck, his collar unfastened, his waistcoat abandoned. The tumbler of brandy had barely been touched. He ignored the glass and continued to stare at the rows of neatly penned numbers in the books that lay on the dark polished wood before him. It did not make any sense, yet Bradley was right: the evidence was there in the figures before him. Had he not instructed the man to audit all of his affairs as part of the process of amending his will in favour of Marianne, the anomaly would never have been discovered.

Marianne. He thought of his wife in bed upstairs and wondered if she would be awake. And the memory of the passion between them the previous night stoked the desire in his blood. She was all that he wanted, all that he needed. She was the light in a lifetime of darkness, the cooling touch to the fire of his anger, the balm to his pain. But always in the background, even though he did not let himself confront it, lurked the shadow of Misbourne and the burden of duty. And Rafe knew he could not hide from it for ever.

A quiet knock sounded at the door and he knew it was her even before she entered.

Her feet were bare, her pale hair hanging long and unbound, soft as silk, and he wanted to wrap his hands in it, bury his face in it. Her nightdress was expensive, embroidered in white work, high-necked and loose, hiding what he knew lay beneath. She had a shawl wrapped around her shoulders, long and silken, the silver-threaded fringes swaying and glinting in the light of the candles from the branch she held in her hand.

He rose to his feet, coming out from behind the

desk. 'The hour is late,' he said. 'I thought you would be sleeping.'

She set the candles down on his desk and looked at him. 'I could not sleep. Not with you out on the streets of London alone at night.'

'You were worried about me,' he said quietly. The thought was so sweet that it made him smile.

'You have a five-thousand-guinea price on your head and my father and brother are sworn to kill you. Of course I was worried.'

He reached to her and, taking her hand, touched his lips to her knuckles. 'But you got my note saying I would be late?' He did not release her hand, just kept it within his own.

She nodded. 'Did you resolve matters with your man of business?'

'Not entirely.'

She glanced over at the ledgers lying open on the desk. 'Was there a problem?'

'It appears there is a discrepancy with the monies in my bank accounts.'

'You mean there is money missing?'

'Quite the opposite,' he said and the worry was back with him again. 'I was the recipient of an inheritance held in trust until I reached my majority. The initial sum was small, but I thought my income through the years came from its successful investment. Now I have discovered the investments were so poorly made that, had someone not been making regular payments into my accounts, I would have very little.'

'How strange,' she said. 'Wouldn't it be possible to check with the bank and find the identity of your mysterious benefactor?'

'Under normal circumstances, yes. But whoever is

behind this has taken great pains to hide their identity. My lawyer has tried every avenue available, but no name is forthcoming.'

'Perhaps it is some relative of yours who wishes to remain anonymous.'

'I have no relatives, Marianne. I am alone in the world.' And he thought of the man who had made it that way.

'Not any longer.' She smiled shyly.

His eyes traced her face, seeing nothing of Misbourne there before meeting her gaze. It was true she had the same dark eyes as her father, but whereas Misbourne's were soulless as the devil's, Marianne's were gentle and filled with passion. 'Not any longer,' he repeated. 'Now that I have you, Marianne.'

They looked at one another. And in the silence he heard the slow steady tick of the clock and the settling of the glowing embers from the hearth.

'Come to bed, Rafe,' she said and he felt the slight squeeze of her fingers around his.

He lifted the branch of candles from his desk and followed her up to their bedchamber.

And so the nights and the days passed. Marianne employed servants who worked with precision, seeing to his every need, and slowly the house began to change from a place where he slept and ate to a home once more. The floors were swept; the furnishings cleaned and tidied. Soon there was the clean sweet smell in the air of beeswax and lavender wood polish, and cut flowers in the vases, and her own sweet scent of violets. The paintwork on the door and windows was pristine. The brass of the door knocker was polished until it gleamed. The house began to take on a

new life, a vibrancy that reminded him of his youth, before his parents had died. Callerton officially became his steward. Every day he watched Marianne's confidence grow and he did not think of Misbourne. And every night he loved her more.

'Not this room, or the adjoining bedchamber. Both are to remain untouched,' said Marianne.

The two maids, clutching their basket of dusters and cloths and polish, bobbed a curtsy each and hurried away.

Marianne stood in the silence of the yellow bedchamber alone and looked around.

The daylight shone in from the landing, exposing what she had only seen by candlelight or the daylight that had stolen through the cracks of the shutters. Since the last time she had been in this room the surfaces had been shrouded with holland covers. Her hand caught at the cream-linen sheet covering the dressing table and let it slither to the floor. The ivory-and-tortoiseshell hairbrush sat in three parts on the exposed mahogany surface of the dressing table, just as she had laid them after gathering them up from the floor. Rafe's mother's brush. She touched her fingers to it and was filled with a feeling of such fierce tenderness, that it took her breath away, and a sadness upon which she did not want to dwell. She could not hide for ever; *they* could not hide for ever. Her father stood between them, an unspoken barricade they could not cross.

She did not know what made her glance round at the doorway, for he made not one noise. But when she did, she saw that Rafe was leaning against the door frame watching her.

'I know it cannot be easy for you, Marianne. The

last time you were in this room, things were very different between us.'

'Very,' she said.

'It was…wrong of me to take you from your father, regardless that I would never have hurt you. I'm sorry that I frightened you.'

'Are you sorry that you took me?'

He looked at her. There was a pause before he answered. 'I have never lied to you, Marianne. I will not start now. So the answer is no. I am not sorry.'

'Even though my father refused to yield you the document?'

'That has nothing to do with it.'

She glanced round at him. 'It has everything to do with it!' she said, shocking herself with the anger in her voice.

'It was the reason I took you, Marianne. It is not the reason I am not sorry.' He paused. 'Nor the reason I made you my wife.'

'We both know why you made me your wife. To save me from ruin.' She wished so hard that it could have been for another reason, the same reason that she felt in every beat of her heart and every breath that filled her lungs.

'You know what is between us. You must know how I feel about you.'

Desire. Attraction. Not love. How could it ever be love considering what lay between Rafe and her father? Yet at his words she felt her heart somersault in her chest, felt it thump harder and a dizziness bubble through her blood.

'Must I?' she said, holding his gaze, willing him to say the words. The silence hummed loud and awk-

ward. She turned away, glancing around the yellow bedchamber. 'It was your mother's room,' she said.

'Yes.'

'The shutters are still nailed closed.'

He said nothing.

'And those in the adjoining bedchamber too. Your father's?'

He nodded.

There was a pause, a quiet in which she could hear the sound of her own heart and, she fancied, his heart too.

'What happened to your parents, Rafe?'

The silence hissed in the room. At first she thought he would not answer, but then he said, 'They were killed—murdered in a robbery.'

'I am sorry for your loss.' She ached with compassion for him.

'The shutters were closed that night. I swore that they would remain so until the man responsible for their deaths was brought to justice.' His voice was calm, controlled, devoid of emotion.

'Justice,' she whispered. *Not vengeance.* An icy finger stole down her spine at the word. And she remembered his strange remark about his parents in her father's study on a night that seemed so long ago.

'Justice,' he said.

'When did they die?' She felt suddenly deeply uneasy.

'1795,' he replied.

'The mausoleum in the burying ground,' she said and saw again in her mind's eye the lettering chiselled into its stone lintel—EDMUND KNIGHT, 1795—only now realising its significance.

'That of my parents.'

There was a cold feeling in her chest, a deep seeping dread. '1795, Hounslow Heath. The document that was taken in exchange for your daughter.' She spoke the words of his ransom demand.

'I am surprised that he showed you.'

'He did not. It was my brother.' Her heart was pounding hard now and there was a sick feeling in her stomach. 'What happened to your parents is at the root of what is between you and my father, is it not?'

He said nothing, but she saw the flicker of tension in the muscle of his jaw and the slight darkening in his eyes.

'He is my father. You are my husband. Surely I have a right to know?'

'You have every right, Marianne. But he *is* your father. Do you think I have no care for you?'

The words were bittersweet, for she understood now why he did not want to tell her, why he had not told her at the start: because he knew she loved her father. 'You do not wish to hurt me.'

'No.'

But she had to know. And she was sure, no matter how much she loved him, that he was wrong about her father. 'My brother is searching through *The London Messenger* archive for all of that year, seeking anything to do with Hounslow Heath. What will he find, Rafe?'

'He will find that my parents were robbed and shot dead by a highwayman upon Hounslow Heath.'

'A highwayman,' she said. 'In the same place that you held up my father.'

His eyes never shifted from hers.

'The same place you took me from him.' And she remembered the words he had answered when she asked him what her father had ever done to him. 'When

you said that my father took from you that which was most precious, you were not talking of the document, were you?'

'No,' he said softly.

'Are you saying that my father was the highwayman?' She could not keep the incredulity from her voice.

He gave a laugh that held nothing of happiness. 'As if Misbourne would dirty his hands.' He shook his head. 'No, Marianne. But your father was behind it. He was the one who paid for it to be done.'

'That is ridiculous! Why on earth would he do such a thing?' The thud of her heart was loud in the silence. His gaze was steady, everything about him so quiet and focused and controlled.

'He wanted the document, and he wanted my father dead. My mother just had the misfortune to be with him at the time.'

'You cannot know that.'

'Oh, but I can, Marianne.'

'How?'

He could see that she didn't believe him, that she still believed in her father over him. And part of him was glad of it and part of him railed against it. He didn't want to tell her, but he needed to. Needed to tell someone after all these years and she was the one, the only one.

'I was there that night,' he said and felt a strange kind of relief in saying the words aloud.

'You witnessed your parents' murder?' He could hear the horror in her voice.

He gave a nod.

'Your fear of highwaymen…' Realisation dawned on her face.

He glanced away to the shadows that edged the room, his face grim. 'I watched what he did to them and there was nothing I could do.'

'Fifteen years ago. You must have been a child at the time.'

'Ten years old. Old enough to understand.' He shook his head again and darkness of the past closed in upon him so that he could see again the nightmare playing out before his eyes. 'He took my mother's jewellery, my father's watch, his purse of money. I thought he would ride away and leave us safe. But he did not.'

He knew that she had come to stand before him, but he did not look up. 'He demanded the document from my father's pocket. But my father would not yield it.'

'Just as mine would not,' she whispered.

'Indeed,' he said. 'I heard him lie and say that he carried nothing. Even with the muzzle of the highwayman's pistol touched to his forehead.' It seemed he was back upon Hounslow Heath, watching the horror unfold before him, and his body felt that same overwhelming fear, that same rage, that same impotence. He could hear again his mother's screams, see the highwayman shoot her, feel the crack of the highwayman's fist against his face. 'When he was dead, the highwayman took the document from his pocket. There was blood on his fingers when he opened it out and showed it to me—my father's blood. I have never forgotten what he said: "These few words, whatever they say, are worth a grand and your pa's life."' He glanced at her with a small tight smile that belied all he was feeling. 'And he rode away and left me there.' He felt the grief raw and ragged as he had done on that day on the moor fifteen years ago and turned away so that she would not see his weakness.

She caught one of his hands, holding it between both of hers.

'I have made it my life's work to find that highwayman…and the man who set a bounty of a thousand pounds on my parents' lives. I traced every link in the chain, all five of them, Marianne, until I found him.' His gaze met hers. *Misbourne.* Her father's name whispered silently between them.

'My father would never sanction murder. Someone has misled you. Whoever gave his name lied.'

But Rafe knew what he had done to the men he had found. 'No, Marianne,' he said gently. 'No one lied… of that I can be certain.'

He saw the small shiver that ran over her. 'There must be some mistake.'

'There is no mistake.' Yet no matter what he said, no matter how much he told her, the denial was still there in her eyes.

'I know my father, Rafe, and he is far from perfect, but to kill an innocent man and woman…?' She shook her head. 'I cannot believe it of him. There is no way back from such a crime.'

'There is not,' he said quietly.

He saw the sudden comprehension in her eyes and the fear that followed in its wake. Justice and all that it implied loomed black as death over both of them. 'He is innocent, Rafe. He has to be.'

He felt his heart ache, for her pain and for his own. She came to him, wrapping her arms around him. Pressing her face to his chest, breathing him, holding him, her eyes shut tight. And they stood like that, entwined, with only the soft sound of their breath and the beat of their hearts, in defiance of the past, in spite

of the future, and all it could bring. They stood there until she turned her face up to his…until she took his hand in hers and led him from the room.

Chapter Thirteen

Marianne led him to their own bedchamber, to their own bed. The daylight was only now beginning to fade, the sky darkening as the night breathed black upon it. She sat him down on the edge of the bed and stood between his legs. There were no words she could offer that would comfort him. Denial would not salve the pain and grief that drove him. Such a strong fearless man, yet he had feared as much as she. He had suffered. He suffered still. She felt his pain worse than any of her own. She stroked his hair, caressed his cheek, placed her lips upon his and kissed him with everything that she felt in her heart, as if by so doing she could draw his hurt into herself and carry it for him. She kissed him once more, then drew back and looked into his face.

'Let me comfort you as you comfort me. Let me pleasure you as you pleasure me. Let me make us forget, even if it is just for this moment, just for this night.'

'Marianne, I...' She saw the turmoil of emotion in his eyes.

'You need me...' she said, 'and I need you.' And she began to loosen his cravat. Together they peeled off

their clothes until he stood there clad only in his black breeches. She looked at him, this big, strong, dauntless man. Invincible. A man like no other. Yet when she looked into his eyes she knew that she had spoken the truth: he needed her every bit as much as she needed him. She reached her fingers to rest lightly against the top of his breeches.

His eyes held hers.

'I want to see you,' she said.

He unbuttoned the fall. Drew them from his hips, easing them down his legs until he could step clear of them. Marianne had never seen the front of a man's underwear before; the white linen covered where his breeches had and reached almost to his knees.

'All of you,' she insisted quietly.

He unfastened the drawers, let them drop to his ankles, and stepped out of them.

She looked at him, at the whole magnificent nakedness of him, her gaze tracing down over his chest, over the hard ribbed stomach and abdomen, following the line of hair that led lower. Down the long muscular lengths of his legs, right down to his toes, then back to the part that made him a man. Masculinity and strength and power. He looked more than she had expected, overwhelmingly so. And beside him she could not fail to be aware of how much slighter she was compared to him, of how much weaker, how vulnerable… and how feminine. Yet when she looked at his body she felt something happening deep down low in her belly, felt a heat stirring through her blood. There was nothing of fear.

She was standing so close that she could smell the scent of his skin and see the pulse that beat at the side of his neck. She looked up into his eyes and saw only

the man that she loved. Her hands slid up his chest, to his shoulders. She reached her mouth to his and kissed him. A soft, sweet kiss. Tasting him. Dipping into his mouth, teasing his tongue. Kissing him while his hands swept a glorious caress against the nakedness of her back. They kissed and then they lay down on the bed together. When he took her breasts in his hands, when his fingers worked their magic upon her nipples, she kissed him harder, more passionately before drawing back with a slight shake of her head.

'Not yet,' she said, just the way he had said to her. She wanted to share the wonder he had given her, wanted to make him forget the pain. This was not about her, only about the man who was her husband. 'May I touch you?'

He nodded and let his hands lie loose by his sides, giving her permission to do what she would.

She knelt over him, her knees straddling one of his thighs, and plucked the pins from her hair, uncoiling its length until it hung free over her shoulders the way she knew he liked it. She ran her fingers down its waves the way he always did, skimming her nipples, her belly, her hip, and saw his eyes darken as he watched. Then she reached out and touched the tips of her fingers lightly against his lips, letting him kiss them, letting him flick his tongue against them, but sliding them beyond his reach when he would have taken them into his mouth. Her fingers trailed over his stubble-roughened chin, before moving down his neck, his Adam's apple bobbing as she caressed it. Her fingers journeyed on, lingering over the small springy hairs on his chest, pressing down on the hard muscle beneath it. His chest was so different to hers—hard, muscular, flat. She laid her palms over it, felt the beat

of his heart. She teased against his nipples, plucking them, rolling the tiny buds between her fingers. Everything she enjoyed, everything that made her blood rush and her heart race, everything that made her breathless. All of it, she would do to him, *for* him.

She lowered her mouth to his nipples and licked, working her tongue over the flat dark skin, and beneath her lips she felt his heart beat harder. She drew back so that she could look down into that most beloved face as he lay there. The man she loved. Slowly she traced her hand lower, feeling his stomach suck in, feeling his rapid inhalation of air. Her fingers caressed each hard band of muscle that lined his abdomen then she paused, feeling the warm steady beat of her heart, knowing how much he had done for her, how much she wanted him. Her hand slid closer to the centre.

'Marianne!' She heard his whispered warning. She hesitated, her gaze meeting his. His eyes looked black in the dusky light. He was breathing harder now, the pulse in his neck visibly throbbing, and she was surprised by how much she could affect him. She looked at him and then down to that part of him that was close to his belly. That part she had so feared. And then she slowly stroked her fingers against it.

He gasped and she felt the slight jerk of him beneath her fingers. But he did not move his hands, nor did he try to stop her.

Contrary to all that she had expected, his skin was silky smooth there—the only place on the entirety of his body that was so. But even beneath the silkiness she could feel the rigidity, the hardness, the strength. She slid her fingers down the length of him from the very tip all the way down to the root. He groaned, a low

guttural sound of need that mirrored those she made when he touched her, mirroring what she felt for him.

She wrapped her hand around the girth of him.

'Marianne,' he gasped and beneath her hand he grew even harder and longer. *Such power wielded by the lightest touch*, she thought. She squeezed him gently and felt the way his whole body stretched and tensed, the muscles of his thigh rippling beneath her.

'A man's weapon,' she said softly, knowing how she had feared it.

'And his weakness,' said Rafe. Her eyes met his. Yet his hands remained by his sides, trusting her. 'You hold the power, Marianne.'

'Yes,' she said. Then she bent and placed a single kiss on the silky skin at the very tip of him.

He groaned and jerked again.

She rubbed her fingers along his length, trying to emulate the way he touched her. And then she stilled and wrapped her fingers around him again, showing that she had no intention of letting him go.

'Show me how,' she said.

His hand moved to cover hers and he showed her.

She watched him while her hand moved on him, watched him with eyes that were dark and burning with desire and felt all that was within herself rise to meet it. Watched him while he shifted his thigh to touch her womanhood, making her gasp and catch her breath—but she did not still her hand.

'Marianne.' It was a plea, a cry from the soul.

'Rafe,' she whispered, needing his body, needing his heart, and she laid her body over his even while her hand still slid upon him.

'Marianne,' he gasped and his arm came around her, freeing her hand from him and rolling her on to her

side, so that their bodies were flush together. And he stared into her eyes as he pulsed against her belly and she felt his warm wetness between their skin.

'Marianne,' he said again, then took her mouth with his and kissed her as if his soul touched hers.

His fingers moved between her legs, slid to one single place and it was enough; she arched against him and felt her heart merge with his in utter ecstasy and joy. And when it eventually rolled away and left her in his arms he rose and she heard him pouring water into the basin. She watched him wring out the cloth. He washed her, gently, with tenderness, as if she were the most precious thing to him in the world, and then he washed himself. They lay down together in the darkness. And he held her as if he would never let her go.

She stood by the bedchamber window and watched the dawn break over the rooftops. From the bed behind her came the sound of Rafe's breathing, soft and even as he slept. As she stood there in the coolness of the new morning there was something on her mind, something of which she could not stop thinking and which made her clutch her shawl more tightly around her shoulders. Her father had the document Rafe sought. She had heard the admission from his own lips. And if he had the document, the question was how it had come into his possession. The unease whispered all around her. He would not murder. He would not kill an innocent man.

And then she thought of his promise to find the highwayman and how he would deal with him and shivered despite the warm wool of her shawl. She heard a slight noise and glanced round to find Rafe watching her.

'Marianne.' His voice was low and husky from sleep, his eyes warm and sensual. Her husband. Her love. She felt like she were standing in a sunbeam with him, but the clouds edged around the sky and soon the shadows would close in upon them. Time was running out on the small haven of happiness, like grains of sand running through a timer.

'I must visit my family today, Rafe.'

'I understand.'

'Do you?' she asked and turned fully to face him, her gaze scanning his.

He nodded.

She wanted to capture this moment in time and preserve it. She wanted to still the clocks and remain here for ever, but she knew she must face the world.

He peeled back the edge of the bedcovers. 'Come back to bed, Marianne. The hour is early enough yet.'

She smiled, but there was a lump of sadness in her throat. She went to the warmth and protection of his arms.

'I have missed you,' her father said and kissed her cheek. He looked well, more than well; he looked like a man from whom the weight of the world had been lifted. 'But it is good that you are married.' He smiled and chucked her beneath the chin as if she were still his little girl. And when she looked up into his eyes, eyes that were so like her own, she thought of what had happened on Hounslow Heath on a night fifteen years ago.

'How do you find married life?' her mother asked.

'I am very happy,' she said.

Her mother leaned closer and lowered her voice slightly. 'You did as I said?'

Marianne felt her face flush warm. 'Mama, that is hardly a topic fit for the drawing room,' she said with a calmness that belied her embarrassment and anger.

Her mother looked unabashed. 'We have been anxious about you.'

'You have no need to be,' said Marianne.

'Then I am relieved,' said her mother and peered more closely at her. 'You look different,' she said. 'Almost…' she angled her head to the side and considered her daughter '…radiant.'

Her father gave a nod of satisfaction. 'Where are your footmen, Marianne? It is not safe these days for a woman to travel with a maid alone. A husband should take care of such things. It is his duty to protect his wife.'

'I am in the process of taking on new staff. The carriage is waiting outside.' She had forgotten how much her family worried over every small thing, their paranoia feeding an atmosphere of fear, coddling her to the point of suffocation.

'You should have a care, Marianne,' her father said. 'Especially when the highwayman is not yet apprehended.'

She felt her cup rattle in its saucer and quickly took a gulp of tea to disguise her response. 'There is such a great price on his head that I am sure he will not dare to show his face in London or the surrounding villages or towns again. We need think no more about him.'

Her father shook his head and gave a grim smile. 'My enquiries are ongoing even as we speak, my dear.'

'Are you close to catching him?' She sipped at her tea as if his answer was not so very important.

'Let us just say I am making progress. But never

fear, Marianne, I shall find him even if it takes me a lifetime.'

'I wish you would not, Papa. Please, do not seek him.'

He peered at her and she could see that she had shocked him. And in the background, where he stood silent and listening, she saw her brother's face sharpen.

She set the cup and saucer down upon the table. 'He is a dangerous man. I do not want you to get hurt.' *And I do not want you to hurt him.*

'My dearest girl, you need have no fear on my account. I have made my preparations to deal with him, most thoroughly.'

She closed her eyes at the menace in his voice.

'You have paled, Marianne. I should not have reminded you of the villain,' he said. 'If you will excuse me, my dearest, I have an appointment I must keep elsewhere. But I am glad that you are married to Knight. He will keep you safe.'

She could have laughed out loud with the irony of it were it not so very terrible. She wondered what he would do if ever he discovered that her husband and the highwayman were one and the same.

And when he had gone her mother chattered over inconsequential fripperies. Marianne was worrying so much over her father's words that it was a struggle to pretend an interest and she was relieved when it came time to leave. But when she would have done so her brother, Francis, drew her into her father's study, with such a dark intense expression upon his face that her stomach knotted and she felt the prickle of foreboding over her scalp.

Once inside he closed the door behind them.

'Does Knight treat you well?'

'He is good to me,' she said. But he would not be good to their father.

'You are certain?'

'Of course. Why do you ask?'

'Because there is something about him…' He glanced away into the distance. 'I do not like him.' His gaze returned to hers. 'And I do not trust him.'

She felt the stir of both anger and fear. 'Have a care how you speak of my husband, Francis.'

'After the way he seduced you at your ball I don't think I need have any care over him.'

'He is my husband.'

'Even so, you barely know the man, Marianne.'

'If that is what you brought me in here to say, you will excuse me.'

'Not so hasty, little sister.' She felt his hand upon her arm. 'There is something that you might want to see.'

Her heart gave a stutter. 'You have found the document?'

'Not yet.' He shook his head. 'Father will discuss little of the highwayman matter with me, so I took the liberty of looking into it myself. Remember the first ransom note that he sent?'

She nodded. The words were engraved upon her heart.

'1795. Hounslow Heath. The document that was taken in exchange for your daughter,' said Francis as if reading them again. He took a piece of paper from his pocket and when he unfolded it she could see that it was a page that had been cut from a newspaper—a newspaper that was yellow with age. He passed it to her. At the top of the page in tiny letters she saw the page was from *The London Messenger*, and the date was June 22nd, 1795.

'1795,' she said and when her eyes dropped lower on the page she saw the article entitled 'Robbery and Murder upon Hounslow Heath'. She swallowed down the nausea.

'Read it,' her brother said.

The names leapt out at her before she even began to read. She read, in silence, a small part of what Rafe had already told her.

'Edmund Knight,' he said slowly. 'And his wife, Catherine.'

'A tragedy,' she said.

'Do you know who they are?'

She nodded, but did not meet his eye, just kept her gaze fixed on the sheet of newsprint before her.

'Rafe Knight's parents,' he said.

The silence hissed between them.

'What is your point, Francis?'

'1795. Hounslow Heath. A highwayman. A strange coincidence, don't you think?'

'What are you suggesting?' She looked at him then. Her heart was thumping so fast, so hard, that it threatened to leap from her throat. 'You think that the man who killed Rafe's parents is the same one who abducted me?' But she knew that was not what he was thinking.

'No. But the two crimes are connected in some way.'

'There must have been hundreds of happenings upon Hounslow Heath in that year.'

'There were not,' said Francis. His gaze held hers and the look in his eyes made her shiver.

'Then maybe the reference is to some event not reported in the newspapers.' She hoped he could not see her nervousness.

He shook his head. 'It is the strangest thing,' he said,

'but when I started asking questions about the murder of Rafe Knight's parents I discovered that no one is willing to answer them.'

'Then maybe you should stop asking questions about something that is long since dead and buried.' The blood was pounding in her head and she felt a fear worse than any she had known, for this fear was not for herself, but for the man she loved. She did not trust herself to raise her eyes to her brother's. She gripped the newspaper page tighter so that he would not see the tremor that ran through her fingers.

'Don't you want us to catch the highwayman, Marianne?'

No! she wanted to shout. 'I want to put the past behind me and move on with my life.'

'Even if he's still out there?'

'There are worse men than him out there, Francis,' she said quietly. She hated to see the pity that flashed in her brother's eyes and wished she had not spoken.

'Not in England,' he reassured her.

She prayed he was right, and when she went to leave this time her brother did not stop her.

Rafe was in his study, discussing matters with Callerton, when Marianne returned from her father's house. Her face was pale and he could see the worry in her eyes. She had not even removed her pelisse, bonnet or gloves when she came to him. He sent Callerton away before coming to stand before her.

'Francis has found it. He knows, Rafe!'

He felt his heart miss a beat. 'The document?' he asked quietly.

She shook her head with impatience. 'The article from *The London Messenger* archives for 1795. He

knows of the murder of your parents.' She untied her bonnet and set it down on his desk.

'It is no great secret, Marianne.'

She peeled off her gloves and thrust them down beside the bonnet. 'No, but it is the only incident reported for Hounslow Heath for 1795.'

The silence hissed between them. He knew what she was saying.

Her eyes held his and he saw the fear in them.

'He has already been asking questions about your parents...about you.'

He had not cared if they caught him before, not as long as he took Misbourne down with him, but things were different now.

'Do not underestimate my brother, Rafe. He seeks to protect me and that makes him tenacious, and determined, ruthless even. He will not let the matter rest, not until he has found all there is to know of you... and the highwayman. We have to go away before he discovers the truth.'

'We can't run from this, Marianne.'

'Why won't you understand?'

'I do understand,' he said softly and drew her into his arms.

She stared up into his face. 'My father will destroy you,' she said. 'And you will destroy him.'

'You know that he has the document, don't you?'

She nodded and he saw tears sheen her eyes.

'And you know what that means, Marianne.'

'I know, but I cannot believe it of him, Rafe.' She shook her head. 'All of this for a sheet of paper. What is written on it that it is worth so many lives? You saw it that night.'

'Only the smallest part of it.' Only the three vowels written large and clear.

She placed her hands on either side of his face and stared up into his eyes. 'He is my father, Rafe, and I love him.' She paused and a single tear overflowed to trickle down her cheek. 'And I love *you*. More than anything.'

'I know.' It seemed he could see right into her very soul. 'I love you, too, Marianne.'

She squeezed her eyes shut at his whispered words, but the tears escaped to flow none the less.

'What are we going to do, Rafe?'

'We are going to face what will come.'

'I cannot,' she sobbed.

'I know that you can, Marianne,' he said.

'If I lose you, Rafe...' The words choked and finished.

He held her in his arms and he could not tell her that everything would be all right, for they both knew the truth: it would be his neck or Misbourne's in the noose and, either way, it would break Marianne's heart.

Chapter Fourteen

They lay in bed together that night. The wind rattled at the window panes and the sky outside was a sheer sheet of black. There was no moonlight, no starlight. Only the glow of the fire's red embers broke the darkness of the room. But there was no need for light. They lay naked and entwined, breast to breast, heart to heart. So close that she could feel his eyelashes against hers, so close that they shared the same breath. Every hour was precious. Every minute. Too precious to waste on the past or on worries of the future. All they had was now.

'Make love to me, Rafe,' she whispered against his lips. 'I am asking you.' Then, remembering the words he had spoken so long ago, 'I am begging you.'

'As I would kneel at your feet and beg you, Marianne.' And then he kissed her and it made all his other kisses fade to oblivion. In his kiss was everything that had been between them and all that love could ever encompass. He kissed her lips and then he kissed her breasts, tenderly, with all of his love, so that it felt like he was worshipping her with his mouth. His breath seared her skin, branding her, making her his, as if

she could ever be another's. Tasting her, touching her, taking them both on a journey that could only have one end.

Their hearts beat in unison. She could feel the rush of his blood as surely as she felt her own, feel the convergence of their desire to a blaze of unimaginable intensity. He kissed her until there was no thought in her mind save for him, kissed her until her body was begging for his. She needed this union with him, wanted it with all her heart, all her soul. To share their bodies. To lose herself in him. For ever. Against her belly she could feel the press of the long thick length of him and between her thighs the dull throbbing ache was almost unbearable. She slid herself against him, needing to feel him between her legs.

'Marianne,' he breathed her name.

'Rafe.' There was nothing else in the world. No fear. No hurt. Only her love for him and his love for her.

He rolled her on to her back, taking his weight on his elbows as their bodies clung together. Her thighs gaped wide, opening herself to him, and she could feel him touching her, letting her taste the place to which he would take them both. A promise. A vow.

'Yes,' she whispered. She wanted to love him in every way she could. She needed him, him and only him, as desperately as if her life depended on it.

His lips brushed hers, their breaths mingling, warm and intimate, and then he slid inside her. It was the most wonderful feeling in the world, being filled with him, as if their bodies had been made to fit together. A sense of coming home. A sense that everything had been made right. She sighed with relief, with delight, the sensation of it making her dizzy. She kissed his mouth and only then felt him begin to move within her.

Thrusting, in long strokes, a rhythm that cemented the love that was between them. Deeper and faster until she was clutching him to her so hard that her fingers dug into his back, into his buttocks. Until she was moving with him, pulling him in even deeper, even harder. Until their breaths panted loud and their skin was slick and sliding with sweat. Faster and faster in a whirlwind that tumbled and turned and drove and urged. Until she arched against him and cried out his name and heard him cry hers, as everything seemed to explode in an ecstasy that stole her breath and stopped her heart, and shattered her body, her very being, into a thousand pieces scattered across the heavens, like stars in the darkness of the night sky. She clung to him, revelling in the heavy weight of his body upon hers, feeling his love all around her, within her, filling her heart and her body and her soul as, together, they floated back down to earth.

They lay there, and he kissed her, a single kiss both tender and possessive, then rolled his weight from her.

She heard him climb from the bed, watched the dark shape of him move across to the fireplace. She saw the tiny flare on the candle he lit from the red embers on the hearth. And the two small flames flicker in the darkness as he used the first candle to light the others. She could see his nakedness as he returned across the room and set the branch of candles down on the bedside cabinet. He did not climb into the bed, but sat on its edge, looking round at her, his eyes very dark, his face shadowed in the flicker of the candlelight.

There was silence, a pure silence, raw and unbroken. And she felt her heart tighten because she only now remembered, and she knew what he was going to say.

* * *

Rafe looked into the eyes of the woman he loved.

'You were not a maid.' The candles flickered in the draught, making shadows dance upon the walls, upon her face.

'No.' Her voice was quiet. She did not try to deny it, made no pretence.

'Why did you not tell me?'

'The right moment never came, and then I…forgot.'

'Forgot?' He raised an eyebrow and looked at her.

'You made me forget,' she said.

'Does your father know?'

She nodded. He closed his eyes, tried to close his ears to the horrible little voice that whispered possibilities of which he could not bear to think.

'The night of your birthday ball, when your father caught us in his study… Was it all a ploy he devised to catch you a husband?'

'No! Never think that!' He saw the shock that flared in her eyes, and the distress that followed in its wake, and he knew that she was telling the truth. And besides, it was too late, because he loved her.

They looked at each other across the small distance.

'Tell me what happened, Marianne,' he said gently.

Her eyes scanned his face as if she were committing him to memory, then she glanced down and began to speak. 'It was the night of my eighteenth birthday. My father wanted it to be a quiet family celebration so we did not even leave the house that day. I retired as usual. My maid helped me change into my nightclothes and put me to bed, and then she left. It was a mild night and the fire had almost died upon the hearth and…' She hesitated, and took a deep breath as if willing herself to continue. He reached his hand across the covers to

take hers. She felt cold to his touch. He folded his fingers around hers to warm them.

'The curtains were drawn,' she said. 'I blew the candle out and it was so dark.' He felt the slight tightening of her fingers. 'He came from behind the curtains. He said he would kill me if I cried out or struggled and I was so shocked, so very afraid, that I made no sound, not until he was gone. I could not see him in the darkness, not until he left and the streetlight shone on his face as he climbed out of the window.'

Rafe felt her pain as raw as if it were his own. His heart was thudding hard in his chest and he was aware of the metallic taste of blood in his mouth. And more than anything of the quiet deadly certainty that he hid from his face and his voice. He placed his other hand over hers, enfolding her one small hand with both of his, protecting it, warming it.

'Monsters in the darkness,' he said quietly.

'Yes.'

He paused. 'Who is he, Marianne?'

'He is gone. Fled to the Continent before my father and brother could find him. They would kill him were he ever to return.'

They would not, for Rafe would get to him first. 'His name, Marianne.'

'The Duke of Rotherham.'

There was a small silence before she said, 'I tried to block him from my mind. I tried not to let myself think of him or what he had done. And then I met you...'

And he had made her father grovel hurt in the dirt while she watched. And he had abducted her at gunpoint and held her prisoner. He only now realised the truth of what he had done.

'I never would have abducted you had I known.'

She looked up at him then and her expression was one of devastation. 'Now you are sorry for it.' And she began to weep.

He moved across the bed, pulling her into his arms, trying to make her understand. 'I can never be sorry for taking you, Marianne. Had I not, you would always just have been Misbourne's daughter. How would I have come to love you? How would I have made you my wife?'

'You made me truly forget what Rotherham had done.'

'I am glad of it,' he whispered.

'My mother told me there was a way that you might never know. To pretend the pain and scratch my skin with a pin so that the blood would mark the bedsheets. But I could not deceive you like that.'

'I know you would not. I love you, Marianne. You are mine. And I am yours. Nothing can ever change that.' He kissed her and took her in his arms and made love to her again, gently, with all that was in his heart, to show her the truth of it, to show her that nothing else mattered.

In the week that followed they lived and loved minute by minute, hour by hour, one day at a time. There was nothing of fear, nothing of darkness, only a love so strong that it seemed to etch itself upon time itself. Marianne knew they could not live like this for ever, that sooner or later, reality must intrude upon the world they had constructed for themselves. And it did.

The note was delivered by hand on Tuesday afternoon. She recognized the neat slope of her mother's handwriting and cracked open the red wax seal of the Earl of Misbourne.

Leicester Square, London,
November 1810
My dearest Marianne
Your father and I would be delighted if you and
your husband would come to tea at three o'clock
tomorrow afternoon. We look forward to seeing
you both.
Ever your loving mother

She passed the note to Rafe, who read it without
a word.

'Will you come?' She knew what she was asking of
him—to take afternoon tea with the man he believed
responsible for the murder of his parents. She hoped
with all her heart that he was wrong and prayed for
the miracle that would prove it both to her and to Rafe.
And deep within her was the small glimmer of hope
that, somehow, the breach between her husband and
her father could be healed.

He nodded.

Her heart gave a little squeeze. She reached her face
up to his and kissed him on the mouth. 'Thank you,'
she whispered.

At three o'clock the next day her father's butler led
them into the drawing room. She knew the minute the
door closed that she had made a mistake in coming
here. There was no sign of her mother. There was no
tea tray. Only her father and on the table, where the tea
cups should have been, a crumple of deep-blue silk and
Mr Pickering's betrothal ring. She felt her heart miss
a beat and her stomach sink down to meet her toes.

'Where is Mama? What is going on?' She played the
game, feigning an indignation and innocence, anything

that would protect Rafe. And even while she played it she prayed and prayed that she was wrong.

'Sit down,' said her father in a voice she barely recognised.

'No.' She manoeuvred herself to stand in front of her husband, as if she could shield him from them. 'We are leaving.'

She tried to back away towards the doorway, but Rafe was solid and unmoving as a rock. Behind them she heard the closing of the door and the key turn in the lock; when she looked Francis was standing there, barring their exit.

'Do you recognise this dress, Marianne?' Her father lifted it from where it lay on the table. And when she said nothing, 'You should do, it is the one the highwayman sent you home in.'

She felt Rafe move, coming to stand slightly in front of her. She swallowed and felt her blood chill. She did not look at him, just kept her eyes on the dress that was gripped so tight within her father's hand that his knuckles shone white.

Her father began to speak. 'Your brother was most interested in this dress. It appears that one can discover so much from a dressmaker's label. The dress was made in March 1795 by Madame Voise of New Bond Street, a dressmaker with a very select clientele.'

She waited, and the sense of dread she had felt on entering the room expanded and grew to fill the entirety of her chest. But she showed nothing of it, determined to yield not one thing that might implicate Rafe.

'Madame Voise died some years ago. Her nephew runs the business now, under the name of Sutton. But he still had his aunt's old records.'

The tension in the room was so tight she thought she could not bear it.

'No one would have anticipated such a thing after all these years,' he said.

She said nothing. She did not dare look at Rafe, but she could sense the strain emanating from his body.

Please, God, she prayed. *Please.*

'The dress is made from Parisian silk,' he said.

Say it if you know, she wanted to shout.

'The material cost one pound, sixteen shillings and thruppence a yard.'

Every word was a torture of waiting, for she had a very good idea of where this was leading.

'And do you know the lady for whom it was made?' He smiled, but it was not a smile of happiness, nor even one of victory.

She held her breath and felt the tremble go through her as the seconds stretched.

'Mrs Catherine Knight.' He paused. 'Your husband's mother.'

In the silence there was only the fast frenzied thud of her heart.

'Rafe Knight is the highwayman who held us up on Hounslow Heath. Rafe Knight is the man who abducted you.'

'What nonsense—' she began, but her father cut her off.

'But then you already know that, don't you, Marianne?'

'This is madness! Rafe has done nothing!'

But her father and brother just looked at her.

'Do you think I would not know if my own husband was the highwayman? Do you think—?' But

Rafe stayed her with the gentle pressure of his hand on her arm.

'They know, Marianne.' His eyes were very dark and his face the sternest she had ever seen it. There was about him such a certainty, such an aura of danger and power, that she feared the terribleness of what was about to be unleashed within this room.

She shook her head as if doing so would deny that he had said the words. 'No,' she whispered, and looked up into his eyes. 'No.' And stroked her fingers against where his hand rested upon her arm.

'Your brother was right,' her father said. 'You love him.'

'Of course I love him,' she said, loud and angry, and faced her father with defiance. 'I love him,' she said again. 'And I will not let you hurt him.'

Her father ignored her and kept his attention focused on Rafe while he spoke to her brother. 'Take your sister upstairs.'

Francis took a step towards her.

'No!' she shouted. 'I am not going anywhere.'

'My wife stays with me,' said Rafe, his voice low and uncompromising.

'Very well,' her father said, but his mouth tightened. 'Are you going to tell me what manner of game you are playing, Mr Knight?'

'There is no game, Misbourne. You know what I want.'

'I am sure I have not the slightest notion. I played along with the highwayman's demands for the sake of my daughter's safety.'

'June 17th, 1795,' said Rafe. 'Hounslow Heath. You may have forgotten that night, Misbourne, but I have not.'

'I am not unaware of the tragedy of your parents' demise, Knight, but I fail to see how their unhappy fate has anything to do with me.' It made sense what her father was saying. He would have been so very plausible, had she not already overheard the betrayal from his own lips.

'I was there that night, Misbourne,' said Rafe in the highwayman's deadly quiet whisper. 'Did not your henchman tell you?' He stepped forwards and his eyes had nothing of gold in them, nothing of lightness, only the promise of death. 'I watched what he did to them. I saw what he took from them.'

Every last vestige of colour washed from her father's face. 'If you believe that I had anything to do with your parents' murder, you are mistak—'

'Five men,' said Rafe. 'Tommy Jones—brother of Billy Jones, the villain who dressed up as a highwayman and did the deed—who you ensured was hanged so that he might never reveal the truth. James Harris—Billy's handler, the one with whom your man made the arrangement. Frederick Linton—your man with whom the liaisons were made. Alan Brown—the corrupt Bow Street Runner who led the investigation—and George Martin Fairclough—the magistrate who was in Linton's pocket.'

Her father swallowed hard. His eyes seemed to bulge as he realised the significance of the names. 'They were the ones you robbed? The ones you…'

'Yes,' said Rafe darkly. 'You paid them well for their silence—they kept it for fifteen years. But they talked to me.' He smiled without humour. 'How they talked.' And those words spoken so quietly sent a chill through the room.

Her father tried to laugh it off as an absurdity, but

the sound was hollow and unconvincing, and across his face was unadulterated fear and a guilt that endorsed Rafe's accusation better than had he held up his hands and admitted it. 'You have got this all wrong, Knight.'

The two men stared at one another.

'Give me the document, Misbourne.'

Her father shook his head.

Rafe slipped the pistol from his pocket and pointed it straight at her father's heart. 'I will not ask you again.'

She saw her brother edging closer to Rafe, positioning himself ready to act.

'Go ahead and pull the trigger, Knight,' her father said.

Marianne saw the slight tightening of Rafe's fingers on the pistol. 'No!' She stared at her husband, at the hardness and the hatred in the focus that held her father. She did not take her eyes from Rafe's face as she moved to stand between him and her father.

Rafe's eyes moved to hers. 'Stand aside, Marianne.'

But she shook her head. 'You know that I cannot let you do this.'

They stared at one another and she knew what she was asking of him. She saw the pain and the anger and the grief and all that he had spent a lifetime working towards. But she could not let him pull the trigger. She stood there, her eyes fixed on his, willing him to understand. Slowly he lowered the pistol.

From the corner of her eye she caught the movement of her brother charging at Rafe. 'No, Francis!' she cried, but it was too late; Francis launched himself at her husband, knocking the pistol from his hand and the two men were down on the floor landing such savage blows on one another that the blood reached to splatter against the hem of her skirt. Crimson against

ivory. So stark and so awful. She stood stock still and stared at it in shock for a moment, while the furore erupted around her. Her brother's blood. Her husband's blood. She bent down and lifted the pistol from where it had landed at her feet, then she pointed it at the sofa behind her and fired.

The noise was deafening. The plume of smoke was acrid and stung her eyes. And when it cleared, both men were on their feet, staring at her with alarm and concern.

'Enough,' she said. 'No more.' She dropped the spent pistol to the floor with an almighty thud. Her ears were still ringing with the echo of the pistol shot. She looked first at her brother, a searing glance that made him look away in shame. And then she looked at her father. She looked him straight in the eyes.

'After what you have done to Rafe, do you not think an explanation is the very least he deserves?' she said quietly.

He stared at her as if he had not thought she knew the awfulness of his crime. As if he only now realised the truth—that she knew what he had done. For a moment there was such a terrible tortured expression in his eyes. It was a pain like none she had ever seen, as if his very soul was writhing in agony. He closed his eyes as if he could not bear for her to see it.

'I am sorry, Marianne,' he said in a voice that was barely above a whisper. 'I am so very sorry, my darling girl. You are right, of course.' There was nothing of fight in him, nothing of his energy and strength. 'I never meant for the Knights to be killed. It was to be a highway robbery only. The fool was supposed to rob them, nothing more.' And then he waved Francis away and looked at Rafe. 'I have spent a lifetime regretting

the loss of their life, what I did to you…' He shook his head. 'I am sorry, truly I am.'

'The document.' Rafe's voice was harsh.

'The damnable document.' Misbourne gave a laugh, except it came out like a sob. 'Your father and I were both members of a particular club…some might call it a secret society. He was taking the document to the Master of the Order. There would have been an investigation. It would have all come out. I could not let that happen.'

'So you killed him that you would not be black-balled from your club?' Rafe said with incredulity.

But her father shook his head. 'I would take the shame on myself a thousand times over, if only it had been that simple.'

'Then what?'

'I could not risk that the document might find its way back to its owner.'

Rafe sneered and shook his head. 'So the document was not even yours to steal?'

'It was not,' said her father. 'But I had to have it,' he added quietly. 'I would have done almost anything in the world to possess it.' He raised his eyes suddenly to Rafe's. 'But it made no difference. I had unleashed a monster and I could not call it back.'

'Where is the document now?'

Her father's eyes flitted to hers before returning to Rafe's. 'I will give it to you. And you may do what you want with me. Only send Marianne upstairs, to sit with her mother, first. I beg you, Knight.'

'I have been treated as a child for too much of my life,' she said. 'I want to know what this document is that cost Rafe's parents their lives and my father his honour.'

'Marianne has every right to see exactly what you refused to bargain for her safe return. She stays.'

Her father seemed to shrink before her eyes. With every breath in the silence he aged a lifetime. His eyes sunk. His cheeks grew gaunt. Her proud strong father looked old, defeated, grey. His gaze moved to hers, and there was in his eyes such a terrible sadness and regret that it broke her heart. He looked at her, drinking in her face as if it were the last time he might look upon her, the seconds stretching too long before he looked at Rafe once more. He said not one word, just turned and walked over to the small boxed bookcase by the fireplace and withdrew a blue leather-bound book that looked like every other in his collection. He hesitated only for a moment, holding the book in his hands as if he had held it a thousand times before, then opening it and turning the pages to find the one he sought. He creased the spine open and she realised that the document had been bound into the book like a proper page. Then he passed the wide-opened book to Rafe, who had moved to stand before the fireplace.

Marianne watched Rafe's eyes scan the page. She waited for him to reveal the document's secrets, but there was only a deafening silence. Her heart beat once, twice, three times. She saw Rafe's eyes widen, saw the way his gaze shot to her father's and the look that was in them—utter incredulity and condemnation and comprehension all rolled into one. The silence was deafening. A piece of coal cracked and hissed upon the fire. And still Marianne waited and her stomach was clenched tight and for all the heat in the room and the sweat that prickled beneath her arms her fingers were chilled to the bone.

'Why the hell have you kept this all these years?'

She could hear the horror in Rafe's whisper and it frightened her more than anything else had done.

'So that I could never forget what I did. So that I would always remember that it was my fault,' said her father, and he seemed a shadow of the man he had been. 'It is my penance, my punishment.'

'Rafe?' she said and began to walk towards her husband. She had a horrible feeling about what was written on that page. A dread like none she had ever known. She feared to discover its terrible dark secret, yet she was drawn to it like a moth to a flame.

She saw the flicker of something in Rafe's eyes. In one rapid move he ripped the page from the book, balled it and threw it into the fire. 'No!' she gasped in disbelief, racing towards it as if to save it from the flames, but Rafe stopped her, capturing her in his arms so that she could only watch the page darken and crinkle and shrink to nothingness within the roar of flames.

'You *do* love her,' whispered her father in his old man's voice as he stared at Rafe.

'The only reason you are still alive is because I love her.'

'What have you done?' she cried and stared up into Rafe's face.

'What your father should have done long ago,' he said.

'Are you mad? After all these years of seeking… after all that you have gone through… Why would you do such a thing?' She shook her head, unable to believe it. 'What was written upon that page?'

The question that Rafe had spent fifteen years asking. The thing he had thought the most important in the world. He understood now how wrong he had been.

He understood now that the most important thing in the world was that Marianne never discovered the answer to that question.

'You must think me the very devil,' said Misbourne.

Rafe did not disagree.

'But you understand, do you not, why I had to move heaven and earth to retrieve it? Why I could not yield it? He needed the paper in his possession to redeem it. I thought that if he did not have it I could stop him.'

Rafe felt sick to the pit of his stomach. Yet he gave a nod. He understood too well.

'What the hell is going on?' Linwood asked.

'Take your sister upstairs to her mother. Then come down and I will tell you,' Misbourne said. 'I owe Knight the truth. And whatever he decides to do, you should know the reason for it.'

Linwood gave a nod.

'You cannot seriously think to send me to another room as if I am of no consequence in any of this. I am not a child.' Marianne looked from her father to her brother and back again. 'I have been as much a part of this as any of you,' she continued.

Rafe saw Misbourne wince as her words struck home. Marianne did not know that she had been at the very centre of the whole thing.

'I shall stay with my husband,' she said and looked to Rafe for support.

'You should see how your mother is, Marianne,' he said quietly.

She looked at him as if he had just slapped her. He knew that she must think he was letting her down, but rather that a thousand times over than she learned the truth.

'Rafe?' She stared at him with shock and hurt in her eyes.

'I'm sorry, Marianne.' God only knew what he would do to protect her. 'Please trust me in this one thing. Believe me, it is for the best.'

'The best?' she said. And she gave him a look of utter strength and anger and disappointment. 'I have spent a lifetime doing what other people deem best for me. I thought you were different, Rafe.'

'Marianne, you do not understand…' But there was nothing he could say to make her see, without telling her the truth.

'You are right, I do not understand at all,' she said, then she turned and strode away, slamming the door behind her.

'Thank you,' said Misbourne.

'Don't thank me,' snarled Rafe, 'I didn't do it for you. I did it for Marianne.'

'I know,' said Misbourne. 'And that is why I thank you.'

'Is someone going to tell me what is going on?' asked Linwood.

Rafe's eyes slid to Misbourne.

The earl slumped down into the chair and in a quiet monotone he began to talk.

Marianne did not make her way up the stairs to her mother's little parlour. She felt angry and hurt beyond belief over Rafe's attitude. Everything had changed in the moment he read the document. What secret did it hold that he would rather ally himself with the man who was behind the murder of his parents than reveal it to her? He said he loved her, but what had just happened in the drawing room did not feel like love. It felt

like betrayal, by both her husband and her father. And what did anything written on a piece of paper mean in comparison to that?

She could not go and sip tea and chat about the latest fashions with her mother, closing her mind to all that was around her, pretending that nothing had happened. She could never be that cosseted, fearful, stifled woman again. Marianne slipped out of the front door, closing it noiselessly behind her.

Callerton had not yet returned with the coach to collect them. She could not very well go back inside and start ringing bells and summoning servants to ready her father's carriage to take her home. Although she was uneasy about the idea of walking alone through the streets of London, she would damn well do it. Better that than the alternative. And then she saw the hackney carriage at the end of the street and her dilemma was solved. She glanced back at the window of the drawing room and was relieved to see that no one was standing there. She squared her shoulders, held her chin up and, with a determined grip on her reticule, headed towards the hackney carriage.

'You bastard!' Linwood landed the blow against his father's chin and Misbourne did not turn away, let alone raise an arm to defend himself. 'How could you do such a thing?'

Misbourne said nothing, just stared at the carpet with deadened eyes as the blood trickled down his chin and his lip began to swell.

The flames had died away within the fireplace. The coal was devoured and in its place was a mass of glowing embers. Rafe did not know how long it had taken for Misbourne to explain every last detail, but he had

done it and the silence that followed had been deafening. He could not blame Linwood. Only the thought of what it would do to Marianne stayed his own fists... and pistol.

'It was you, wasn't it?' he said. 'Paying the money into my account. Trying to appease your conscience.'

'I had taken your parents from you. Paying for your education, ensuring that you would never want for money—these were the only things I could do. I stood in the shadows and watched you grow from a boy to a man, easing your way when I could, safeguarding you when it was necessary.'

Rafe felt sick.

'I was right,' said Linwood. 'You would have married her to anyone.'

Misbourne nodded. 'Anyone to save her from him.'

'It is why he fought so hard to secure first Arlesford, then Pickering—why he had me wed her so quickly,' said Rafe. 'It had to be by her twenty-first birthday.'

'He would have come for her otherwise,' Misbourne said, 'and no matter what protection I built around her he would have found a way to breach it.'

Rafe balled his fingers into a fist at the thought.

The door slammed closed and the hackney carriage drew away. It stopped again a few minutes later; the coachman was speaking to someone, declining a fare. And then they were off again, making their way steadily through the streets.

Marianne thought about Rafe. And in her mind all she could see was the look in his eyes when he had sent her away, a look she did not understand and yet seemed to reach into the very core of her and touch where no other could. A look that had such a grim

irascibility about it that she knew he would not falter. Whatever he had read upon that page, he was never going to tell her. He was shutting her out. Treating her as her father had done all of these years. Overruling her, without discussion or explanation. Always knowing what was best for her. Marianne knew she could not just sit back and let that happen. She knew she had to fight for what was between them. And just as she thought it, the sun peeped from behind the clouds, lifting away the heavy dull greyness and shadow that hung over the day. She glanced out of the window at the patch of blue sky above and the beautiful shimmer of the sunlight upon the water below and felt the finger of unease down her spine. She moved closer to the window, looked out properly, focusing on the route the carriage was taking and saw they were on London Bridge, crossing the Thames…heading in the opposite direction to St Luke's and Rafe's town house. The panic was sudden, like a fist slamming into her stomach, making her catch her breath, making her feel sick. She banged a hand on the door and called out to the driver in a loud clear voice.

'Stop this carriage at once.'

But the carriage did not stop.

She told herself that the driver was just a villain chancing to fleece her for a higher fare by taking her on a longer route. She prayed to God that that was the case. But in her heart she knew, even though she did not want to believe it. She felt the panic roil, felt her limbs stiffen with terrible fear so that she could not move, could not make a sound. And then she heard the whisper of Rafe's words. *Running from fear only makes it chase you. Hiding from it only makes it seek you. You have to face fear.*

She stopped struggling inside herself and stilled the turmoil of her thoughts. With traffic as it was in London it was only a matter of time before the coach had to stop. But the carriage did not slow. Instead its speed increased until it was rattling dangerously fast over the pot holes and ruts of the poorly kept road. Marianne gripped tight to the securing strap and knew there was no chance of jumping from the speeding vehicle.

She shouted as loud as she could, thudded her free hand against the glass of the window, anything to attract attention. But the carriage driver was taking her through a place where there were no houses or shops, only large warehouses and derelict-looking manufactories. There was no one to see, no one to hear. She stopped shouting and saved her energy for the fight ahead.

The carriage eventually came to a halt outside a seedy tavern. There were men on the narrow street, unshaven, unkempt, with bloodshot eyes and blackened teeth, sitting on steps and old broken wooden crates, drinking from dark and dirty bottles. And women, too, women who lounged in doorways with their petticoats showing and grimy skin beneath, who looked at her with malice and amusement in their eyes. There would be no help here. It reminded her of the rookery in St Giles from which Rafe had saved her. But he would not save her now. He thought she was upstairs in her father's house, drinking tea with her mother. She had only herself to rely on. She sat very still, watching, waiting for what was going to happen.

The door opened and it was not the carriage driver that stood there, but a tall thin gentleman, as old as her father. A gentleman with a black lacquered walking cane, who had just climbed down from his seat beside

the coachman. He was impeccably dressed, as out of place in this seedy place as she was herself. He climbed inside, sat down opposite her and made himself comfortable. And she knew even before he looked round to face her who he was. There had been no imagining in the botanical gardens, or that night in her bedchamber. She looked across the hackney carriage into the cold pale eyes of the Duke of Rotherham.

'What do you mean, Lady Marianne is not there?' Misbourne demanded of the footman.

But Lady Misbourne was hurrying down the staircase at that very moment, running up to her husband, breathless and uncaring of social graces. 'I thought she was down here with you! She did not come upstairs.'

Rafe saw the whites around Misbourne's eyes grow larger. The fear that crept across the man's face was transparent. He sent his wife and servants away. 'Oh, my God, he has come for her!' he whispered as if to himself. 'It cannot be…' He stared at Rafe. 'I thought she would be safe once she was wed. He is such a stickler for precision. Everything to the letter. Everything just as was agreed. I thought once she was married he could not…' He clutched his hands to his face and could not continue.

Rafe looked at Misbourne and the man quailed beneath the look in his eyes. 'You should have warned me that he was coming back for her, that I could have guarded her against him,' he said in a deathly quiet voice. 'Had you shown me the document…'

'Had he shown you the document you would have killed him for the bastard he is and what would that have done to Marianne? Besides, we are jumping the

gun,' said Linwood. 'She was angry and upset with us all.'

But most of all with Rafe. He knew it was the truth. From Marianne's point of view he had let her down when she had needed him most.

'She has probably returned to Knight's house,' continued Linwood, but Rafe could see the fear in Linwood's eyes. And he felt a ripple of the same fear.

He strode to the front door and opened it. His carriage sat waiting directly outside in the street, with Callerton standing by the horses. Callerton moved to open the carriage door when he saw Rafe, slipping the step down into place. By that one small action Rafe knew that Marianne was not within the carriage, that Callerton was expecting her to emerge from the house on his arm. The dread pierced right through him, sharp and cold as the blade of his sword. And he knew in that moment that Misbourne was right. The fact that the document was destroyed and that Marianne was his wife changed nothing. Misbourne had made a pact with the devil, and the final day of reckoning had arrived. Misbourne had indeed unleashed a monster. And the monster had come for Marianne.

Chapter Fifteen

'Rotherham,' Rafe whispered and the intensity of the word cut through the room like the lash of a whip.

'How could he have slipped back into the country? I have eyes and ears at every port,' said Misbourne.

'Men that can be so easily bought are always open to a deeper pocket,' said Rafe.

'He has her and there is nothing we can do.' Misbourne crumpled to his knees, his face ashen, a stricken look in his eyes.

'On your feet, Misbourne,' Rafe snapped and dragged him up with nothing of compassion. 'Where is his town house?'

'It no longer exists. It was burned to the ground the week after he fled to the Continent.' It was Linwood who answered, and there was something in his voice that meant Rafe did not have to ask who lay behind the property's destruction.

'She is already wed to Knight.' Misbourne seemed to be talking to himself. 'He cannot marry her. But he means to have her regardless. I had not thought he would deviate from what was agreed.'

Rafe thought of the words written upon the second

half of the page he had torn from the book. *I give to you my daughter, Marianne, once she has reached her twenty-first year, to be your wife.* Rotherham was a man who wanted precisely what he had been promised. And if that were the case then Rafe thought he understood what the villain was doing.

'He could have her anywhere,' said Misbourne and covered his face with his hands. 'We haven't a hope in hell of finding them.'

'We do not need to find them,' said Rafe.

'What do you mean?' Misbourne let his hands fall away and stared at Rafe.

'I think we will hear from Rotherham before the afternoon is out.'

'Good afternoon, Marianne,' Rotherham said in the soft voice that had so haunted her nightmares. 'We meet again, just as I said we would.'

'How did you…?'

'I have been watching you, my dear. How very fortuitous that you escaped your "guard" to travel all alone and by hackney coach…when the coachmen are so easily and quickly persuaded. All the money in my purse and the promise of even more when we reach home.' He leaned forwards and dropped his voice slightly, as if he were telling her a secret. 'Although he might be in for something of a surprise when we get there.'

'You villain!'

'Come now, my dear, that is no way to speak to me when I have come all this way to rectify a little misunderstanding.'

'Misunderstanding? It was hardly that, sir.'

'I wish only to make my apology and put matters right.'

'I do not want your apology! Take it and return whence you came.'

The cool pale gaze flickered over her face, appraising her. 'How much you have changed, Marianne, in three short years. You are not afraid of me.'

'You are the one who should be afraid,' she said. 'You should be very afraid.'

He smiled in a condescending way as if she were a simpleton who did not understand the words she was saying. 'And why exactly should I be so fearful? Hmm?' He wetted his narrow lips.

'Because if you do not release me, there is a man who shall not rest until he has hunted you down.'

'Really.' He seemed amused, more than anything else.

'And when he catches you…'

'If he were to catch me…' Rotherham sat forwards in his seat as if riveted by her words. 'What would he do, Marianne?'

Marianne thought of Rafe in the rookery and what he had done to the men who had stood in his way. She thought of the burying ground and the bullets and the blood. And most of all she thought of the way a city of thieves and villains had parted to let him pass.

'You think you are dangerous,' she said and shook her head. 'But you have not met my husband.'

'Rafe Knight,' said Rotherham and something of the smile vanished from his face.

She laughed to see it and felt Rotherham's eyes shift to hers, and in them for the first time was a flicker of anger. 'How hoydenish you have become, my dear. You should learn to mind your manners.'

'I do not think so, your Grace,' she said. 'My husband likes them just the way they are.'

He paused, then said very carefully, 'Then Rafe Knight is an unfortunate fool. Just like his father before him.'

The wind dropped from her sails. 'His father? What do you mean?'

'Poking his nose into affairs that were none of his concern, taking documents that were not his to take. It was Knight who stole the original document from me, you know. Once it was in my possession again, I had a copy made. A precise replica, so good that Misbourne could not even tell it apart from the one he had written with his own hand when he went to such lengths to retrieve it. I take it your husband has told you the story of how his parents met their death?'

She gave a single stiff nod.

'Billy Jones, the highwayman that night, worked for me, of course. I always remembered him with a degree of affection as a reliable sort of man, until Rafe Knight started asking questions and I realised that Jones had not been so very reliable after all.'

She stared at him, unable to believe what she was hearing. 'It was you who ordered the murder of Rafe's parents!'

'Indeed, my dear. But it would have been so much harder to silence Edmund Knight had your father not arranged the robbery.'

'And why was it necessary to silence Rafe's father?'

'Knight was taking the matter that very night to those who would have made what was agreed within that piece of paper impossible. And I had to have you, my dear.'

Everything in the world seemed to pause in that moment. She thought she must have misheard him, but when she looked at his face she knew that she had not.

'The piece of paper…' she began, but her lips felt too stiff to form the words.

'Did your father not show you?' He arched his thin grey brows. 'You know he should not have let you marry Knight, and so slyly done. No betrothal, no courtship, not even a hint of gossip. I had no idea. I thought I was coming back to the matter of Pickering. I hope you have recovered from your little coaching accident.' He smiled, but the look in his eyes was one of anger. 'I really am most disappointed in Misbourne.' From the inside pocket of his waistcoat he produced a sheet of paper folded like a letter except it bore no name or direction, and no seal. 'A gentleman's gaming debt is a matter of honour, after all, and your father has more than proven he has none of that attribute.' His eyes dropped to the paper in his hand.

Marianne's gaze followed.

'Do you know what this is?'

She could hazard a very good guess.

'It is the original document written in your father's very own hand.' He offered it to her.

She stared at the folded paper, but made no move to take it. She knew that within that document lay the explanation for all that had happened.

'Do you not wish to read it? Do you not wish to know what your father gambled on a turn of the cards? What he staked when he was in his cups?'

She had a horrible, horrible feeling. Inside, she was trembling, but when she reached out and took the document from him her hands were still and calm. The paper betrayed not so much as a quiver as she opened it out and read it. It consisted of two separate IOUs written by her father to Rotherham in 1795. In the first he had given her maidenhead—to be claimed when she

turned eighteen. In the second he had given her hand in marriage, if Rotherham so wished it, redeemable when she turned twenty-one.

She stared at the sprawl of her father's handwriting, and in that moment everything ceased to be. Whatever she had imagined had been written in the document, whatever she might have expected, the truth was a zenith away. Nothing could have prepared her for it. Those few seconds seemed to last an eternity. Her mind was thick and slow-witted, unable to comprehend, unwilling to accept the magnitude of what he had done. She could feel the beat of her heart and hear the sound of her breath within the silence of the carriage. Her eyes blinked. From outside came the sound of a man's whistle, followed by a woman's coarse laughter. A seagull cried. Her father, whom she thought had loved her. Her father, who had always tried to protect her. All of her beliefs shattered and cracked apart. She could not weep a single tear. She could not utter even one word. She just sat there, frozen in the likeness of the woman she had been.

'I thought you would understand, my dear,' Rotherham said, taking the document from where it lay in her hands and folding it neatly once more into his pocket. Then he gave a single thud upon the roof with the head of his walking cane and the carriage moved off, swaying and dipping over the uneven surface of the narrow road.

The curtains were drawn within the study of Rafe's town house. Four men stood around the desk: Rafe, Callerton, Linwood and Misbourne. Four men with cold determined eyes. A letter lay discarded on the desk between them.

London, November 1810

My dear Mr Knight

The lady that you seek is within my care. I hold her for one reason and one reason only. That is, to bring about an end to that which was agreed between the lady's father and myself fifteen years ago.

I am grown old, and my health feeble of late, and with each day that passes the burden of guilt over my part in it weighs heavier upon my soul. I wish to return abroad unhindered, to live out the rest of what days I may have in solitude and penitence for my sins. You are husband to the lady at the centre of this tangled web and thus I make my proposal to you, and you alone. I will release her only in exchange for the document that her father still holds, that I might destroy the last evidence of our wickedness...and my guilt.

I seek to avoid capture only that the noble name of Rotherham is not blighted. Therefore there can be no question of involvement of the law, or otherwise. Come alone to Hounslow Heath at four this afternoon with the document, if you wish to proceed as I have suggested. If not, I will be forced to revise my plans for the lady and myself.

Your remorseful servant

Rotherham

The letter had been addressed to Rafe and marked private, yet every man in the room knew the words that Rotherham had written upon it. They had spent the last hours readying themselves.

Misbourne checked the ink was dry, then folded the

freshly written piece of paper and passed it to Rafe. 'You will find it faithful to the page you burned in every word and every stroke of the pen. Their very image is engraved upon my memory, for there has not been a day in the last fifteen years that I did not force myself to look at them.' He paused and then said, 'Thank you for doing this for my daughter.'

Rafe looked into Misbourne's eyes, the eyes of the man he had spent a lifetime hunting and hating, the man whom he would never forgive for what he had done to his parents and to Marianne, and he gave a nod of acknowledgement.

'It has been an honour to know you, Knight.' Misbourne's voice was quiet within the room; respect burned in his eyes. 'For all that you have done for my daughter. For all that you would do for her this night. I thank you, sir.' Misbourne held out his hand to Rafe.

Rafe looked at Misbourne's hand and only the ticking of the clock punctuated the silence. Sometimes a man had to make sacrifices for the woman he loved. Even if it meant sacrificing all that he believed in. Even if it meant sacrificing his own life.

For Marianne, only for Marianne, he thought. He met Misbourne's gaze and took his father-in-law's hand within his own. And it was done.

The men moved to leave for Hounslow Heath.

The late afternoon air grew damp as the sun began to set, casting Hounslow Heath in an orange-tinged hue and silhouetting the hackney carriage to a black-blocked shape that was as dark and sinister as Rotherham himself by her side. Her shawl was lost within the carriage, and the cold seeped through the thin muslin sleeves of her gown, right through her skin to chill her

very bones. The rope that Rotherham had used to bind her wrists behind her back was immovable. No matter how hard she strained against it, or stretched her fingers to reach the knots, it gave no sign of yielding. The coach driver had long since been dispensed with, leaving them to travel here alone.

Rotherham checked his pocket watch again. 'Five minutes before four o'clock. Not much longer now, my dear. And then all of this…fiasco…will be over and you shall be with your husband.'

She wanted to believe him. She prayed that he was telling the truth. But she could not trust him. Not for one second, not for all that calm measured look upon his face, or the soft reassuring lilt of his voice. And even if he was telling the truth, there was the small matter of the document her father had held, the document upon which all of this centred, the document that was now ash within the ashes tray of a fireplace. But Rafe would think of a way round that problem, she did not doubt it for a second.

The globe of the sun began to sink down beneath the horizon, firing the sky a vivid pink. The heath was silent in its waiting; not a bird called, not a bat fluttered. Even the distant streets of Hounslow that bordered it were hushed as if holding their breath. Four faint chimes of a church bell sounded, and as she watched the sun slip lower and the glorious glow of light begin to fade, a solitary horseman appeared on the horizon, riding straight out of the sun so that it seemed he had been born of the sun itself; a dark-caped figure galloping fast towards them, with such purpose, with such lack of fear. And as he came closer she saw the old-fashioned tricorn hat that she knew so well, and the dark silk kerchief across his face…and the pistol held

high in one hand. And she felt her heart lift. Rafe had
come for her.

Rotherham grabbed at her arm, pulling her before
him as a shield for any bullets that Rafe might fire and
producing a pistol of his own to hold against her head.
'Very amusing,' said Rotherham and his eyes flicked
over Rafe's highwayman attire as her husband brought
the horse to a halt fifty yards away. 'And somewhat
appropriate.'

Rafe slipped down from the beast's back.

'Please divest yourself of the weapon. Over there.'
Rotherham indicated a spot some distance away, where
the gun could not be readily reached.

Rafe hesitated, as Marianne knew that he would
over such an order.

'I am aware of the fragility of trust, Mr Knight, but
I am afraid I cannot dispense with my own pistol until
I know you are unarmed. I would not wish my finger
to grow tired where it is positioned upon the trigger…
not when Lady Marianne is in such proximity.'

Rafe threw the pistol to the place Rotherham had
gestured.

'And the rest of them, if you would be so kind, sir.'
Rotherham's voice was smooth, his hand held across
her *décolletage* cold and calm. She could smell the
sweet scent of tobacco that came from his coat and
the familiar heavy scent of his cologne.

Rafe took two pistols from his pocket and threw
them to land by the first. He stood facing Rotherham,
unarmed and unafraid if the defiant tilt of his head
beneath his low-slung hat was anything to judge by.
Marianne felt her stomach grip in fear, and not for
herself. Her focus was fixed firmly on Rafe and the
danger that he was in. The touch of muzzle was light

against her hair, yet she could feel the prickle of her scalp beneath and a gladness in her heart, for all the while Rotherham aimed his pistol at her he could not shoot Rafe. She watched her husband intently, while every nerve in her body was poised and alert, ready for that first hint of movement in Rotherham's hand.

Rafe held his hands up to show there was nothing in them, then, with slow clear movements so that Rotherham could see exactly what he was doing, he produced the document from within his greatcoat.

'Open it. Lay it down on the ground before me. But do not make the mistake of coming too close.'

Rotherham cannot be trusted, the little voice whispered in her head. And every nerve in her body strained to free herself from her ropes that she might save Rafe. Rotherham must have felt her surreptitious movement, for his arm tightened ever so slightly around her.

'Patience, my dear,' he whispered in her ear.

Rafe walked closer; she held her breath, waiting for him to produce another pistol from some unknown hiding place and shoot Rotherham. Or for him to move fast, landing a blow that would send Rotherham reeling. But the man from whom the worst of villains had scurried, the man who could best seven men with his fists alone, did only as Rotherham instructed. She realised in that moment that he would do nothing to endanger her life.

The IOU looked very convincing where it lay upon the grass. *A copy of a copy*, she thought, and prayed that Rotherham would not realise.

Please, God, she prayed for her husband's safety. *Please*. She prayed that somehow this mess would all work out for the best.

'Thank you, Mr Knight.' Rotherham gave a sigh as if in relief.

Rafe said not one word, just faced him with a steady determined patience.

This was the moment. Rotherham thought he had the document. He had Marianne and a loaded pistol, and Rafe unarmed before him. Every muscle in her body tightened. The breath stayed lodged in her throat. Her heart gave a stutter.

'It is over,' Rotherham said, 'at last.' She waited for him to squeeze the trigger, for the roar of the pistol as it fired its bullet. But whether it would be into her head, or Rafe's chest, she did not know. She felt the slight movement in Rotherham's arm and she closed her eyes and prayed his aim would find her.

But there was no explosion, no plume of gunpowder. Rotherham's grip slackened and dropped away. She opened her eyes and for a moment she just stood there, unable to believe it. And then Rotherham gave her a little nudge forwards.

'Take her,' he said in a soft voice in which the regret was unmistakable.

Marianne ran the small distance to her husband.

Rafe swung her behind him, shielding her from Rotherham. He gave a grim nod at Rotherham and then turned to her, urging her forward towards his horse, always keeping himself between her and the duke.

They walked away and Rotherham let them go, just as he had said he would. They were almost free. Five paces and they would be on Rafe's horse. And for the first time since Rafe had placed the document down she allowed herself to hope. Maybe Rotherham was telling the truth, maybe both she and Rafe could escape this nightmare alive.

Four paces. Maybe Rotherham did mean to go back to the Continent and never return.

Three paces. Maybe it really was going to be all right.

She wanted to look round at Rafe, to look into his eyes. Two more paces and she could do it. Two paces and they would be upon the horse's back. Two paces and they would be safe.

The shot rang out, ripping through the quietness of the heath.

'No!' She turned to see Rafe collapsing down on to his knees, his gloved hand clutched to his chest. 'No!' But he was already face down upon the grass and in her line of vision, through the haze of drifting white-blue smoke, was Rotherham, standing where she had left him, the pistol still smoking in his hand.

She chafed at the ropes that bound her until her wrists bled, but it made no difference, she could not free herself to help her husband. She dropped to kneel by his side.

'Rafe!' Her voice was guttural and ragged. 'Rafe!' she cried, but his body lay still and unmoving.

'What have you done?' she yelled at Rotherham.

'I have made you a widow, my dear,' he said in a voice devoid of all emotion, 'a widow who is set to re-marry with indecent haste.' He dropped the pistol and produced another from his pocket. 'But let us take no chances.'

Marianne had not thought it was possible to feel such pain, such rage, such madness.

'No!' she shouted. 'You are the vilest of creatures to have walked this earth!'

'That is no way to speak to your future husband, Marianne,' he said and began to walk towards her.

The tears were streaming down her face. She wanted to launch herself at him. She wanted to kill him. Rotherham smiled at her. She stared and could not look away. She stared and thought that what had just happened had driven her mad, in truth, for behind Rotherham a man was crawling closer on his belly. And as she watched the man rose up to his feet and the man was tall and dark and powerful. He was a man who wore no hat or dark silk kerchief around his face, yet had seemingly risen from the dead—the man was her husband.

She did not know if his image was the product of her own imagining or the soul of her husband come back to save her from beyond the grave.

She saw him aim his pistol and heard him call Rotherham's name in his own strong harsh voice.

'He has a pistol!' she yelled in warning.

Rotherham turned and fired at the man who looked like Rafe. But he was not fast enough. Rafe's bullet landed in Rotherham's thigh, sending the duke sprawling on the grass.

'Rafe?' She was on her feet, running towards the spectre before it could vanish.

'Marianne.' He reached her, cutting the ropes from her wrists, hugging her briefly against him, his body warm and hard and strong.

She glanced back at the fallen body of the high-wayman in confusion, but Rafe grabbed her hand and ran to the man.

She watched while he rolled the man over so that he lay on his back. And the man gave a grunt and opened his eyes.

'Did you get him?' The words were muffled behind his mask.

'Rest easy,' said Rafe and freed the hat from the man's head and the mask from his face that he might breathe easier, and checked the wound to the man's shoulder. At first she did not recognise him, for the beard had been shaved from his chin and the moustache from his lip. And then the man's eyes met hers.

'Papa,' she whispered.

'My daughter,' he said and his voice was thick with emotion. 'Whatever you think of me, it is deserved. But know that I love you and that I have spent a lifetime ruing those vowels so wickedly and thoughtlessly and drunkenly written.'

She clutched his hand in hers, feeling the wet blood that smeared upon it.

'I love you, too, Papa.'

He wept at that, silent tears rolling down his cheeks.

Rafe pulled her aside, speaking quiet words for her ears only. 'We have to get him home. There is a doctor waiting ready.'

'Was there no other way?'

'None that would not endanger your life all the more. And none of us would risk that. He wanted to do this for you, Marianne. I could not deny him the chance to regain some measure of honour.'

She nodded.

'Help me get him into the carriage.' Together they moved her father into the hackney, supporting him as best they could and laying him across the seats. Then Rafe tied her father's horse on a lead to the carriage.

Rafe walked over to Rotherham and grabbed him, flipping the man to lie flat on his back. He took a fresh pistol from his pocket and pressed the barrel against Rotherham's temple.

Rotherham paled even more and gave a whimper.

'No.' Marianne came to stand by Rafe's side, touching her hand to the tight tense muscle in the curve of his arm. 'Do not do this, Rafe.'

'For what he has done to you he deserves to die.'

'If you kill him, they will hunt you down and hang you.'

'It is a price I would willingly pay.'

'But I would not.'

She felt the tremble that ran through Rafe's arm.

'He is nothing to me. And you are everything.' It was true, she thought. Rotherham no longer held any power over her. She was not afraid of him. 'And besides,' she said in a quiet voice, 'you once told me that you were not a murderer.'

He closed his eyes at that and she knew that he understood the truth of it—that if he killed Rotherham in that moment he would be no better than the villain himself.

'Do not give him the power to change the man you are.'

Rafe lowered the pistol, but he did not shift his eyes from Rotherham. 'The document,' he growled.

Rotherham scrabbled in his pocket and passed him the copy.

'He has the original too,' she said. 'He has had it all along.'

'Then the one in your father's possession…?'

'A copy Rotherham had made. Billy Jones was Rotherham's man. He killed your father under Rotherham's instruction.'

She saw the darkening in Rafe's eyes and wished she had not blurted the truth here and now, when the pistol was still in Rafe's hand and Rotherham lying helpless before him.

'Rafe,' she said softly. And he looked round at her. Their gazes met and held. All that was in her heart reached out to him. He touched his fingers gently to her cheek. Then he took the original document, the one her father had written all those years ago, and stuffed it into his pocket. Taking Marianne's hand in his, he turned and led her away towards the carriage.

'You cannot mean to leave me here?' said Rotherham.

'I shall not kill you, Rotherham. But neither shall I help you.' Rafe's voice was quiet and controlled.

'This place is not safe. And my leg...'

'Nowhere in England is safe for you, Rotherham.' Rafe's voice was grim and dark and filled with promise. 'In the eventuality that you escape this heath you would do well to remember that.'

'Damn you, Knight!'

But Rafe had already turned and was helping Marianne into the carriage. She sat beside her father, whose face was white and strained from Rotherham's bullet lodged in his shoulder, and held his hand in hers. And as the darkness of the night began to close in, Rafe drove them home.

'Now that Mama and Francis are not present to hear, tell me honestly...' Marianne paused briefly '...will he survive the wound?'

'There is likely to be some impairment in his left arm, but aside from that, and assuming that he takes no fever, then your father should make a good recovery.'

She nodded and closed her eyes; when she opened them again they were blurry with tears.

'I should not have let him do it,' Rafe said, misunderstanding why she was weeping. 'I should have—'

But she did not let him go on. 'I thought it was you,' she whispered and the tears flowed harder. 'I thought Rotherham had killed you.'

'Marianne.' Her name was like a sigh on his lips. He took her into his arms, trying to hold her against him, but she did not yield, just stared up into his face, determined to tell him.

'I thought it was you, and I could not bear it.'

'I'm sorry, Marianne. If there had been another way…' He traced the outline of her face with his eyes. 'But I did what I had to, to save you. And I will always do that. Because I love you.'

His words were a whisper, the same whisper a highwayman had used on a heath what seemed an eternity ago. And they meant more to Marianne than anything else in the world. She stared into his eyes.

She reached up and touched her fingers to his lips and there was no more need for words, only the need of a woman for her man. After all that they had been through, after all the day had brought. They undressed each other, one garment at a time. And then he carried her to their bed, and he made love to her, and the union of their bodies, the physical manifestation of a love that had been born in spite of vengeance and hatred and wickedness, began to heal their hurts.

It was two weeks after that fateful day upon Hounslow Heath. The house was very different from the one that the highwayman had first brought her to. There was a full staff of servants. The shutters had been opened in the yellow and master bedchambers and the rooms were filled with late autumn sunshine as she and Rafe carefully packed away his parents' possessions.

'You must choose the paints and wallpapers, and

materials, Marianne. I would fill this house with light and laughter…and children.'

She smiled and gave a nod. 'Most definitely.'

'I will hold you to that, my love,' he said.

'Please see that you do.' She leaned across and kissed him on the mouth, and everything in the world was right.

* * * * *

REQUEST YOUR FREE BOOKS!

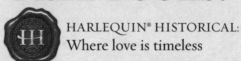

HARLEQUIN® HISTORICAL:
Where love is timeless

2 FREE NOVELS PLUS 2 FREE GIFTS!

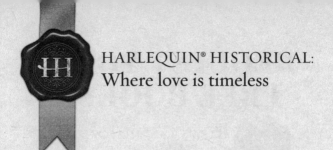

HARLEQUIN® HISTORICAL:
Where love is timeless

BOUND BY ROYAL COMMAND!

A dangerous mission at Queen Elizabeth's bidding is Celia Sutton's chance to erase the taint of her brother's treason. Her life is at risk if she's discovered—and so is her heart when she learns her co-conspirator is also her one-time seducer: brooding and mysterious John Brandon!

Will Celia fulfill her duty to Queen and Country or risk it all for love?

Find out in

Tarnished Rose of the Court

by Amanda McCabe

**Available October 2012
from Harlequin® Historical**

*Introducing fan-favorite Harlequin® Historical author
Christine Merrill's latest sexy, witty Regency romance.*

Read on for a sneak peek of
TWO WRONGS MAKE A MARRIAGE

Kidnapped! Dishonored! Forced to marry one's abductor to avoid the scandal!

It was almost too perfect. Jack Briggs could hardly contain his glee, though this was not the moment to reveal it. The plans he'd set in motion at the beginning of the London Season were coming together, suddenly, unexpectedly and in a way almost too perfect for words. He would have a rich and well-born wife and he'd have her months ahead of schedule.

Miss Cynthia Banester was not the woman he'd expected to catch. But she was everything that the Earl of Spayne had requested Jack bring to his family by marrying. And now that weapons had been drawn, there could be no turning back. He would have her, whether the earl liked her or not.

She smiled at him in a hopeful, rather worried way, as though her own happiness depended on his cooperation. "I am sorry, Lord Kenton, but I cannot permit you to leave. If you attempt it, I will be forced to shoot you."

Jack watched the barrel of the pistol moving in twitching figure eights as she tried to keep it steady. If the gun fired, by accident or with intent, Miss Banester would become the second most beautiful woman to have shot him. But if she did not control her aim, it could prove more damaging than a hurried leap from a courtesan's boudoir window. At such close range, there was a very real chance she might hit something he wished to keep whole.

He kept his hands raised, put on his best smile and worked his magic upon her. "I would not dream of leaving.

Did I not come willingly to this spot, when you requested me to follow you away from the other guests?"

"You thought me foolish enough to leave a crowded ballroom to go walking in a dark garden with a man who is nearly a stranger to me." She tightened her grip on the pistol and for a moment, it stilled, before the muzzle drooped alarmingly in the direction of his manhood.

Don't miss this lively tale of deception,
desire and matrimony!

They've made their bed… So they might as well lie in it!

TWO WRONGS MAKE A MARRIAGE
by Christine Merrill.

Available October 2012

HARLEQUIN® Blaze™

red-hot reads

Two sizzling fairy tales with men straight from your wildest dreams...

Fan-favorite authors

Rhonda Nelson & Karen Foley

bring readers another installment of

Blazing Bedtime Stories, Volume IX

THE EQUALIZER

Modern-day righter of wrongs, Robin Sherwood is a man on a mission and will do everything necessary to see that through, especially when that means catching the eye of a fair maiden.

GOD'S GIFT TO WOMEN

Sculptor Lexi Adams decides there is no such thing as the perfect man, until she catches sight of Nikos Christakos, the sexy builder next door. She convinces herself that she only wants to sculpt him, but soon finds a cold stone statue is a poor substitute for the real deal.

Available October 2013...

www.